NB Winner of the NorthBound Book Award 2022

"Careful and compassionat_e_ ... so moving ... around im_____ attitudes towards older peo___ and meaningful, but also fu____ and beautiful description ... _a really_ lovely read.
—EMMA HEALEY, author of *Elizabeth Is Missing*

"A study of empathy and compassion, in lyrical prose. It examines human connections and asks how we should care for others, and be cared for ourselves ... There is a luminous, shimmering sense of place – unforgettable ... the beauty, the drama and the dangers of *The Bay* linger with me still." —CATHERINE SIMPSON, author of *One Body*

"This is a beautifully crafted and utterly absorbing story about the ever-present and ever-hopeful possibilities for human connection ... From the moment I started reading this book – with its sweeping, textured, and harrowing seascapes – I knew [I] would love it." —JANINE BRADBURY, University of York

"A truly remarkable book, with lightning characterisation and such extraordinary compassion. I loved every page."
—KATE SIMANTS, author of *A Ruined Girl*

"A perceptive, beautifully sculpted and moving novel about the loneliness and difficulty of being an outsider."
—EMMA BAMFORD, author of *Deep Water*

"An evocative, weather-lashed story of an unlikely duo, raising urgent questions about how we treat those who cross borders. Heart-wrenching and hopeful in equal measure."
—THE BATH NOVEL AWARD

"An important story deftly told in spare, affecting prose."
—JOANNA BARNARD, author of *Precocious* and *Hush Litle Baby*

Published by Saraband
3 Clairmont Gardens
Glasgow, G3 7LW

ISBN: 9781913393762
eISBN: 9781913393977

The author would like to acknowledge the financial support
of the NorthBound Award from New Writing North
and Saraband, funded by the University of York.

10 9 8 7 6 5 4 3 2 1
Printed and bound in Great Britain by Clays Ltd, Elcograf SpA.

*This is an entirely fictional story. It was inspired in part by real
events in Morecambe Bay in 2004, but no resemblance to any
actual person, living or dead, is intended or should be inferred.*

The Bay

A novel by

Julia Rampen

With an afterword by
Hsiao-Hung Pai

Saraband

To my grandparents,
the ones who crossed continents
and the ones who loved the bay.

Chapter One

"You know what General Cockle says? Once they're in your hands, they're completely trapped." Changfa dug a dark shell out of the sand and passed it to Suling. "You just need to find them first."

Suling felt the weight of the mollusc in her gloved palm. "Fine," she told him. "You find them." They were surrounded on all sides by a vast plain of sand. In the distance it looked smooth, but under her boots it was oozing and uneven. She'd raked like the others, bent down like the others, scooped up shells like the others, and stuffed them into the orange plastic net. But it was only half full. She was never going to earn her life back.

"Hey, be patient," Changfa said with a smile. "It's only your first week." He squinted at the shore and picked up his own, full net. "The minivan's here."

All around them, the cocklers were hoisting bulging nets onto their shoulders. Last night they had been companions sharing nicknames and oolong tea. Now, anonymous in their waterproofs, they seemed like hardened soldiers.

Birds plunged after clouds in the huge sky. Suling didn't recognise any of their cries.

"You were supposed to get us good jobs," she said, as they started to walk. "I might as well be picking rice. At least I'd be warm."

The wind moaned in her ear like an endless tannoy instruction she couldn't understand. Each gust made her twitch, and then she felt pain of the day's labour rip through her muscles, and the blister on her hand where her glove had worn through. She wanted to collapse on her dirty old mattress and sleep.

Changfa only laughed. "You'll get more for one cockle out here than a whole day of picking rice," he said. "You should hear where Huimei worked before. This is practically VIP. In a few years, we could actually make money."

He was always going on about Huimei, like the pretty single mum was some kind of model worker. She hated how cheerful he sounded. "Years?" she said.

"Once the debt is paid off."

The broker in Putian had made her debt seem manageable, like a crop you sowed one year knowing you'd harvest it the next. But in a dark car park in France, a snakehead had doubled it. Now the debt was out of control. It stalked her each day and smothered her at night. There was no use telling Changfa – he had his own arrangements to worry about. There were dark circles under his eyes.

"I'll ask General Cockle," Changfa said. "He'll be able to sort something out."

"Not for me," she said. "He already thinks I'm useless."

Ahead of them, the cocklers dragged their nets towards shore. They were tough, but not as tough as General Cockle. He'd arrived in a Fujian shipping crate and raked and stamped and haggled his way up. He never smiled, except when he threatened you. The only people he seemed to care about were the ghosts, the English bosses who rang him on his fancy mobile phone. And all they seemed to care about was how many nets he'd sold.

Changfa's gloved hand squeezed hers. "I'll talk to him," he said.

Another promise. He made so many he should start a factory.

They reached the marsh grass. It was more solid than the sand but pockmarked with tiny streams they had to jump between. The other cocklers had already formed a huddle by the minivan. "Hey," General Cockle shouted. "What took you so long? You discover a cockle mine or something?" Unlike the others, he wasn't wrapped up – at some point he'd become so stony he no longer noticed the cold. He leapt down the bank to peer into their nets and spat. "Changfa, you need to find yourself a faster girlfriend."

Changfa laughed, as if the joke was funny. General Cockle marched back to the minivan.

Suling tried to hide her hurt. She knew she was supposed to laugh too. *He breaks you like an animal*, the cocklers had whispered as they served up noodles the previous night. *This is your life now.*

It wasn't. It couldn't be. She stopped.

"He's right," she said.

Changfa stared at her. "What do you mean?"

"I'm no good at this job. I should try somewhere different. Like London."

There, she'd said it. Made it real.

Changfa was shaking his head. "You're crazy."

"I was crazy to come here." *To listen to you*, she almost added. She looked around at the strange landscape again. It might as well be a different planet. "I thought we'd be in a city. Learning English. Creating real futures for ourselves." She felt the lump of the dictionary in her coat pocket. She'd planned to learn as she worked. Then she'd picked up the rake and she was just muscles and nerves in a race against time. "This is worse than the factory."

3

He winced as if struck by the wind. But it was the truth. She'd listened to his stories for years, caught the bus to Putian with them, cashed them in for a ticket to England. Now they were on the windy, never-ending sand and he was still trying to peddle his fantasies.

The factory girls used to laugh sometimes. "Even my supervisor was better than General Cockle," she said.

"But Susu." He lowered his voice. "It's not just General Cockle. The debt collectors – they'll come looking for you."

Thugs hammering on her mother's door. Smashing up their only furniture. She pushed the thought out of her head. "The debt collectors only care about money," she said. London was rich, with palaces and lucky red phone boxes. She held up the net so the wind rattled the cockles. "I'm not paying them with this, am I?"

They stared at each other for a moment, long enough for her to notice the sand in his eyelashes and the cracks in his lips, and the lines of failure already appearing on his forehead.

"I've got enough cash for the bus fare," she said, her heart speeding up like a drumbeat. Three crisp notes, still carefully wrapped and tucked under the mattress. "For both of us. Unless you prefer General Cockle."

Changfa looked up at the vast sky before replying. For a few seconds the world teetered on its axis.

"General Cockle is too ugly for me," he said eventually.

She laughed, relieved.

"Let's talk it over in the minivan," he said. "We shouldn't make a decision too quickly."

She shook her head. In the minivan, the other cocklers would chip in, with all their reasons to stay. She didn't want to hear their sad, tired stories. "I'll walk back."

Changfa frowned. "You could get lost."

"I'll follow the road," she said.

He looked down at his boots. "OK, so we'll take different paths, I guess."

She handed him her net. "To the same place," she said. She couldn't bring herself to call the damp, crowded room they slept in home.

He nodded like he understood. "You've got my number. See you," he said, and scrambled up the bank after General Cockle. Before he followed the others into the minivan, he stopped and turned.

"Remember – stay invisible," he shouted.

That was the last thing he said before the minivan door shut behind him.

Chapter Two

The postcard showed one of those black and white photographs of the town, girls in swirling skirts and bold lipstick, boys with rolled-up shirt sleeves, preserved in time by dark room chemicals. Arthur turned it over. "Dear Gertie," the card began. "Wishing you a happy birthday from the USA. Found this gem at the bottom of my stationary drawer. Brought back memories of your English hospitality, when I so needed it. Love, Nancy."

Oh, bugger. Another one he would have to write to. It was surprising how bad news failed to spread. Was she the American Gertie once brought back from church? He'd thought they all knew by now, but then, Gertie was very good at maintaining all kinds of distant friends. She would spend evenings at her bureau, carefully distilling their lives into letter form. "Dear Nancy. Please send me her letters." No, he couldn't bring himself to write that yet.

He stood up and wandered into the living room. The tweedy light fell through the window, illuminating the bookshelves, the framed picture of Gertie, her smile wide, hair still a tawny brown. He stared through the sliding-glass door at the balcony. He remembered the American sitting there, the sacrilege of her mixing his single malt with coke.

Beyond the balcony, the town clung like a barnacle to the coastline, the last frontier before the Irish Sea. Arthur's bungalow was built on a hill above the town. From where he stood, he could see the whole of the garden below, in shades of rust ahead of autumn's approach, and as the hill grew steeper the roofs of the houses, and beyond that, the milky surface of the bay. The tide was coming in. Soon it would be a shimmer of grey, and after that, darkness.

Monday, October 20th, 2003. This was the first of Gertie's birthdays he hadn't needed to fuss around looking for a present or find an excuse to pop out for the cake, which he would drive so very carefully back and reveal after tea, a candle for each decade twinkling on the top. Last year, he'd got the dates mixed up, and Gertie had spent most of the evening testing him with questions. He'd been defensive and she'd been concerned, and neither of them realised that it was her they needed to worry about.

Perhaps he should have invited his daughter round to mark the occasion. Margaret was unlikely to be busy. But she would almost certainly turn up with an inferior cake, insist on eating it and loudly cry.

No – he had to accept it; Gertie's birthday was just a day like any other day now.

He crumpled up the card in his palm and dropped it in the wastepaper basket. He'd work out what to say to Nancy later. He pulled on his coat and let himself out of the house. It was October and there were leaves to rake; big soggy clumps of them. He started under the apple tree and moved slowly down the garden as the light expired. At the end, screened by the beech hedge's coppery leaves, he paused to listen to the sounds of the unseen street: a car sliding into a driveway, a woman calling for her cat, "Dimples, Dimples". Then a passer-by, talking to himself, quite mad, until Arthur peered over the hedge and saw it was just a bloody foreigner talking on one of those bloody phones.

He turned around and began working his way back. On the other side of the fence, Reggie O'Brien's grass was overgrown. It had been that way ever since he was carted off to a care home, but there were lights on in the house. The long-lost son must be back from Australia. Arthur shook the leaves off the rake and rested against it for a moment.

In the upstairs window of the O'Brien house, a blonde-haired boy appeared, nose pressed against the glass. It seemed only a few years ago that Reggie had come round excitedly with pictures of the new-born grandson. "You'll meet him soon," he'd said, but he never did.

The boy vanished.

The paving stones were speckled with rain. He put the rake in the garage and went back into the house.

It was a quarter past four. If he wrote the letter now, he'd have time to send it before the post office closed. He could drive back the way Gertie loved, along the bay. He opened Gertie's bureau and sat down awkwardly. His handwriting was so straggly these days – his teachers would have rapped him over the knuckles. But his teachers were safely six feet under. He wrote: "I am sorry to tell you that my wife Gertie passed away in July. Thank you for your letter – it was a kind thought. All the best, Arthur."

He folded up the piece of paper and pushed it into an envelope. He wanted to get it out of his house as quickly as possible. He put on his hat and headed to the car.

*

Sending the letter to America took longer than Arthur expected. First because he needed a special stamp for which he had to queue. Then he had to weigh it, and all of this had to

8

be communicated to the woman behind the counter, who had a thick Indian accent and was talking through a glass pane.

"What did you say?" Arthur said, after she waved stickers at him.

"Do. You. Want. An. Airmail. Sticker?" she shouted slowly, as if he was the one who needed help.

"She's asking if you want an airmail sticker," the man behind him in the queue said.

"I'm not deaf," he said.

"I think you want one," the man in the queue said, and nodded at the woman behind the counter, who slapped a blue sticker on the envelope and dropped it into some unseen bag.

"Next!" she said.

"I wasn't finished," Arthur protested, but the man had already heaved a parcel onto the counter and was saying: "First Class to France, please."

By the time Arthur was in the car again it was almost dark and pouring with rain. The people in the post office itched at him like an insect bite. He was done with this day. There was hardly any point driving along the coastal road.

But it was Gertie's birthday. How many times had they taken that route together? Only last year, when Gertie had said one afternoon she felt like a drive. "Gar on, git gan," she had joked in the language of their childhood. He turned left at the junction.

On the country roads a little pressure on the accelerator sent the car leaping. The itch began to fade. He loved driving. It was a strange thing, that even as his body got more unpredictable, the cars he drove got smoother, more supple to the touch. There was even something comforting about the rain on his windshield, as if the sky was summing up his mood.

Outside the window, the tarry bay slipped by. Ahead of him were the fells, half devoured by dark clouds. He fantasised about disappearing into the night sky. If only he still had his knees.

He was so swept up in his thoughts that the blue lights took him by surprise. He slowed down just in time to see the police car parked on the side of the road, two figures silhouetted in its vivid flashes.

If it had been anywhere else, he wouldn't have thought twice.

But this was the bay road. The Wet Sahara swallowed horses and their owners whole. He'd worked on it long enough to know it was hungry. When you were on the sand, you were walking on other men's graves. Or your own. He remembered that sunny afternoon when he and Sid's shadows were like giants and shivered.

More blue lights. He slowed to a crawl. There was only one reason police could be out on a road like this. But what did they know about the bay? They sat in their little offices and caught shoplifters – they knew nothing about the old spots, and the hidden rivers tide. How a solid sandbank could disappear in seconds. It was ancient, this bay – it didn't play by the laws they had drawn up for the land.

The police were no doubt clueless. Just their luck that one of the only people left who understood the bay was driving straight towards them.

Chapter Three

Suling had lived her whole life – all seventeen years of it – with someone jostling at her elbow. The kids in her village, the factory girls gossiping in the dorms, the silent men slumped against her in the dark of the van as it drove through countries they never saw. Now she was alone.

She was less sure of the way than she'd pretended to Changfa. In Putian, they'd wander the malls on their days off, gaze through the shop windows at their dreams. It was different in England. She never left the house except to climb into the minivan. She had her tiny English dictionary in her pocket, with her notes on asking directions, but Changfa had warned her not to draw attention to herself. Still, the road ran parallel with the shore for some time. She kept walking along the marsh grass to avoid General Cockle, but the sputter of an engine confirmed he hadn't waited long. No doubt he was already thinking about how he could fill her empty seat.

The sound of the minivan died away. She walked to the beat of her heart. Maybe Changfa did think it would all blow over by the morning. But she would pack their bags as soon as she was in the house. And once they were on the bus, he would forget the cockles and become his old self again, the one who wasn't going to stop until he'd found his ticket to a better life. She smiled just picturing him building his palaces in the air.

A gust of wind knocked her sideways. This place shrank everyone. The tree-less hills rose around the shore like ogres. On her right, somewhere beyond the sand, was the sea.

Thinking of it made her walk faster. The evening was smudging the details of the landscape and the sky above was filling with clouds, black and thick like weeds. But she was walking into her future. Soon she'd be out of this backwater, in a city where opportunities flashed above your head on every street.

A car's headlights illuminated the grass at the top of the rocky bank. The others would probably be at the car park by now, no doubt listening to General Cockle curse her as the redhead saw the empty net and hammered down his price. A drop of rain landed on her nose, and she yanked up her hood.

Behind her, she heard a roar. For a moment she pictured General Cockle, foot down on the minivan accelerator. Then she turned and saw in the dusk the white teeth of the waves. The tide was coming in.

She scrambled up to the rocks. When the cocklers had talked about the tide in hushed voices, she had thought they were exaggerating. Now she saw it for herself. The bright line of spray swept across the grey sand like a sickle. The dark sea fell in sheaves behind it. Within minutes the seabed she had been walking on had vanished into the deepness of the night.

If she'd hesitated or taken a less direct route – or, worse, got lost – she could have drowned.

The thought made her shiver, and she turned away. There was no point dwelling on it. She'd be out of this place soon.

By the time she reached the road, the rain was like artillery fire. In the distance was a scattering of orange lights: the town.

She pictured the cocklers slurping noodles in the lamplit room, in those precious hours after General Cockle drove off to whatever restaurant he was playing mahjong in that night. They were not bad people – just tired and beaten down by the wind and rain. She would enjoy spending one last evening with them. And then she would quietly pack her bag and go.

Whee-whaw, whee-whaw – a car was hurtling towards her, swathed in blue light. She jumped onto the verge, but the car didn't even slow down. *Whee-whaw, whee-whaw.* The blades of grass flickered blue. There was something evil about its cry.

"Stay invisible," Changfa had said. The car had passed her now and was twisting around the coast, but she could still hear its shriek. The cocklers had told her about a man who was hired to water plants in a warehouse, who ended up jailed for supplying cannabis after his bosses ran away. But at least they knew where he went. Most of the time, no-one knew where they took you. The one thing everyone agreed on was no-one ever came back.

She looked behind her. The car had disappeared behind a hill, but then she saw its blue lights again. The siren stopped. The blue lights remained though. They were not warm, but icy, like the water trickling down her back.

A glimmer of golden light appeared on the road's wet surface. At the top of the hill, there was a building made from old stone. Inside the house, perfectly framed by the window, a long-nosed woman stood washing dishes. She had bare arms, as if it was warm, and yet on the other side of the window, Suling was cold to her bones.

She stood there for a moment, watching. If the woman looked – really looked – she would see her, only a pane of glass away. But she didn't.

Then Suling turned a corner and knew immediately where she was. The tall, crumbling stone buildings had lantern-like windows, and there was that green lettered sign, still flickering enigmatically. Changfa had said these streets were the terraces, a hard-to-pronounce word that, unusually for this flat language, shifted tones. She'd remembered it by imagining lights in the windows turning on, first the middle floor, then the top, then the basement. "Teh Ah Seh." But tonight, most of the windows on the street were in darkness.

Behind the terraces was a lane, with wooden fences dividing one back door from another. She pushed through the gate into the back yard of the cocklers' house, knocked on the door and waited.

No-one answered. She knocked again. Silence. She tried the handle, but it was locked and she didn't have a key – the cocklers so rarely did anything alone. The kitchen window was dark.

She shook the handle. Everything she owned was in that house. Her notes of cash, pictures of home, her mobile phone, carefully wrapped up in its charger, her dry clothes. "Let me in," she said, daring to raise her voice. "Hey, let me in." Even if they were crowded in some unseen room, Changfa should be listening out for her knock at the door.

Perhaps it was the wrong house. But no, through a gap in the curtains she could see the empty bunkbeds, the mattresses propped up in the corner, a discarded blanket. A single light from the hall.

"See you," Changfa had said, before following General Cockle. "We'll take different paths," he'd said. She'd thought he'd been talking about the way back to the house. But General Cockle had contacts all over the place. The others had warned her that he sometimes moved them to other jobs at short notice. It was to do with the tides, they'd said, or sometimes just because he liked to play games, show who was boss. Perhaps he'd heard her talking him down.

Even still, why hadn't Changfa waited? Couldn't he have found some excuse? If it was too good an opportunity to refuse, surely he'd leave her a note?

She looked around the dark back yard, at the rain-streaked windows. No note. "You've got my number," he'd said. Not much use with her phone locked up inside the house.

Had she driven him away with her complaints? In Putian they were lost together. But this new country made her feel stupid, like she was trying to learn to read all over again. He'd been there two months already, got to know the other cocklers. He was always laughing and joking with Huimei.

Whee-whaw, whee-whaw.

Another screeching cry. The upstairs windows catching the blue light as the car passed. Changfa and his promises had caused her enough trouble already. It wasn't safe to stay outside with the police on patrol. She had to find somewhere to shelter, quick.

Once the car's cry had died away, she let herself into the lane again. A streetlight at the far end flicked on and off, as if powered by some more ancient force than electricity. The street dived under a bridge.

When she emerged at the other end, she was standing on a wide, empty road, with railings on one side and a huge expanse of blackness beyond it. The bay. Like staring at the edge of the world.

Then she heard the rattling. A different sound to the wind, the sound of wood on wood. The old concrete building jutting out into the bay was so dark and abandoned looking, she might never have noticed it if not for the loose board where the door had once been. That was what was making the racket.

She'd never forced her way into a building before. But the night was snarling in her face, and she had nowhere else to go. She dug her fingernails into the gap between the wood and the concrete and tugged. It moved a little. She pictured General Cockle and summoned all her fury. It didn't take her long to push through.

Chapter Four

It was pouring with rain. The road had become a gravelly track. Arthur pulled up to a halt and got out.

"Excuse me, can I help you?"

The lad was young, so young Arthur wouldn't have believed he was a police officer had it not been for the uniform. He even had spots, confirmed every few seconds by the blue lights.

"I know the bay," Arthur said. "Who's in charge? I should let them know I'm here."

Spotty scratched his head. They weren't very bright these days. "Which organisation are you from?"

It took sixty seconds for a man to drown, thirty for a child. "We don't have much time to lose," he said, trying to keep the impatience out of his voice.

"It's just…" Spotty said.

"What's happening?" A second policeman appeared. He looked slightly older – he had stubble at least – but he spoke with a self-satisfied briskness that made Arthur immediately want to shake him.

"Who's this?"

"I've come to help," Arthur said. "I used to work on the sands. Do you know where they are?"

"What?" Stubble said to his doltish colleague.

The lad shrugged. "I didn't understand either."

"I'll handle this," Stubble said. Before Arthur could stop him, he put a hand on his shoulder. "Look, sir, we appreciate your offer of help, but we've got plenty of officers here. On a rainy night like this, you should really be inside."

First the man in the Post Office, now this. He was being treated like a babby. He imagined knocking off Stubble's daft little cap. But all he said was: "I'll decide if I'm inside or outside."

Stubble smiled. "Of course you will," he said. "If you just go back to your car, you can do whatever you want. But right now—"

He'd seen Sid drown, his hands twitching and grasping in the water. Sid could knock a man flat at just fifteen, but he was no match for the sands. That was the year before the war. Arthur didn't mind signing up after that.

"I know what I'm talking about," he said. "Once the sand gets you, it won't let you go. And then the tide – there isn't another tide like it. You don't even…"

He paused to catch his breath. The policemen were staring at him. They had a strange expression on their faces, and he wondered if they were about to arrest him.

But then they started to laugh. Cackling like spotty, stubbly gargoyles in their daft, luminous uniforms.

"Oh, there's no-one out on the bay," Stubble said. "You don't need to worry about that."

"What?" Arthur said. "So why is the car here?"

Stubble wiped something from his eye. If Arthur had more strength, he would have clouted him. The policeman said, "It's nothing serious. Just some cocklers braying in the car park. They're very territorial, the old lot – don't like this new breed from abroad."

He nodded down the hill, but all Arthur could see were the lights and the rain. "Nothing serious?" he said. "You mean to tell me there are foreigners running around that bay and it's nothing serious?"

"That's racist," Spotty said. Stubble was still chuckling.

"It's not bloody racist – it's..." Arthur stopped. They weren't going to listen. "You're clearing them out now, though, surely?"

"It's been dealt with," the younger one said stiffly.

"Let's just say they won't be hitting each other again," said Stubble. "We don't discriminate." He had managed to stop laughing. "It's best if you go," he said with a wink. "Before you say anything you might regret."

"For God's sake," Arthur said. There was no point talking to these donnats any longer. The wind ripped through his mackintosh. Beyond them, somewhere, were the foreigners. Who had apparently been merrily wandering around the sands when they weren't clouting one another. Foreigners! Even a local-born man was a foreigner in that bay. But more and more, he felt like a foreigner on dry land as well. He could still hear the policemen snickering.

For the first time, he realised how wet he was. The car windshield was smeared with rain. He turned the key, put his foot down and waited for the engine to bite. He'd done it a million times, but somehow this time he couldn't find it.

He sank into the seat, his feet slipping off the pedals. For decades, the cocklers had passed down their knowledge of the bay, father to son, uncle to nephew. And all for what? Now that Gertie was gone, the facts became plain – no one cared about his knowledge anymore. Those policemen treated him like he was daft. He tried the clutch again and this time the car stirred into life. Well, those know-it-all coppers could be damned.

He drove away from the blue lights along the dark coastal road, the bay sullen on his right-hand side. It was hungry for prey.

The clusters of houses marked the outskirts of town. If he turned up the hill, he could be back in front of the TV, but somehow this didn't seem satisfying. He wanted someone to talk to, someone who could understand what eejits those whippersnapper policemen were. Then it hit him: Jack.

Of course, it was late to knock on someone's door, but Jack was always a night owl. No doubt he was sitting on his sofa, watching TV. They had worked on the cockle beds together, goddammit.

He kept driving. The terraces around here were bed and breakfasts once, all stuffed with holidaymakers and "No Vacancies" signs, but these days most had fallen into other hands. One sign flashed H-tel mournfully in the rain. Yes, those young upstarts had nothing to be smug about.

Jack had always hated upstarts, along with budget package holidays, immigrants, feminists, traffic wardens and microwaves. Arthur cheered up just thinking about him. He turned left into a quiet square and parked. Jack would understand. He got out of the car and walked up the path beside the scrawny garden, which Jack had really let get to ruin, and rang the doorbell.

After Arthur pressed the button, there was silence. Then he heard the turn of metal, and the door opened. It wasn't Jack.

"Hey-lo?" the man said in a funny accent. He was young and dressed in nothing but cotton shorts and a vest.

"Is Jack there?" Arthur asked. "Where's Jack?"

The man frowned. "You know what time it is?"

Arthur glanced at the number again. It was 44. Jack's

number. There was even the same cracked paving stone. He felt a surge of anger at this stupid man. "Get me Jack," he said.

"There is no Jack."

"I told you – get me Jack."

"What's the matter?" another voice said. A woman in a raincoat was letting herself into the house next door. She stopped fiddling with the keys to peer at them in the rain.

"You know Jack?" Stupid Shorts said.

"Oh, Jack," the raincoat said. "Well, yes. But he's dead." She leaned over the wall and tapped Arthur on the arm. "He's dead, I'm afraid."

She might as well have knocked him down. His head whirled. He was vaguely aware of a door shutting, and Stupid Shorts retreating from view, while the rain kept up its infernal racket. The woman in the raincoat tapped him on the arm again. She had a sagging mouth and dark circles under her eyes. "Aren't you Margaret's dad?" she said. "Look, do you need a lift?"

Arthur shook off her touch. "I'm fine," he managed to say. "Thank you."

So Jack was dead. Why had nobody told him? But now he was remembering a pub with the afternoon light streaming in, and everyone clad in black. Jack's wake. Had he been there? Had he walked to the grave, thrown dirt and flowers on the coffin? Was all he had left of this an image of the afternoon light in the pub?

The rain slid down his neck. The rage in him stiffened to fear.

"Are you sure?" the woman was shouting behind him. He got into the car, slammed the door and drove off before she could stop him.

Chapter Five

Suling's cheek was pressed against something cold and hard. She opened her eyes and saw it was sparkling with sun. She sneezed.

The first thing she remembered was the rain. She felt her hair. It was dry but tangled. She brushed it out with her fingers. Her comb, along with her toothbrush, was in her little red bag, locked inside the house in the terraces.

Now all she had were the grey sweater and leggings she was wearing, and her waterproofs and boots, piled in a heap by her feet like a cast-off skin. The sweater was Changfa's. He had given it to her when he saw how cold she was in this country. "I'll keep you warm," he'd said.

If he wanted to keep her warm, he should have come with her, rather than running after General Cockle. They could be in a city by now.

Instead, she was – somewhere. She propped herself up on her elbows.

She had fumbled her way into a room. The ceiling was grey, with flakes of plaster dangling like fish scales. The wooden surface she had collapsed on last night was a bench, and the coolness she had felt against her cheek was the wall, which, like the floor, was tiled. Rusty metal cupboards stood on either side. There were no windows. The light snaked in from a corridor and forged a path across the grubby tiles. They might have been white once. It was hard to imagine what the place had been used for.

"We'll build your mother the biggest house," Changfa had said when they caught the first bus from the village. "Three floors, south-facing, everything."

She sneezed again. Her body felt like it had been washed out and wrung. The rain here got under your skin. It seeped into your bones, your heart, until you didn't know what to feel any more. It dissolved things you thought were solid. Her connection to Changfa. His promises. Her arms prickled with cold. She forced herself to her feet – she needed to keep moving to stay warm.

The doorway summoned her in a blaze of light. She tiptoed barefoot across the tiles towards it and passed through into a strange kind of courtyard.

Here too the floor was tiled, but in the centre was a large, rectangular pit filled with rainwater. It was open to the sky and ringed with a high concrete wall, like a fortress.

Slowly, it began to fall into place. The room she had slept in, with all the metal cupboards, was a changing room. The courtyard was the pool – and that long plank of wood at the end a diving board. Suling felt the thrill of being an explorer. Only there was no-one to share her discovery with.

She sat down at the edge of the pool. The sun clanged on the cloudy water. On one of her father's rare visits, he took her to visit relatives in a nearby town, and they all went swimming. He'd left soon after, and that time he didn't come back.

Her frowning reflection stretched and wobbled on the water's surface. Black, shoulder-length hair that kept escaping her ears. The face Changfa's mother had muttered was too square.

The wind chipped the water and the reflection vanished. Voices swooped over the high wall. There must be people walking along the promenade. They would drift up and down, unaware of the girl who had given up on the other side of the wall, unaware of her wasting away, until she was just a body in a fortress tomb. When they pushed open the boards in years to come, all they would find would be her plastic permit. A fake.

*

Changfa was an optimist. "Beach holiday," he'd shouted to her above the wind on that first day she joined him on the sand. She pictured him in the minivan rattling off to another coastline, already friends with the workers sitting on either side. No doubt he'd convinced himself that she was fine, that she had a key to the terraces, or whatever other story allowed him to get on with the job at hand.

A scratching sound broke through her thoughts. The voices had gone. The sky was bloody, her stomach a cavern. In the half light of the courtyard, she saw a mouse. It had large black eyes like berries and neat brown fur, and a tail like a flick of ink. Its tiny hands scrabbled at the tiles.

They were always battling with mice at home. There were too many cracks, too many crumbling bricks. But now she had nothing to defend. She lay still and watched him.

The mouse was tearing a napkin into shreds. The wind must have ripped it from someone's hand – now it was his bed for the night.

She pushed her lips apart. "What's your name, Mousy?" she asked. The creature paused, as if he understood, and stared at her slumped figure with bright eyes. Then he went back to the napkin again, his miniature paws grabbing and tearing like a machine on a production line.

It was night now, the time when the hidden creatures of the world hunted. If that mouse could find everything it needed, at a fraction of her size, then she could too.

She got up slowly. "Nice to meet you, Little Bandit," she said to the mouse. He scurried back to wherever he came from.

Her waterproofs were dry. She pulled them on, eased open the boards and stepped onto the long, dark, empty promenade. Lamplight fell in tidy, orange pools, as if last night's gale never happened.

She went first to the terraces. She had to, just in case the cocklers had returned and everything was back in its place, slivers of light and chatter falling onto the paving stones in the back yard. Perhaps they would open the door and let her in with a nod, and she would find Changfa packing their bags.

But the back yard was silent, and the house was still in darkness. Through a crack in the blinds, she could see the mattresses and someone's crumpled jacket. The way it lay on the floor gave her a desolate feeling. In the factory in Putian, people constantly came and went, but she'd always had Changfa. What had General Cockle said to him, to convince him to disappear without a word?

Or maybe he didn't need to be convinced. She'd thought she was forcing him to choose, but she'd offered him an excuse. What if he really preferred sharing the back of the minivan with Huimei?

She slumped against the wooden fence. All these thoughts made her weak. The one thing she knew for sure was that she was alone, with no money or friends or mobile phone. She needed to be strong if she was to survive in this country.

She closed the gate behind her. A narrow alleyway led to what looked like a high street. At the end was a modern building, a supermarket, its bright logo suspended in the dark like a guiding star. Behind its glass walls were shelves and shelves of food. If she could just pass through the thin panes, she would have everything she wanted.

A sudden rustling made her jump. She turned, but the street was deserted.

Another rustle. It was coming from a dark square behind the supermarket, where cars were parked.

Moving very slowly, she passed through a gap in the hedge and into the square. On the far side, a hooded figure was leaning over a bin, its hands rummaging through the junk

It was a figure she'd seen many times before. Not here, but in Putian, and even in her village from time to time. She had always seen it out of the corner of her eye, and then tried to pretend she hadn't, because no one wants a reminder of what they could become.

Now, though, she was starving. She crouched behind a car and waited. After that journey across Europe, she knew how to be silent. The figure straightened up and left. When she was certain the car park was empty, she crossed over to the bin.

It was stuffed with plastic wrappers and packages of food. She had written a note to her mother when she left her village: "I will take care of you". But she was already tugging the package out, tearing off the wrapper and sinking her teeth into what was beneath. Each bite of bread made her feel sick and alive again at the same time. There was egg, and salad, and something that tasted rotten, but she didn't care – it was the energy she craved. And she had it, gulp after gulp.

She unwrapped another sandwich, some sort of pork this time, and ate it. Then she grabbed as many as she could and stuffed them under her sweater. There were some newspapers jammed into the bin as well, and she took those too. Her mattress for the night.

The courtyard was still when she returned, the lychee moon rattling about the bottom of the night sky. Suling dumped everything on the tiles.

"See, Little Bandit, you're not the only one who can fend for yourself," she said into the dark.

Chapter Six

Arthur dreamed of Gertie. She'd been cross about something, in that cool, understated way of hers that he only noticed when it was too late. He lay there for a few minutes after waking, eyes stubbornly shut against the sun. She could be up already (she was the early riser), boiling the kettle for a cup of tea in the kitchen, and then, while it was steeping, drawing the curtains in every room. But what if she never came back, but wandered from room to room, retreating further as his memories cracked and broke? The thought pushed him out of bed and into the kitchen, where he flicked on the radio and made tea with as much clatter as he could.

The radio was playing the news – Tony Blair this, Tony Blair that. Some nonsense about women in the boardroom. A strike at an airport he'd never been to. No mention of the foreigners turning up at the bay. Not cocklers. He refused to call them that. The real cocklers had been proud, tanned men who downed their pints after coming in with the catch. They might not have been able to spell much more than their names, but they knew the difference between a bar and an old spot and taught it to him over many years. As a boy, he picked up stray cockles, and later he raked, and finally he was allowed to stir the sand with the jumbo. In those final years before the war, he had believed he would do this forever.

The way he had been brushed off by those plods. He bristled with anger. There was a time in his career when he could walk into the accountancy office and say something, and it was as solid and serious as if it were carved in stone. Now, despite all his experience, he was a laughingstock.

The doorbell rang. He glanced at the calendar. Today's square, like all the others, was blank. Had he made arrangements and forgotten them? He stopped by the hallway mirror to check he didn't have a smear of cream on his cheek or some other evidence of senility. An old, bald man looked warily back.

But the door handle was already turning.

"Hi, Dad," Margaret said, dropping her handbag on the hall table. She was wearing a purple quilted body warmer over a greyish fleece, neither of which suited her and looked far too warm. Her short, frizzy brown hair was escaping its clips. "Patsy called. She said you were wandering around in the rain, all confused."

He knew the doorbell was bad news. "Patsy should mind her own business," he said. "I was visiting a friend."

His daughter marched into the kitchen, checked to see if the teapot was warm and poured herself a cup.

"She said you were trying to visit a man who was dead."

"I don't know where she gets these ideas from."

"Dad, I'm only telling you because she was concerned." Margaret opened the fridge, sniffed the milk, and put it back again. "I know I haven't been around as much as I should – it's this new order from Japan. I've been flat out trying to find suppliers." She peered up at the cupboard and tested its door. "That looks like it'll come off its hinges at any moment."

"It will if you keep bending it like that," Arthur said.

"This house is falling apart." Margaret spoke if she hadn't heard a word. She jiggled the tap. "Sink's going rotten. You need a tap that doesn't spray everywhere."

"It's served me perfectly well for 50 years," Arthur said. They'd bought the house on the hill as newlyweds, after his promotion at the factory. Gertie had liked the idea of looking down at the bay. He'd liked the indoor toilet. He had ways of managing the kitchen tap.

"You just have to turn it on carefully," he said.

But she was already tapping on the cupboards. "We should think about getting you a walk-in shower. It might be safer than a bath."

"Yes, baths are real killers these days," Arthur said.

Margaret kept tapping. "I know you've always coped," she said. "But it's different now. You're alone. And frail."

Arthur felt his temper slipping away from him like a soapy glass. "You're alone too," he said before he could stop himself.

The tapping stopped. Gertie never liked to tease Margaret. "She's got other interests," she'd say firmly when the lack of a husband came up. But if Arthur had hurt his daughter's feelings, she didn't show it. Instead, she reached into her pocket and pulled out a silver mobile phone.

"Look," she said. "I was just stopping by to give you this."

"Why are you wasting money?" Arthur protested. "I already have a telephone."

"It wasn't expensive, Dad. All it means is that you have a way to call me, if you were to get lost, like the other night. Or if you fall." She put it on the table. "It's simple to use. Look, I'll show—"

"I don't want it," Arthur snapped.

"Dad, I took a morning off to check up on you," Margaret said, her voice breaking. "I'm only trying to help."

"Well, you don't have to," Arthur said. He left the room before he said anything more.

He sought refuge in the garden. The autumn air was crisp, the chrysanthemums in bloom. They had planted for everyone – a pear tree for Gertie, a rhubarb patch for him, roses for Margaret. Just a few of the red ones remained. He walked between the flowerbeds, inhaling the scent. A bitter note crept in.

"Arthur."

For a second he thought it was Reggie, smoking in the garden on the other side of the fence like the old days. But the voice was a woman's. He turned around. Her skin was pale and wrinkled, and she was sitting in an electric wheelchair, but he still recognised Reggie's ex-wife. "Angela?" he said.

"That's right," she said with a smile. She tapped the ash from her cigarette. "I asked them to leave me alone in the garden. God knows how many years it was since I was last here."

Arthur thought of Reggie leaning on his spade. "You don't remember when you upped and left?"

The smile twisted. "I see you got Reggie's side of the story," Angela said. "Well, I'm pleased to see you, Arthur, even if you don't feel the same. How's Gertie?"

"She's dead," Arthur said.

The smile vanished. "Oh, I'm so sorry," Angela said. "I didn't know."

He wasn't going to spare her. "It was a stroke. Three months ago."

"I wish – I mean – I would have come to the funeral," Angela said. She pressed a button on the arm of her chair and moved closer to the fence. "I liked Gertie a lot, you know. We used to do things together, with the kids. I missed her when I left."

I bet you did, Arthur thought. Angela had always been a troublemaker, always saying awkward things at dinner that Gertie had to smooth over. She read a lot of books, but not the kind everyone else liked. She talked openly about sex – once, after a few glasses of wine, about pleasure. And when she started talking, she never stopped. Sometimes Arthur would come home on summer evenings and find she had invited herself into the garden for such a long chat with Gertie that his poor wife hadn't even had the chance to start the tea. And then there had been the letter he'd found stuffed in their bookshelf, in Angela's hand, with that casual phrase: *you can always leave.*

"I know I should prepare myself for news like this," Angela said softly. "But she was such a sparky woman." She traced a pattern on the side of the wheelchair. "I often wonder what we'd have done if we'd been born at a different time."

She was doing it again – stirring things up. "What do you mean by that?" he asked.

Angela looked up, surprised, as if she'd forgotten he was there.

"Oh, you know," she said. "If we'd had the opportunities our daughters had. University. Maybe having careers." She smiled. "I always thought Gertie would be a great town mayor."

"A politician?" Arthur didn't like the idea of Gertie getting dragged into the mud with all those eejits. "She had more sense than that."

"Sorry," she said, with a tiny smile. "I've offended you."

Even in the early days, she always had that little smile, as if she was secretly laughing at him.

"So who did you run off with?" he asked. Reggie had never

gone into any detail, and he hadn't liked to clout a man while he was down. But she couldn't avoid the question.

The smile broadened. "No-one," Angela said. "I ran off with no-one." She laughed, a laugh that turned into a cough. "How boring." Her eyes flickered back to the house. "Luckily, my children came to understand. They are so much more open minded than I was."

He stared at her. To think this woman had been Gertie's friend, had played with his daughter. She could destroy everything – for nothing – and she was laughing about it. Even now, a shrivelled-up hag in a wheelchair, she was laughing.

"I'll get back to raking," he said.

"Of course," Angela said. "Well, it was good to talk, Arthur, one last time." She rolled her eyes. "I've got my own marching orders. Lung cancer."

"Sorry," he said, automatically. Of course, that hadn't stopped her smoking. She'd always carried her fags in a turquoise cigarette case. He could see it now, tucked into the side of her wheelchair.

"Too late to give up now," Angela said with a shrug. "See you, Arthur."

She pressed the arm of the wheelchair and began to glide away across the grass. He watched her go. She had caused so much mayhem once. It was hard to make sense of the fact that soon she simply would not exist.

She still nettled him, all the same. That day he'd found the letter, Gertie had walked into the room. For a second, he'd met her eyes, and the life they'd built tumbled around them. Then he'd tossed it into the fire, she'd stepped forward, and he'd clung to her arms.

He went to get a pair of secateurs from the garage. On the way back, he saw Margaret through the kitchen window, her face buried in one of Gertie's jumpers. For all his daughter's awkwardness, he'd never questioned her love for her parents. At least, until one of them had gone.

Margaret's shoulders stirred. He went hastily back to the flower beds. To his relief, the next-door garden was empty once more. *See you, Arthur*, Angela had said. But all he wanted was to be left in peace with his memories.

He picked up the secateurs and chopped the dead heads off the roses.

Chapter Seven

From the top of the diving board, Suling could see the trains. Their lights glinted in the distance as they curved around the edge of the coast, the clatter of wheels floating across the bay. They vanished, only to reappear on the far side of the bay before hurtling into the darkness again. They ran until the time when the lights of the town started to disappear, and the moon had climbed as high as the hills.

"There are trains that travel hundreds of kilometres an hour," Changfa used to say as they walked home from school. He'd grin. "One day, I'll buy us tickets and we'll speed away."

But you didn't need tickets when it was easy to slip onto a train unnoticed. "We'll pay when we're rich," her father had said on that trip to the swimming pool, his big hand enclosing her small one, his eyes flicking back and forth. She imagined stepping onto a carriage, sitting down by a window and watching her future come into view.

*

The town was full of absent-minded people. They left their hats and scarves and shoes without thinking about what the rain would do to them, whether the gulls would pull them apart. But each little thing Suling discovered felt like a treasure.

The supermarket bin was also refilled daily, it seemed. After sunset, she rooted through it and then made her way back through the alleyway behind the terraces. It wasn't the fastest way to go. She just hated the thought that the lights could come back on without her knowing. That they might be back in the cramped terraced house with the kettle bubbling away and the windows steamed up with their chatter. But the yard was always in darkness.

On the fourth night, though, she found the blinds were up. The cocklers always kept them closed. She let herself into the back yard and crept forward until her nose touched the cold window and she could see inside.

Someone had tidied up. The room she used to sleep in was completely bare – even the mattresses had gone. Only a dark smudge on the carpet hinted at the pile of rakes and nets that once lay there. The kitchen was stripped of food, a mop propped up against the door.

The blinds were up because there was nothing to hide. Wherever the cocklers were, they weren't coming back.

It was as she turned to go that she noticed the comb, lying in between some old cardboard boxes on the paving stones. It was just an ordinary plastic brown comb, but she recognised it immediately as the one she had given Changfa. "For when your hair turns grey," she'd joked, as she'd pressed it into his hands outside the factory. But they both knew it was a charm.

Only, at some point, somewhere during the time he'd arrived in England and she had found herself bargaining in the back of a lorry, the magic had worn off. Now it just lay there like another bit of rubbish. Discarded, just like her.

Her mother had spent her life waiting for a man who never came back. "That's your father's radio," she'd protested, years later, when Suling twiddled the dusty knob to find a different station. For a moment, she imagined running the comb against the wall until the teeth were ragged and split. But her hair was tangled, so she picked it up and pocketed it.

*

The shuttered shop windows turned blue as the car screamed past. She turned sharply round the corner. Stay invisible.

A dog barked. She halted on the dark street. The man from the supermarket bin was crouched over something on the ground, and he was looking directly at her.

He was the first person she'd seen up close in days. He looked as if he'd been chewed up and spat out. His eyes moved this way and that, and the muscles in his cheeks danced in an unpredictable way. He had a brown beard, gloves with holes in them, and a heavy jacket.

The dog barked again. The man hushed it, and she saw for the first time it was on a lead. He nodded at her and said something. She didn't understand any of his words, so she just repeated the phrase she knew: "Good day."

He was standing over a pile of black plastic bags. One was open, and as she watched, he pulled something from it. A pair of jeans.

"You," he said. He was holding them out to her.

They were women's jeans, with a glittery edge around the pockets. The kind of jeans you'd go to the cinema in, lick ice cream in, stroll along the promenade with your boyfriend in.

She reached out her hand. "Thank you," she said, as the language books had instructed her. He pulled out a pair of red socks, sniffed them, and stowed them away in a pocket of his raincoat. Then he said: "Where you from?"

She had practised this phrase many times, before she got to this country, when she still imagined she might have red-head friends. She shook her head. She had taken too many risks already.

The man shrugged. He pointed to himself. "Kee Teh," he said. Then he pointed at the bag, gesturing it was hers, and started to lope away.

She watched him go, the jeans hugged to her chest, and suddenly she remembered the word she had been repeating all day. "Hey! Where – train?"

He paused. "Train?"

She nodded.

His dirty finger pointed along the promenade. He said something that she didn't understand, but she caught the word that mattered. "Train."

"Thank you."

She waited until he had disappeared around the corner. Then she grabbed the bag and ran. Who left clothes on the street? What a strange country this was.

*

She wrote a note to Changfa on the back of a poster she'd found flapping on a wall. *I waited a long time and then I caught the train. I am going to London. Ask for me there.* There it was, an ultimatum clearly written in blue ink. She couldn't waste any more time – the debt collectors wouldn't. It was up to him now. If he loved her, it was enough for him to find her. She folded it carefully and posted it through the letter box of the terraced house.

The next morning, she dressed in jeans from the bag, a smart-looking shirt and a woollen jumper. Everything else that fitted, she packed into a plastic shopping bag. Each change of clothes was a gateway to a different job. She'd pick an English name – Chloe maybe, or Jenny. In a few days, she'd be chopping onions, or scrubbing plates, or vacuuming hotel rooms. Her boss would be tough but fair. She'd start paying off her debt straight away. If Changfa eventually turned up, they could work things out. They could still be good for each other, so long as General Cockle wasn't around.

The sunset smouldered in the sky. She left crumbs for Little Bandit. "Restaurant's closing," she told him. The evening was turning to ash above them. It was still early, for the voices of people on the promenade fluttered on the wind, but she didn't want to miss her chance.

She pressed her eye to the crack in the boards and waited until no one was in sight.

It was a mild night. The moon was low. She tried to be as inconspicuous as she could as she walked past the boarded-up buildings – another person with their hood up, eyes on the ground, weighed down by shopping. At the end of the promenade, an old sign was tacked to a stone wall, beside some steps.

No-one was around, so she pulled out her dictionary and translated it. The sign said "Station Road".

She was close. The knowledge propelled her up the steps and along the dark road. At the end was a building with a grand-looking stone arch and, set in gold above the door, the word S T A T I O N.

If there were barriers, she'd have to wait out of sight and jump them when the time came. Avoid the attendant's eye. Still, they were just flimsy gates, compared to the rest of her life.

But as she drew near, she saw that there were no barriers at all, and no sign of an attendant either. She passed through the archway and found herself on the platform.

Near the factory, they had been building a metro with neat, clean ticket halls and shiny trains. This station looked like something out of the past. Despite the arch's grandeur, it was really just two platforms divided by the rails. At one point the roof had a delicate wooden fringe, but in some places it was missing or rotting. A wooden bench was rotten too, and none of the lamps were working.

Just as well she was getting out of this place. She sat down on the crumbling bench and waited. The moon was only at the trees – there were at least four more trains.

It was on a night like this that she and Changfa had caught the bus to Putian. She'd been dumb with guilt about leaving her mother. He'd filled the silence with his plans. "In the city you can reinvent yourself. Anyone can be an expert. Not like here where they squabble over whose kid married well." He'd reached for her hand and squeezed it. "You and me together."

An owl hooted. She must have waited a long time now, yet no-one else had come. There was a rickety wooden bridge that crossed the tracks, and she climbed it and rested her arms over the side. The moon cast a silvery sheen over the water of the bay.

And then she heard it – a clickety-rickety sound, at first very faint, but impossible to mistake. She saw the tiny gold disc of light. The train was curving around the coast.

Her future was coming to meet her. She clattered down the wooden steps of the bridge, grabbed the plastic shopping bag and stood on the platform. In a moment, the train would sweep into sight, carriages glowing, and she would step on.

But it didn't come. The sound stopped. She peered down the track, at the rails snaking away into the darkness. The grass growing between the tracks was long, and she'd still not seen a single other passenger.

The station was not quiet. It was abandoned, just like the pool. How had she not realised it? The train she had seen must be on a different set of tracks.

She'd trusted Changfa's patter about how their lives were going to change. In the cramped dark of the van across Europe, she'd shut her eyes and imagined the house they would build on their return home. How she'd wake up in the morning and step onto the balcony in a fine silk dressing gown and breathe the morning air.

The lights of the houses were starting to disappear, one by one, the town erasing itself into the dark night. Wherever the train stopped, it wasn't here. She'd spent so much money to go nowhere. All Changfa had done was swap one backwater for another.

She watched the moon until it rose above the hills before walking back to the swimming pool.

Chapter Eight

Money – that was all Margaret cared about. It was a Sunday morning and the promenade glistened with the sun slick of freshly fallen rain. Margaret and her friend marched in matching Gore-Tex jackets. She kept just a step or two ahead of Arthur, but he knew she was cross.

Well, so was he. She'd turned up in the middle of his breakfast and started asking him about his finances. She had no business poking around in his affairs. He'd first made a will in his twenties, when she was just a bundle in his arms. He kept his bank statements. What more did she need to know? He'd said as much and she'd stomped around, tidying up his breakfast things before he'd even finished.

Now they were on the way to church – "It'll remind us of Mum," Margaret had said. But having needed to get out of the house, they had time to kill, so he parked the car in town and they took the long walk by the promenade. The sky was blue, with scudding clouds. Grass waved at the edge of the sands. The gusts reminded him he was skin and bone these days.

"This is the time to re-mortgage," Margaret was saying to her friend, some girl from school who was now a woman with dyed hair and lines under her eyes. She had a flat half an hour's drive away, close to the steel plant where she worked. Years ago, Arthur had stood on this promenade in the twilight and lifted her as she stretched her hands to the stars. Now she wanted to talk about bloody house prices.

It was then he spotted Angela. Her chair was pushed up against the iron railings of the promenade, a red hat masking her thinning hair, a cigarette between her lips. The wind flapped her beige coat. She didn't seem to have noticed him, or perhaps she was pretending, the way he used to pretend not to see colleagues if they made an appearance at the weekend.

It was probably better if he pretended not to see Angela too. One conversation was enough. But then the red hat, caught by the wind, came tearing over the promenade in front of him.

"You're still nimble," Angela said, with a hint of envy in her voice. "Thank you for returning it."

He shrugged. Old reflexes. "It looked like an expensive hat."

"It was." She cradled it in her arms for a moment. "Istanbul. 1976. I hadn't expected it to be cold."

"What are you doing out here anyway?" Arthur asked. He didn't care for Angela's stories of Life After Reggie.

"Watching a grandson." Angela pointed to the playpark, and Arthur caught a flash of a trainer disappearing up a climbing frame. "What about you?"

"What do you think?" He nodded at Margaret's receding figure. "Avoiding a conversation about house prices."

Angela peered down the prom. "Mind if I join you? It's years since I've been down there."

Arthur stalled. "Don't you need to watch your grandson?"

"Oh, it's only his mother who thinks he needs watching." Angela said. "She's from Sydney." She switched her cigarette to the other hand, put two fingers in her mouth and whistled. "Back soon," she yelled at the climbing frame. Then she put the cigarette in her mouth, tugged the hat back on and began to roll down the promenade.

Margaret and her friend were now distant figures silhouetted against the vast sky.

"House prices are so dull," Angela said.

Arthur felt a strange defensiveness on behalf of his daughter. "You found everything dull," he said.

"Well, they are. I've only got a bit of time left in this world and I've spent most of it listening to my son and daughter-in-law talk about valuations." She cast a sideways glance at him. "They're going to sell the house, you know."

"I guessed," Arthur bluffed. But he'd imagined Reggie's shed slowly sinking into the overgrown grass forever.

"She keeps complaining about the weather," Angela said, and he knew from the emphasis that she was talking about her daughter-in-law. "He's busy catching up with friends. But my grandson, he likes it here. All the old stuff. Crumbling away." She laughed, hoarse like an old engine. "Like me."

Everything was a joke to her. "It used to be smart round here," Arthur said. The promenade was curving round, like the prow of a ship. Birds swooped to land on the old boating pond. At one time, the place would be filled with crowds. For a moment, he could almost hear them.

Angela coughed. "What changed, do you think?" she asked.

"Hmmph," Arthur said. "It's Spain this, Turkey that." He eyed her hat. "The only holidays that count. But if you took the time to look properly, you're standing in one of the most beautiful places in the world."

He waited for Angela to protest, mention some wonder from her travels, but she didn't. They were approaching the hulk of the swimming pool, its windows all boarded up.

"Gertie, though," Arthur said. "She liked to dive." He pictured the lido, sun jiving on the water, the girl in the polka dot bikini disappearing in a splash.

"She must have been hardy," Angela said, tightening her scarf. "I always stayed on the deck chairs."

"She had nerves of steel," Arthur said proudly. He'd watched her all afternoon, without a clue of how he might start talking to her. And then she appeared by the side of the pool, shouted: "Areet, lad, can thee give me a hand out?" He still remembered the warmth of her palm and the coolness of the drops on it.

Angela cleared her throat. "I met Reggie at a meeting of the Communist Party," she said.

He laughed, and then stopped, thinking of Reggie, alone in some anonymous care home room.

"It's alright, it is funny," Angela said. "We weren't very good revolutionaries. I liked buying things too much." She smiled. "Reggie was always talking about bringing you along a meeting, but I persuaded him you were a lost cause."

He thought of his well-tended garden, his wife and daughter in their Sunday best. "You were right," he said shortly. They were coming to the end of the promenade, where the old boating pond stood. It was empty now, except for a puddle of rainwater reflecting the sky. Margaret and her friend had already climbed the bridge that led to the church. His daughter was peering down at the overgrown train tracks.

"She used to do that when she was a little girl," Angela said. "The trains were still running then. I'd take the kids together down here. They were quite good friends for a while."

It annoyed Arthur, that she held this memory of his daughter that should rightfully be his. She was trespassing on his past again.

"Don't you feel bad?" he asked abruptly. "Staying in his house, after you abandoned him?"

Angela's eyes narrowed. "I didn't abandon him, Arthur. We divorced." She coughed. "He wanted a wife that wore pretty dresses and made the tea. Very bourgeois if you ask me. I wanted something different."

"What, buying hats?"

Another cough. "Freedom, Arthur. Freedom to be an individual. To see the world. I'm sorry if you don't understand the concept."

She had never grasped what was precious to other people. She was always bored, always casting her eyes to the ceiling.

"Gertie was happy," he said.

"Was she?"

Arthur felt like giving the wheelchair a shove, but it was already clipping along at quite a pace.

"Gertie knew you were a bad influence," he said. After burning the letter, he'd asked his wife not to invite Angela round again. "That's why Margaret stopped coming on your little walks."

He'd crossed a line. The wheelchair stopped. The papery hands fumbled for another cigarette.

"Well, that's ironic then, because Margaret seems to value my family's advice," Angela said when she eventually spoke. She flicked an old silver lighter and cupped her hand to shelter the flame. "After all, she's been asking my son about care homes." She dragged on the cigarette.

"Care homes?" Arthur tried to hide his alarm. "What do you mean?"

Angela looked at him. It was a look he remembered; a cool, forensic sort of glance that made him feel very small.

"I won't go any further," she said. "There's no ramp up the bridge."

He couldn't let her go. Not without knowing.

"Come on, Angela. What has Margaret been asking?"

But all she said was: "I have to get back to my grandson."

She pressed a button and the wheelchair did a U-turn. He grabbed a railing for support and watched her zoom away, until she had vanished around the curve of the prom.

*

So Margaret was plotting against him. The questions about money. The conversations with old schoolfriends about his whereabouts. It could not be denied. The thought made him both furious and nervous, but the church bell was ringing and the same Margaret, at the vestry, beckoned impatiently and then disappeared. An organ started up, and the voices of the congregation sawed through a hymn.

He hadn't been to church since Gertie's funeral. Ahead of him bobbed a platoon of white heads, with the occasional blonde grandchild and the dark tresses of the foreign nurses from the care home. Margaret and her friend were perched on a pew at the back. Better to pretend he didn't know her schemes, at least until he'd found a way to beat them. He sat down and picked up a service book.

Quavering voices rose and fell with each line of the hymns. Arthur mouthed the words when they came to him and moved his lips when they didn't. Next to him, Margaret's flat tones tramped over the delicate notes. Her eyes were squeezed shut. It was like she was channelling some power he could not see or feel.

Father Mulroney read his sermon, but Arthur was too distracted to listen. Angela's words played in his head on repeat. *Asking my son about care homes.* Across the aisle, the awful Amelia Clancy caught his eye. She'd shuffled poor Mr Clancy off to some padded room years ago. Her lipstick smile gave him the shivers.

Candles flickered behind the church flowers. Lilies and incense summoned him like some old perfume.

The body of Christ, the body of Christ. It was communion now, but he wasn't ready to join the line weaving towards the altar. When Margaret stood up, he shook his head and mouthed "Stiff legs". With the two women gone he had the pew to himself, and he did feel like he was on the brink of some understanding now – not Christian, but a heathen revelation. He shut his eyes, imagined Gertie sitting next to him in her usual spot. To his annoyance, the look on her face was faintly disapproving, as if she knew he'd dragged her into his fight with Angela. He opened his eyes again and saw Margaret at the altar, her hands outstretched for the body of Christ like a suspect waiting to be judged. Only she was the judge and he was the suspect, and the small disc in her palms was only a wafer.

They reached the last hymn. The priest disappeared and everyone swept out of the church hall.

Chapter Nine

The light, like Suling's hopefulness, was disappearing. Every morning, she woke to find the courtyard a little more in shadow, and every evening the sun dropped a little earlier behind the rim of the bay. One night she let herself out onto the promenade shortly after sunset, only to realise there were still crowds milling around, as if it wasn't late at all. She pulled up her hood and trudged up and down the promenade until the last of them had gone.

Although she was in a cold country, it was getting colder still. She hunted for things to keep her warm – plastic bags, newspaper, bubble wrap, a tarpaulin to shelter her from the rain. She explored the town's gardens while its residents slept. In one, she found sheets hanging on a line, and took as many as she dared. But still she was kept awake by the dull ache of the cold, and in the morning her breath was all smoke.

A few days after the disappointment at the train station she packed the shopping bag again, dropped crumbs for Little Bandit and walked inland. The train didn't come to this town, but it must go somewhere, and if she walked and walked and walked, she might find it.

The town was on the side of a hill. As the road got steeper, her muscles ignited. She savoured the warmth. The houses here were bigger, each one nestled in its own shadowy garden. Some overflowed with light, and she caught glimpses through the bushes of hands pouring wine, bookshelves, the spark of a chandelier. Others, despite their size, were dark and empty, like great husks of families now departed.

At the top of the hill, the tarmac road curved back down again towards the high street, but a gravel track turned off it, into the darkness. The edge of town. Suling hoisted the shopping bag onto her shoulder and followed it.

There were no more houses, only the trees weaving their walls around her. The night was suddenly full of sounds. Down by the promenade, everything was drowned out by the wind and the occasional purr of a car, but the woods were orchestral, the trees whispering and fluttering and creaking as the leaves crackled underfoot. Something bounded away in the dark, but it was just an animal. She kept her eyes on the dim outline of the path. It felt like the kind of place that could tangle you up forever.

Then, to her relief, the path led out from the trees and onto the open hill. The track here was just a muddy line through the grass, no more sophisticated than the ones in her village, trodden by generations of farmers hurrying from one task to the next. It did not feel like the way to a train station, but at least there would be a view from the summit. If she saw the lights of the next town, she could find her way across the fields to it, and even the next town after that.

Reaching the top of the hill, she found only the carcass of a sheep, its skull picked clean. Beyond it was a wild land, the hills rising and falling like waves on a shadowy sea.

A little way from the carcass was a small square building made of old stone. She walked slowly towards it. Perhaps a farmer lived there, or someone like Kee Teh. It was a risk to approach them, but if they gave her directions, she could be on her way before they asked any questions of their own.

But when she walked around and found the open doorway, there was only the rest of the flock of sheep inside, huddled together for warmth.

*

There was one place that always looked warm – the only lively place she'd seen since moving to this country. It was a tavern of sorts, with old-fashioned lanterns, and baskets of flowers that seemed to hang from nowhere, voices buzzing around them like insects. When its coloured glass doors opened, the sound of music and laughter wafted out. If Changfa had been there, he would have promised to take her there on a date. But she knew now not to trust a fantasy.

Behind the tavern was an unlit lane, and sometimes she paused at the end of it to watch the smokers huddle. One night there was a big group of them, including two young women who must be crazy because their legs and arms were entirely bare.

She moved a little down the lane, to a doorway half hidden by a metal bin. Only prostitutes would wear such skimpy clothes in this damp and cold weather. And yet, while the women's legs trembled, they seemed to be happy, their conversation flaring into wild, untamed laughter. There was something otherworldly about their glittery, low-cut tops and high heels, like the flowers she'd once found in the sodden supermarket bin. A man pulled out his lighter, and they craned their necks towards the secret of his flame.

She thought with an ache of Changfa in the summer dark, a cherry-red stub between his lips.

Then the song drifting out of the doors changed to something slow and grand. One of the smokers began singing in a hoarse voice, and the next thing Suling knew the group had their arms around each other and were swaying back and forth. She was surprised by how deep the song seemed to shake them, like trees in a powerful wind. They were drunk, no doubt, but all the same, she envied them.

Suddenly the song stopped, as if the singers had realised they were in a cold coastal town after all. She crouched further behind the bin, but they were looking the other way, at a figure in the darkness. Some backed away, others leaned forward, as if curious. The figure stepped towards the light of the door, and she saw it was Kee Teh.

He asked them for something, money probably, his brown-haired dog straining on its lead. They shook their heads, suddenly alert. But seemingly he was used to being treated like that because he nodded and drifted on. She didn't realise he'd spotted her until he came close to the bin and stopped.

"Come," he said.

It was her turn to shake her head. His world was not her world.

"Come," Kee Teh said again. He grinned and opened his palm to show her a lighter. He must have swiped it from one of the smokers.

She was searching for the words to refuse him when his dog nudged her and looked at her with big brown eyes.

Kee Teh could pull a knife on her and she'd be helpless. But if that was what he wanted, he could do it now. Instead, he reached down to pat his dog. Changfa would have put his arm around her and hurried them both away, but Changfa wasn't here any more. And he had been kind to her before.

"OK," she said.

The chatter of the tavern faded. She followed Kee Teh along

the back lanes to an old building which looked as if it had been grand once, with a paved stone yard around it. Just like the swimming pool, there were boards in the windows and graffiti on the old stone walls.

Kee Teh put his hand to his chest and warbled. "Music," he said while she scrabbled through her dictionary. "Hall."

He hopped the fence and beckoned for her to follow. She could hear voices rising on the cold air.

"Come," he said.

She hesitated. But the fence was low – if she needed to, she could run. She put two hands on the railings and vaulted over. Kee Teh was already disappearing round the back of the building. Despite the dark, she could see there were others there – a man and a woman, she thought, from their shapes.

"Hello," they said, as if they expected her.

Kee Teh knelt and flicked the lighter. Out of nowhere, there was a flame. A newspaper caught fire, then twigs, then branches, until she was sitting around a bonfire. The heat was luxurious. She opened her palms and surrendered to it.

"Anna," the woman said.

"Tam," the man said.

They were offering their names. They didn't have much else. In the firelight, she could see everything about them was shabby. The woman's hair was a mass of yellow matted braids. The man had hungry cheeks and a large rucksack. They looked like they were on a journey, Suling thought, although where they were coming from and where they were going was hard to tell. They were certainly not the kind of people she'd imagined when Changfa first talked about England.

Kee Teh pulled a can from his pocket, snapped the ring and took a swig before handing it to her. She took a sip and reeled at the fizzy richness of it. The girl laughed, a throaty, hoarse kind of laugh. But it wasn't an unfriendly laugh.

Kee Teh was saying something, his dog now lying patiently by the fire, gesturing with his gloved hand – here, and here, and here. She thought it might be his own story. She didn't need to understand the words to know it was a sad one. Tam twitched. Anna poked the fire and said "yeah" as she disturbed the sparks.

Suling listened. The dog crept over and slid its head into her lap, as if they had known each other a long time. She reached out hesitantly and patted its brown hair. Its trust in her was so unexpected, she felt overwhelmed by it.

The world rearranged itself around the fire. Its golden embers were the anchor of everything, the voices rocking her gently. They were soft and low, the tones of disappointment, of failure.

The others fell silent. Kee Teh passed her the can again. It was her turn.

"I'm the stupidest person alive," she said in Hokkien. "I trusted him. I followed him to Putian and then I followed him here. I took out such a big loan I can't even think about it."

The dog's belly was warm beneath her fingers. Her eyes swam, and she hastily wiped the tears away.

"I used to think it didn't matter how hard we had to work, or how many risks we took, because there were two of us. Watching out for each other. We were going to get married one day."

The hollow cheeks twitched.

"Anyway, what does it matter? I'm alone in this country."

Anna gave the fire another prod. The sparks soared up and disappeared in the black sky.

Suling felt the comb in her pocket.

She gave the can back to Kee Teh. "Now I realise the only person I can rely on is me," she said.

The others nodded, as if they understood, and then Anna pulled out a slip of paper and began crumbling a dark substance onto it. The air sweetened as she lit it on the fire. She smoked her strange, hand-rolled cigarette for a moment and then passed it to Tam, who shut his eyes and pressed it to his lips before offering it to Suling. There was something so kind about the gesture that it was only after she inhaled, coughed and passed it on that she thought of how much her mother would have disapproved.

They sat like that for some time, the fragrant cigarette passing around the circle, the sparks rising into the night sky. Eventually the cigarette became a stub, and the fire embers. Then the couple stood up and raised their hands in farewell, and Kee Teh called his dog to him.

Suling didn't want to let the dog go. She wished she could take it with her, a companion for the walk back along the promenade, a warm belly to rub in the cold of the morning.

Kee Teh must have understood something of what she was feeling, because as she stood up to go, he threw something at her. "Here," he said. When she caught it, she saw it was the lighter.

Chapter Ten

Bzz. Whack, whack, whack. Bzz. Whack, whack. Bzz. Why was it that people spoke quieter and quieter, but when it came to disrupting his life, they were noisier than ever? Arthur watched the surface of his teacup tremble. Then he got up from the armchair where he'd been trying to eat his breakfast on a tray and went through to the kitchen to give Margaret's builder friend a long, hard stare.

Whack, whack, whack. He wasn't even looking, just attacking the cupboard with a hammer as if it had insulted his mam. Thank God he had removed all the plates. Arthur coughed and found he couldn't stop. Finally, the hammer came to rest, and the red face came up. "You OK, partner?"

He'd heard of cowboy builders, but this one really thought he was a cowboy. He wore tight jeans and leather boots and he'd even asked for coffee rather than tea. Luckily there was a jar of the instant stuff at the back of the pantry. Apparently his brother worked with Margaret and she'd managed to pull in a favour, but it didn't feel that way. The mug of coffee was still half-full on the table.

Arthur managed to stop coughing. "It's the dust," he said. "How long is this going to take?"

The cowboy pushed sweat off his forehead. "Well, these cupboards will take another half hour, and then I'll get onto the bathroom. It's a rail so you can get out of the bath, yeah? It'll be a couple of hours, I reckon." He took a slurp of the coffee and grimaced. "Then you'll be all set." He picked up his hammer again.

Arthur shut the door quickly. *Whack, whack. Bzz.* He went back into the lounge and opened the big sliding glass door that opened onto the balcony. The sky was a faint blue today, and the bay a pearly white. The garden was heavy with dew. Reggie's garden was empty – he'd seen the Australians' red Volkswagen pull out of the drive. It was the perfect opportunity to do some weeding, safe from the risk of bumping into Angela, but he didn't trust the cowboy an inch.

Instead, he sat back down in the armchair and picked up his telescope. The circle framed a flock of birds on the bay – he would have been able to name them once. Something startled them and they rocketed like a platoon into the sky. Now he was lost among the wisps of cloud. He brought the telescope down again, found the grey steelworks where Margaret worked, on the far side of the bay. Supply chain manager or some other jargon-filled title. Gertie had been so pleased when she got that job, because it meant she wouldn't leave, like so many of their friends' children had.

He felt a twang of regret at his resentment and moved the telescope on. There was the hill where it was said the last wolf of England was killed. And further along the bay, the beach Gertie loved so much, the one they'd walk on summer evenings or stop with a flask in winter and watch the sun go down.

Screeewaaaaah. What the hell was that cowboy up to now? The telescope wobbled. Damn it, he'd lost his place. Now he was staring at some dots in the bay – cocklers, perhaps, but when he took his eye away, he couldn't see anything at all. Once you were out far enough, you were swallowed by the landscape. There was a tale that in the old days, a whole coach party went down, horses and passengers and all. They must still be there somewhere, preserved under the sand.

He moved closer to shore. There were those birds again. Gertie would have known the name in an instant. She kept a book with all the species in the spare room. He put the telescope aside and got up to check it.

The cowboy's noises had moved to the bathroom. He closed the door of the spare room behind him and took a moment to breath. But everything here was a jumble too. The bird book should be on top of the dresser, but it wasn't – only a vase he hadn't seen for years and that daft mobile phone he didn't want. The chair looked like it had been moved as well. He began to open the drawers, one by one, looking for the book, but there was only Gertie's silk scarves, a bundle of letters and some of Margaret's old clothes. It was as if someone had deliberately rearranged everything to throw him off balance. He was lost in his own house. He yanked the drawers open again and began to scrabble through them.

There was an almighty bang. That's it, he'd had it. He marched into the bathroom, where the cowboy was starting up a drill dangerously close to the mirror. "What the hell have you done to the spare room?" he shouted over the noise. "Nothing's in the right place."

The drill had stopped, but he was still shouting. "I can't find anything. What the hell have you done?"

And now the cowboy was shouting. "I haven't been in the spare room. Did you hear me, partner? I haven't been in that room at all."

*

Later it was Margaret's turn to shout, this time down the telephone. "He did that job for free, Dad – he did it because he wanted to help you. And you were so rude to him." She sounded close to tears. "What am I going to say?"

"Tell him your father's a decrepit old bugger who doesn't like people invading his home," Arthur said.

"Thanks, Dad, that's really helpful," Margaret snapped. The phone clicked. Arthur listened to the dial tone for a moment, relieved it was over. At least they hadn't got onto the jumbled-up room. She couldn't send him to a care home just for being a bastard. He put the receiver down and went back to putting plates in the cupboards. Every time he slipped one back on the stack it felt like a piece of a jigsaw puzzle clicking into place. But his hand was shaking after the call, and the next plate went careering towards the linoleum.

"Goddammit," he said, looking at the pieces. Sweeping them up was an ordeal in itself. When he was finished, his back aching, he abandoned the rest and went back to the lounge. He opened a whisky he'd been saving for an evening that never came and poured himself a dram.

The drink smouldered. He held the glass up to the lamplight. When had he bought it? The answer came back clear and golden, like memories should do. On holiday in Scotland, years ago. The woman at the counter had had freckles, a tartan ribbon falling out of her black hair.

The sun disappeared in a rusty sky. In the dark, the world became a photo negative – the resort on the peninsula, usually a smudge, became a line of snarling lights. The sky was a cloudy black nothing, the fells a blurry darkness. He should get up, turn the TV on, heat up a tin of soup, but the whisky bound him to the chair.

He poured another dram. "The problem with you, ol' fella," Gertie said once, "you miss people, but you can't stand them either." There was dust on her empty chair. He felt the silence of the room like an ache. That night was her exit, but it should have been his. All he'd done since was anger people. Margaret, the cowboy – even Angela, on the promenade. That conversation was the first time he'd felt himself for a long time, and then he'd gone and ruined it.

He took a swig of whisky and put his telescope to his eye. The bay was dark and blank, so he drifted towards the lights of the town. A window showed a family at dinner, all eyes centred on the tiny grandchild in the highchair. The babby waved his spoon around and kicked his legs, and every time he did a ripple of smiles went round the room.

He tugged his telescope away. An elderly woman sat in a chair in a darkened room by a lamp. He wondered if she also knew what it was like to be alone, but then the door opened and her equally elderly husband came in.

In a third window, a middle-aged man in his undies rubbed deodorant energetically into his armpits. Arthur couldn't hear, but he imagined him to be whistling. The man danced his way into a pair of trousers. That was enough of him.

The next window was dark. It was the O'Brien's house – they must still be out. If only the telescope could look back into the past. He saw them as if from a distance, at one of the O'Briens' dinner parties, Gertie laughing in her summer dress, he in his newly bought suit, the jacket hung over the chair. Reggie dealing cards around the pudding bowls and Angela, all lacquered nails and black dress, surveying the scene. The kids tucked up in bed in some hidden room of the house.

Angela... Only she had an inkling of how it felt to be surrounded by the past, and he'd driven her away. Soon she'd be gone too.

He needed a piss. With a deep breath, he propelled himself out of the chair. The door to the spare room was open, Gertie's scarves strewn on the floor like the aftermath of a crime scene. He stooped to pick them up. One of them was the same turquoise shade as Angela's cigarette case.

On his way back, he picked up the phone in the hall, and dialled the O'Briens' number.

"Hello?" Reggie said.

He jumped. "What are you—"

But Reggie's voice interrupted him. "I can't come to the phone right now, so please leave a message after the tone." A beep prodded his ear.

Damn it, he'd fallen for one of those bloody automated voices again. He obeyed the instruction, but Reggie's voice had put him off and his message was a mess. "It's Arthur. I want to speak to Angela. I mean – there's some things of Gertie's I want to give her. Look, never mind, she knows where I live."

After he'd finished, he sat down at the kitchen table and wiped his brow. Those bloody automated messages. It was indecent, when Reggie was locked up like that. They probably wouldn't even check it. Maybe that was better all round. He put the glass in the sink and turned off the light before he went to bed.

Chapter Eleven

Suling never saw the couple again. Perhaps they had drifted on to another town, safe in the knowledge they had each other. But Kee Teh was hard to miss. He walked around the streets like he was their custodian, helping himself at the supermarket before stopping to chat to the smokers outside the tavern, his dog tugging him this way and that.

Of course, she watched all this from a distance. She was still supposed to be invisible. But when he saw her, he would bow his head and she would bow hers back.

As for the old swimming pool, it was all hers. Stocks of supermarket food piled neatly under the diving board; a tarpaulin lashed to it to make a shelter from the rain. A mattress in the old locker room that she'd found in an alley and lugged back. Often, late at night, when the town's residents were asleep, she'd light a fire and heat up something from the supermarket feeding Little Bandit the crumbs.

One evening, though she could still hear voices rising from the prom, the air smelled so strongly of smoke that an earlier fire seemed unlikely to be noticed. She clicked the lighter and watched the flame spread from the newspaper to branches.

"This is the kind of fire you'd tell stories around," she told Little Bandit. The embers glittered. She longed to reach in and pick one up. It would be a gold and ruby charm against the coldness of this country.

A bang interrupted her thoughts. There was a faint screech

and then another bang. She froze. Had someone noticed the fire? But then a crackle in the sky made her look up, in time to see a diamond-like light. Fireworks. She climbed up onto the diving board for a better view. There were dozens of them, far away across the bay, unfurling like white flowers. She turned her head and saw more, these ones red and blue, whirling like feathers in a cockfight. There had been fireworks like this at New Year, when Changfa pulled her out of sight of the crowd and kissed her.

But it wasn't New Year, not her New Year, and it seemed too early to be theirs either. The truth was, she had no idea what they were celebrating. No idea what plans they were making, who they were falling in love with, how they measured themselves against time.

*

She was perched on the diving board, watching the fireworks rat-a-tatting across the sky, when she heard a different kind of noise. At first she thought she thought it was just the fire, but then she heard it again. It was more animal-like, and it seemed to be coming from the passageway.

She climbed down from the diving board and stared at the dark hole of the passageway. The wall was too high to jump – the only way out was where the noises were coming from. She picked up one of the burning branches and waited.

A man emerged from the darkness. It was Kee Teh, his dog padding after him. He retreated slightly when he saw her, and as he did, she noticed a plastic wrapper in his hands – an offering. She lowered the branch.

He said something, opened the plastic, and stepped forward. The gift was bread. She took it.

"Hello," she said in English. She gestured for him to sit by the fire. But just then there was another rustling, and this time a Chinese man in a black waterproof jacket and some dull-looking jeans emerged from the passageway.

"Hello," he said in Hokkien.

"You're from Fujian?" she said, amazed.

The man nodded. "Jinjiang."

"Incredible," she said, dazed. It was a special night, after all.

Kee Teh flung out his hand. "Friend," he said, before sitting down and tearing into the bread. Suling's mind whirled. Had he understood her, that night around the fire, when she confessed her loneliness? How could he have? It didn't make sense.

Anyway, this man wasn't a friend, he was a stranger. She could ask his name, but that would mean sharing hers. "Are you a cockler?" she asked.

The man sat down before replying.

"No, I'm just passing through," he said as he broke off a chunk of bread. "Selling DVDs."

"Oh." Changfa had told her about the DVD sellers. A job for desperate people, he'd said. The bosses are mixed up in bad things. She sat down next to the stranger. He had tired-looking eyes, and lines tugging down the side of his mouth. She began to feel a little sorry for him.

"You have to be careful," she said. His weary smile told her he knew the risks.

Kee Teh opened a can of something, lifted it and said a few words in English before gulping it down. Perhaps he had brought her a friend after all. She turned back to the DVD seller. "How do you know Kee Teh?" she asked.

"We got talking," the man said. He smelled faintly of soap.

It was a scent she'd never noticed before, and she wondered if it meant she stank. If the man thought so, he didn't show it. Instead he chewed slowly, as if he wanted each bite to last a long time.

The dog stretched its head over the tiles and lapped at the pool. The water glimmered with the firelight. Suling thought hard. If this man was moving from town to town, he must know a lot of people, and surely one of them would know where Changfa had gone.

"There were cocklers in this town," she said slowly. "Mostly from Fujian. Did you know any of them?"

The man nodded, as if he had expected her question. "They vanished."

She stared at him. "How did you know?"

He shrugged. "People talk. I heard that a group were picked up by police. Some of the locals were jealous, so they beat them up and then reported them."

Changfa had never mentioned an incident like that. Why wouldn't he tell her? Unless–

"What next?" she asked.

He swallowed. "They were arrested," he said. "They didn't have papers."

The blue lights on the shore road. Beyond the bend. Just about where the car park would be.

She tried to keep her voice steady. "When did that happen?"

The stranger shrugged. "Two weeks back. Maybe more."

She had stopped counting the days. But the moon was half-full when she first arrived at the swimming pool, and it was half-full again now. Two weeks or more of thinking Changfa had abandoned her, not realising she had abandoned him.

"Where were they taken?" she asked. Her voice sounded

high, like a child's. She poked the fire. An ember disintegrated like a burnt-out heart.

"To a prison about fifty kilometres north of here," the man said. "The red heads call it a detention centre, but it's the same thing. There's barbed wire, and guards. You can't go in and can't go out." He shrugged. "Some people are held there for years. That's all I know."

Changfa, locked up. His mother, half a world away, wondering why he'd stopped sending money without a word. And her, thinking the worst of him. What if he had been trying to contact her? "Can they get in touch with their friends?" she asked.

He shook his head. "The guards take away their phones. The only way for them to send a message is the pay phone, if they can afford it. And most of them have no numbers to call."

He seemed to know a lot for a DVD seller, but she had to keep asking, for Changfa's sake. "So they are still close by?" Perhaps she could get a message to him. There must be a way. It was unbearable to think of him alone.

"The women were taken to another prison, hundreds of miles away," the man said. "As for the men... One of them finished off his life." He paused. "Easy way out for him. Bad for business and bad for his family."

He laughed. It was a strange kind of joke to make, and something about the way he said it made her think it wasn't a joke at all. What if he was talking about Changfa? But no, Changfa was always cheerful. Surely he would find a way to cope.

On the other side of the fire, Kee Teh was murmuring to his dog. A firework scattered stars in the night sky.

She tried to stay calm.

"Who are you?" she said, as evenly as she could. "Why are you really here?"

The man tore off another chunk of bread and ate it. "All those cocklers borrowed money," he said, through bites. "And in the last month, none of them have paid their debts." He took a swig from Kee Teh's can. "This world is an unpredictable place. Even today. It was cold, then sunny, then fireworks started going off. You can end up in a prison or become a millionaire. But there's one certainty. Debts must be repaid."

He looked directly at her. "Yours too."

She jumped to her feet. "You're a snakehead."

But he was on his feet too. The weary DVD seller had vanished. The man looking at her moved like a fighter. His eyes flicked from side to side, as if he'd already anticipated her every move.

"I'm just collecting what's due," he said. "It was very clever of you to avoid the police. Or maybe you were just lucky. But you can't escape your debt."

He lowered his voice. Kee Teh put down his can. The dog's brown eyes were on her.

"My car's outside," the debt collector whispered, as if she hadn't spoken. "You can get in it nice and quiet, and you'll be paying off yours by tomorrow." He gripped her arm, and she felt his strength. If she screamed, perhaps Kee Teh would understand what was happening, and his dog would come to her side. But that wouldn't stop him bringing her crashing to the ground. And she knew the kind of business they put girls in.

"Come with me," the debt collector said. "Otherwise I'll have to make you, and you'll pay for it all the same."

The grip tightened. "Forget that boyfriend of yours. You can't help him. You can only help yourself."

It was then she remembered the water behind her. The one thing he wouldn't expect. She hurled herself backwards.

The man's grip had gone. She saw Kee Teh lurch upwards. Then everything was freezing, bubbly, quiet. She needed to move – she wouldn't last long in the deadening cold. And he must be just a few feet away on the tiles. She touched the wall of the far side of the pool and crashed through the surface of the water. She looked for the debt collector, but he wasn't there yet, so she braced herself, found the tiles under her fingertips and forced herself out of the water.

Once on her feet, she saw the source of the light – Kee Teh was crouched over the bonfire, holding the tarpaulin, and the flames were shooting skywards. The courtyard echoed with the barking of his dog. The tarpaulin was already curling around the edges, a foul black smoke filling the air. The wind sent a cloud of it over her, and for a moment she could taste ash.

The debt collector was bent double coughing from the smoke, but then he looked towards her, a flaming branch in his hand. She ran. Through the smoky air, to the passageway, into the dark, away from everything she had built up and made. She thought she heard the man howl, a long, drawn-out screech. Her hands were against the plywood and she tried to force it open, but it seemed to be stuck, and he howled again. She scrabbled at the plywood. Why couldn't she open it? In a moment the debt collector would be upright again, would be thundering down the passageway behind her. She would be caught like a rat in a trap. But no, she couldn't go back to that life. She rushed at the plywood with her shoulder. Suddenly it gave way, and she burst out into the cold night air.

Chapter Twelve

It was Guy Fawkes' night. Arthur had barely left the house since his humiliation outside Jack's door, but he'd never missed the fireworks. He pulled on his great coat, eventually found his hat, and drove as he always had down to the promenade. It was unusually busy on the roads, the main street choked with cars, and he was forced to take a detour to the far end of the prom to park.

Once out of the car, he bent his watch towards the streetlight. Six fifty. "Bugger," he cursed out loud. The fireworks would be starting in just ten minutes,

The prom was long – it stretched for a mile or more. He stopped when he was some distance from the main crowd, a mix of adults in raincoats and a few excited children racing back and forth, just like Margaret had done when she was young.

Six fifty-eight. There was an ongoing rumour that the fireworks display would be retired due to budget cuts or some other excuse. But it had been a fixture since the days of the holidaymakers, so much so that the nickname for the area where the crowd had gathered was Sparks Point.

Gunfire tore through the sky. Enemy fire. Where was he? But no – the kids were cheering. He gripped the railing to steady himself, and the world levelled out again. Red lozenges scattered and were replaced by fizzling plumes and blue carousels. Fireworks.

The confusion passed. The fireworks were still whizzing across the night sky. The family next to him clapped. He was back in the world of seaside amusements, the days when this place was filled with razzmatazz.

Back then, the promenade had been lined with music halls, their stern Victorian facades guarding the decadence within. The cocklers had scoffed at the motts in feathers and men with sly grins and elaborate top hats, called them hoors and tappers. He had too, all the time curious about their soft, pale hands, their made-up faces, the world they came from.

One time, on leave from the Navy, he'd taken the lads to watch. Even though it was wartime, the town was swarming with boys in uniform gagging for some scantily clad dancers. Oh, it had been a wonderful night. They all knew they could die young, of course. But pleasure thrived on danger. That's what Margaret, with her talk of bath rails, didn't understand.

There was a burst of clapping, and he realised the fireworks had ended. The crowd started to disperse. Like milk in a teacup, it was only a few seconds before they would disappear into the thickness of the night. There was a cold wind whipping along the promenade.

"Arthur."

He was perplexed, and then he saw the figure in the chair with the thick scarf round her neck. Angela. He wondered how long she'd been watching him for.

"Fabulous, eh?"

"What?"

"The fireworks," she said. "I got your message."

"What message?"

She coughed. "The one you left."

"Oh." Arthur pulled his hat down to hide his embarrassment. He'd wanted to apologise. But he hadn't. Had he?

"I hope it made sense," he lied.

"I deciphered it." She shivered. "They say snow's coming. How are you getting home?"

"My car's at the other end of the prom. How about you?"

She brandished a small plastic mobile phone. "One of these portable telephone things. I call them on this and they come and collect me. They wanted to climb the railway bridge for a better view."

"So we're going the same way," Arthur said.

They began to follow the crowd back along the promenade. It was rowdier now, as if it had absorbed some of the sparks and bangs, and Arthur noticed how many of the young ones had cans in their hands.

"Oi!" Angela said. One of the can holders had barged into her chair. Arthur wished he was still strong enough to grab him by the shoulders of his silly blue jacket. But the lad was already striding on in the direction of the Star and Rake pub.

"He must really want a drink," Angela said, rubbing her arm.

"He's not getting away with it," Arthur said.

Angela laughed. "I hate to break it to you, but chivalry is dead."

The man turned off the promenade and disappeared through the pub doors. Arthur turned too.

"Where are you going?" she asked.

"I mean it," he said.

"Oh, don't bother about him," Angela protested, but when he held open the door of the pub, she glided right in. It was a long time since Arthur had been there, but it was almost the same: the brown carpet and frayed pub stools, brown wallpaper with raised patterns and etched glass mirrors, and the bar in pride of place, with its shiny brass taps.

The air was thick with smoke and noise. Blue Jacket was at the bar, ordering. He looked about six-feet tall. But Arthur had promised Angela he'd have a word. He sidled up to the bar and waited while Blue Jacket tapped his wallet on the table. Finally, the harassed-looking bartender came up.

"Two of the Wastwater," the Blue Jacket shouted in an out-of-town voice, "Three Biglands and a glass of...what was it again, darling?"

"White wine," a woman with blonde hair bellowed.

Arthur watched them, disgusted. The city visitors always plonked themselves on the best chairs and pulled out wads of cash to buy drinks. They assumed the pub existed to serve them. And yet they only appeared on rare occasions – the races, the fireworks. On Monday, no doubt, it would be almost empty again.

The bartender came back with three pints, their glass frosting with the cold drink inside.

"Don't forget Sandra's G&T," the woman with blonde hair shouted.

"Oh, damn." The Blue Jacket gestured to the bartender, who was by the till. "Hey – hey, wait a sec."

Arthur saw his chance. While Blue Jacket was gesturing, he picked up two of the pints and walked off slowly to the corner where Angela had wedged her chair.

"Revenge is best served cold," he said, putting them down.

"You didn't."

"There are benefits to being old." He felt giddy now. "Come on, let's find out if he has good taste."

They sipped their pints. Angela, who had the better view, kept up a running commentary.

"He's just realised the pints are gone – he's asking if they picked them up already. Oh, now they've clocked that they've disappeared. He's looking around, he's looking around – he's asking a lad in a suit. Seems like that didn't go down very well. Now he's asking a woman, and she's waving her wine glass at him." She sipped her beer. "If he accuses you, what are you going to say?"

"Well, he'd have to prove it first. But I'm very forgetful these days. And people hardly notice me."

"Oh, he's storming out the door to ask the people outside." She smiled and lifted her glass. "Cheers."

*

After watching the man in the blue jacket shout at the bartenders for ten minutes, begrudgingly order another round and then stomp around looking for a table, they left. It had been a good pint.

On the promenade, the sky still crackled with fireworks. Angela sniffed and wrinkled her nose. "These bonfires are really something."

Arthur envied the acuteness of her senses. "I can't smell much any more," he said.

"Walking must be some consolation," Angela said. "Oh, and not dying in the next year."

They kept going. The crowd was thinning now, and old leaves whirled across the tarmac. The town's curtains had been drawn against the autumn night.

"I like the bangs," Angela said. "Reminds me of the war. Bloody exciting that was."

Arthur looked out at the darkness of the bay. "Did you ever see the foxfire?" he asked. "It's like the bay is made of fireworks."

"I didn't know it existed," Angela said. He heard a note of sadness in her voice.

"Well, fireworks are better anyway," he said hastily.

The night of the foxfire he had gone out shrimping. His horse had been terrified. Every movement of Penny's hooves in the water was like a sparkler in the dark. Even the shrimps glowed. He hadn't had a camera in those days. The next year, he joined up, and he never saw it again.

There were just a few other people on the prom now, anonymous in their hoods and scarves. Ahead of them was the hulk of the old lido. "Why did you park all the way along here?" Angela asked.

"It was busy in town."

She sniffed again. "You really can't smell the bonfires? The whole place reeks."

He was about to tell her he couldn't, but then a gust of wind hit them and suddenly he was immersed in a sour, dusty pungency.

"Smells like burning plastic," he said. "The kids these days. That's the problem with this town – the only ones born now are little scruffs."

Angela pulled out the mobile phone. "I'd better ring them." She jabbed at it and pressed it to her ear. "Hello, darling? Yes, I'm near the car park. Just come and get me."

She dropped the phone into her lap. "They'll be here in a minute," she said.

The long walk had gone by without him noticing. And now he only had a minute to ask her. She could do what she did before and throw it back to him, but he had to try. "So my daughter is looking for a care home."

"Sheltered housing," Angela said, her eyes flicking along

the promenade. "I heard it from my son, who heard it from Margaret."

"Bloody nonsense," Arthur said. "I'm managing fine on my own."

"Tell me about it," Angela said. Her eyes crinkled and for a second, he felt as he had all those years ago with the Navy lads – that they were allies, arms linked against the world.

"The thing is," Arthur said. "It was Gertie she was close to. And now she's gone – sometimes I feel like she has a grudge against me. Like she's looking for an excuse."

Angela coughed. "Then don't give her one," she said. "Look, here they are." She waved at three figures in the darkness. She held out a hand, and Arthur took it. "Think of it a different way. Think how loyal to her mother she must be."

She let go of his hand. "Thanks for the pint," she said, and she motored off towards her family.

Chapter Thirteen

The sky was still exploding with bangs and stars and whistles, and there were people on the promenade. Every move they made was menacing, like they might reach out and grab Suling at any moment. The debt collector could be one of them. He could have pushed through the boards; he could be right behind her. Suling darted through the people and under the bridge which led to the streets of the town. It was quieter here, except for the occasional shriek and explosion above the roofs. The thudding of her shoes betrayed her. She needed to go somewhere quieter still, somewhere secret, where she could become invisible again.

She'd found the sheets in a garden. It was too small, too close to the house to risk except in the dead of night. But up on the hill there were other gardens, rambling ones where the grass grew tall, as if no one had thought about cutting it for a long time. Perhaps there was a corner there she could curl up in, where no one could touch her.

She trudged up the hill, her eyes on the ground to avoid attracting attention. She was soaking wet, and only the burn of her muscles kept her warm. As the hill grew steeper, the street emptied. The fireworks were less frequent too, although every now and then she turned her head to see stars exploding over the town.

At the top of the hill, she found the garden she was thinking of. Long grass soaked her ankles when she let herself in by the back gate. But the house itself blazed with light. She slumped against the garden fence. Only a few hours ago, she'd had a fire, provisions and a mattress to bed down on afterwards. Now all she had was this body, rapidly cooling in the night air.

Something cold landed on her neck. Snow. She had seen pictures, but it was still a shock to feel it, so light, on her skin. She put her hand out and marvelled at the flakes. Once she'd imagined making snowmen with Changfa, wrapped up in a hat and scarf amid the Christmas lights.

But Changfa was locked up. That was what the debt collector said. He had nowhere to hide. His life was over before it had even begun.

She shivered. If she stayed here, she would freeze. She needed to find somewhere to shelter for the night, fast. She peered over the fence at the garden next door. She had been there before too – the vegetable patch had potatoes she'd unearthed and later roasted on a fire. She knew little about the house itself. Someone lived there, because there was always one or two lamps on, but she'd never seen them. Perhaps they preferred being invisible too.

The house had a wooden outbuilding – a garage, perhaps. It would be warmer than out here, at least. She took a run at the fence and jumped over.

The outbuilding looked like it could collapse at any moment. Its wooden walls had once been painted – it was hard to tell exactly what colour in the dark – but now it was flaking and rotten. The corrugated metal door was locked, but a window was open. She wedged her feet into the branches of a nearby bush, and using all her remaining strength, hauled herself in.

The dark smelled of engine oil and wood shavings. It was still cold, but there was no wind, no wet kiss of snow.

Something gleamed in the dark. She felt metal under dust, the rubber tires of a bicycle.

A clatter. She froze. Then silence again. She must have just knocked something over. She felt slowly around the room. It was satisfying to hold so many objects again, to stroke the man-made smoothness of a hammer handle, to trace the preciseness of a length of twine. And, finally, to touch what she was looking for – the plastic switch of a torch.

She pressed it and saw where she was for the first time. She was standing in some sort of garage, filled by the clutter of time – the bicycle, its front wheel missing, a spade, a confusion of tools, yellowed newspapers covered with broken bits of plant pot and under them, to her delight, a couch. On the floor was a rake, the source of the clatter.

She cleared the newspapers off the couch, swapped her wet clothes for a dusty jumper, unhooked some coats hanging on a peg by the door and lay down under them. The couch was worn and uneven, but it was the comfiest she had been in a long time. With the coats over her head, and her eyes shut, she could almost imagine she was in a bed of her own. It would do for a night, at least – she'd be able to think more clearly in the morning. For now, her mind was assaulted by unhappy facts. The man hunting her. The debt she owed. Changfa caught. Not a prison, but like a prison. Was he one of the ones beaten by the locals? Did he think of her when the police arrived?

You can't help him, the debt collector had said. You can only help yourself. She pulled the coats tighter and imagined a high-speed train carrying her away into a tunnel of sleep.

Chapter Fourteen

It was after Arthur finally started the car that the snow began to fall. Just the odd flake at first, but soon clumps in the corner of his windscreen. When he reached the house, it was cold. "Damn nuisance," he cursed the boiler. This central heating timing thing was so fiddly. But when he looked closely, it seemed the problem was to do with the pressure.

He was too tired to look at manuals that night, so he opened the airing cupboard and took out the woollen blankets. They were thick, woven ones – blankets he'd had since he was a child, before central heating existed, in the days when every working person was locked in a common battle with the cold. He spread them on the bed and fell asleep with the fireworks still ringing in his ears.

The next morning it was very hard to get out of bed, its cosiness intensified by the sharpness of the air. When he finally made a pot of tea, he saw it was still snowing. "Damn nuisance." He liked the snow – when it was warm inside. But of course the boiler would choose this moment to have a razzie. He knew it well – over the years he'd built up a relationship with it, come to recognise its tempers and tantrums. You had to if you were the man of the house, at least in his day. Not like Margaret, with her list of people to call if the slightest thing went wrong.

He got dressed in extra layers. The snow was falling thickly now, rubbing out the winter colours with each flake. Watching it, he couldn't help feeling a bit excited. The phone rang. He thought of Angela waving goodbye on the promenade. It had been good to have some company. She'd promised to visit soon. But it was Margaret. It was always Margaret. He tried to repress his agitation.

"Hi, Dad, how are you?" she said. "Just thought I'd give you a ring." He could hear the chatter of her office in the background.

"I'm fine," Arthur said.

"We've had some weather warnings here," she continued as if he hadn't spoken. "Be careful on the pavements, it's very slippery. There's a service the church runs delivering shopping for the elderly. I'll put you—"

"No," Arthur cut in before she could say any more. "I'll do my own shopping."

"But—"

"No-one knows the things I like," he said.

Margaret huffed. "You like the same as everyone else, Dad. Tuna, and cheddar cheese, and white bread—"

"There are lots of different types of bread."

"You eat the regular kind," Margaret said. "Look, I was just checking in as I'm getting seconded to Hull for a fortnight, but if you need me to drop—"

"I'm fine." Arthur remembered Angela's warning. Don't give her an excuse. "Thank you," he added carefully.

"I'd better go. I'm off my break," Margaret said.

"Bye."

"Bye."

He put the phone down and went back to watching the swirling sky outside. But Margaret's phone call had spoiled it.

Well, at least he could still mend a boiler. He pulled on his jacket and wellies. The steps outside were slippery but nothing he couldn't manage. He tipped his head back, and for a second he was eight again, sticking out his tongue to taste the snow. He walked carefully to the garage and let himself in. Honestly, Margaret was worrying for nothing. He'd manoeuvred through that snow as skilfully as he used to navigate the sands. He was a country lad, after all. And the toolbox was on the shelf – he'd just grab it, and –

BAM.

Chapter Fifteen

Suling heard the racket first. It was only when she peeked out from under the coats she saw the man, lying face down, very still. She could see he'd hit his head, and the blood was already starting to spread across the dusty floor.

Next to him lay the rake, the one she had toppled the night before. *I killed him, I killed him*, she thought.

But then she heard him moan. Before she had time to think, she was off the couch and crouched beside him.

"Don't die," she told him in Hokkien. "Are you alright? You can't die."

He was alive. It scared her to look at him, so she stared straight ahead. A rag stuffed in the bicycle basket caught her eye. It would stop the bleeding, at least. She grabbed it and held it against his head.

"Don't worry," she said. "I'm here."

The man's fingers trembled. She patted his shoulder, the way she would a small child, and this seemed to calm him. Very gently, still holding the rag to his head, she guided him to a seated position. The skin of his hand was loose, and she could feel the bones. Now she saw he was old, old enough to have a face that was told in wrinkles, like a shadow of the bigger, fatter person he once was. Blood trickled down the lines. His nose and ears seemed too big. He had light grey eyes and only a little hair left around his ears. With his blood-red face and twisted mouth, he looked like a demon on a temple wall. Yet she felt only pity.

"Okay," she said, in English this time, and she draped the coats from the couch around him. There was a scarf in one of the pockets, and she wrapped it round his head to hold the bandage in place while she hunted for something better. When she had fallen off a bicycle as a child, her mother had known exactly what to do. Now she was in a strange country, clueless.

"Hold still while I clean the wound," her mother had scolded as she squirmed under a water tap. "You don't know what's climbing in there." She opened drawers full of rusty nails and screws, all the while aware of the blood quietly seeping out of the man slumped nearby. Finally, she found some old sticking plasters in a green bag, and a tube that looked like antiseptic cream. When she unwrapped the bandage, the wound in his forehead stared at her like an accusing third eye. She hid it with the plasters as best she could.

That day of the bike fall, her mother had checked nothing was broken. Now it was Suling's turn to check the old man. First she held his hands, then she gently moved his arms, and shoulders.

The man let her do it. He had stopped moaning, but seemed in shock. His skin was clammy. "Can we go to the house?" she asked him in Hokkien, as she checked his knees. His face contorted in pain. "Not yet," she answered herself. After her own fall, her mother had held her close. She would have to stay with him at least a little longer. There were so many ways an old man could die.

She shut the door on the whirling snow. There was a stove in the corner. With some old newspapers and a box of matches, it didn't take her long to get it going. Then she wheeled the bike out of the way and helped him onto the couch. It was only once he was lying there and she was squatting next to him, squeezing his hand, that she wondered what she had done.

Chapter Sixteen

Blasted eejit, Arthur thought. What a way to go – Margaret coming back from her business trip to find him cowped over on the floor. But he was sitting upright now, and someone had their hands on his shoulders. Was he being attacked? He didn't understand what they were saying. He was in pain, as if the floor had clouted him with a concrete fist. Which, in fact, it had.

It was hard to see out of his left eye. It seemed to be swelling, and his right was very short-sighted. His glasses had broken in the fall. He could make out a person with dark hair, a girl or a youngish lad, moving with purpose around him. If he could, he would have stood up and shouted. But when he opened his mouth, no words came out, and the next thing he knew the stranger was pressing a cloth against his lip, and when they pulled it away he saw it was bloody.

Now he was on an old couch, which had somehow hopped out of the corner and placed itself in front of a burning fire.

He shut his eyes. He thought of Gertie, *that* night, the moment he realised something was wrong. He had been consumed with his own horror at what was happening. It was only later that he thought about how she might have felt. The doctors had assured him it was painless, that many people longed to die in their sleep, but that was the kind thing to say to a widower. And Sid? What was worse, the knowledge that oblivion was rolling towards you, or the moment it crashed into your mouth?

The stranger patted his shoulder. He forced his eyes open. They were holding his hand, moving it between theirs, keeping it warm. Who were they? Had they come from next door? He stared at the flames. He had gone into the garage to get the tools to fix the boiler. It was snowy outside. He had tripped. And then this nervous, twitchy person had come out of nowhere to help him.

Watching the fireworks with Angela seemed a long time ago. He saw himself moving through the pub, dodging the drinkers, as if in an old film.

The stranger let go of his hand. They put another log on the fire and mumbled something. He realised that he didn't want the stranger to go, but he couldn't move from the couch. "Who are you?" he asked, through his bust lip.

He felt the stranger's hand on his shoulder, as if they were trying to reassure him, and then the hand lifted, leaving only the draught.

Chapter Seventeen

The door to the house was unlocked. Suling hesitated on the threshold. Even in the confusion of the last few hours, she couldn't help feeling a sense of anticipation. She'd never stepped inside a house in this country before. The miserable place where the cocklers lived didn't really count.

She pushed the door open slowly. Although she felt sure the uncle lived alone, she stopped and listened for footsteps, just in case. All was quiet. She kicked off her shoes and stood on the soft, carpeted floor.

It was the grandest house she'd ever entered. The ceiling was high, the walls patterned with an imprint of flowers. When she flicked the light switch, a crystal lampshade cast triangular shadows onto the wall. Somewhere down the corridor, she could hear the tick tock of a clock.

She padded slowly through the house, opening one door after another. There was a kitchen lined with cupboards and a fridge, a half-drunk cup of tea on the table. The old man must have made it that morning, just before he decided to go into the garage. There were two bedrooms, both carpeted. One was almost empty, but for a bed and a photograph of a girl on the wall. There was an abacus on the window ledge. She pushed the wooden beads back and forth. If she made enough money here, she could build her mother a house like this back home. And yet so far in this country she was penniless.

The other room was strewn with socks and books, and woollen blankets. She thought of the old man hunched on the couch and gathered them up in her arms.

A telephone stood on a table in the hall. She picked it up and listened to the dial tone. It thrummed with possibility. If she knew the number for a doctor, she could ring them and leave before they arrived. But she knew no numbers in this country.

There was a bathroom, with a throne-like toilet and a bath and a mirror. The stranger looking out of it made her freeze. They had brown skin, crow feather hair, and cheekbones where soft, fat cheeks used to be. The stranger looked hungry.

"Get a haircut," Suling told the stranger in Hokkien, and the stranger mouthed the same thing back at her.

There was a frosted door that opened into a big, light-filled room with a huge window looking over the town. The house was on the side of a hill, and the view was so striking she dropped the blankets on a chair and just took it all in. Everything that day was white. The sky was white, the sand of the bay was white, and the roofs of the town, with dark chasms in between, were white. It was as if the town was mourning for summer, or whatever the time with green leaves could be called. Changfa had told her it was like jade then – green and beautiful and cold. He'd promised to take her for a walk in the park when that season came around again, in the early morning before the ghosts rose.

Ghosts like the old uncle, alone in the garage. She got to work. The water coming out of the taps was cold, so she boiled the kettle and filled a bowl with hot water, then soaked the noodles she'd found in a cupboard until they were soft enough to eat. She picked up as many blankets as she could carry and crossed back to the garage where the old uncle was still on the couch.

"Here," she said in her own tongue, putting down the bowls of noodles. "Eat."

He seemed to understand. She handed him a wet cloth, and he wiped his face slowly, until he no longer looked like a demon but just a pinkish old man. They ate their plain noodles together. Suling wished she'd hunted for some sauces, but the old uncle slurped them down. Then he pulled the woollen blankets around him and shut his eyes.

Chapter Eighteen

Arthur woke to the flicker of the fire in the stove. It must be almost dark again. The stranger – a girl, he thought, as they had cooked noodles – was somewhere in the shadows. His eyes rose to the snow-covered windowpane. In the old days, when the snow came, everything ground to a halt. The schools would close because children didn't have the boots to get there, the fishermen became whittlers, close to the fire, and there would always be someone who got stranded. His parents would stay up late talking in hushed voices about how much food they had left. Even though they were dead and gone, the memory made him shiver.

The stranger crouched by the fire.

"Hey," he said. "Who are you?"

She didn't reply at first. He tried again. "What is your name?"

This time she looked at him, and he could make out the blur of two dark eyes. "Sue," she said. At least it sounded like that.

"What are you doing here?" he asked. "Why were you in my garage?"

But she shook her head. Either she didn't understand, or she didn't want to answer. He realised with a chill that she didn't have to. He could barely move from the couch, and she was young and strong and nimble. She could do anything she wanted.

The stranger stood up abruptly. Had his questions angered her? She prowled around the garage, and in every deft, firm step he heard the sureness of her youth. He hadn't realised youth had a sound until he lost his own, nor how threatening it could be. Where the hell had she appeared from, anyway? He didn't remember seeing anyone when he left his house. How long had she been in the garage? Or was his memory playing tricks on him? He didn't like either possibility.

The steps were a little too fast now, as if the stranger was restless, or frustrated. Something hadn't gone to plan. But what? Had she just been mucking around? A robbery? She could have run and left him on the floor.

Before he could think of any more scenarios, she was looming over him. She placed a hand on his arm. Her touch was gentle.

"Yes?" she said.

She crouched down so he could grip her arm. Slowly, she raised him to his feet. Everything ached. He tried not to black out as the blood rushed to his head. Then he took a step forward. He was walking. One foot in front of another, into the unknown.

They reached the garage door and stepped out into the snow. Sue's arm was everything now, the ground beneath him threatening to unravel at any moment. His first footsteps in the snow must still be there, dimples filled in by the flakes. He felt a hundred years older than when he'd made them. Then they were through the door and – without even taking off his boots – into the living room.

His armchair was waiting. He collapsed onto it, reached for his spare pair of glasses, and looked at Sue properly for the first time.

He knew immediately she could not be from the house next door. She was a foreigner – oriental. Just a girl, a small one at that, her dark hair level with the top of the armchair. And she looked poor, not in the tracksuit-and-belly fat way that passed for being poor now, but the way being poor looked in his childhood. She was scrawny, with hollowed out cheeks, and she had a wary expression, like she might flit at any moment. She was biting her lip, the way Margaret used to do when she was nervous.

Poor and foreign and scared – she was too helpless to be a robber. Only homeless, if she was sleeping in his garage.

But she had picked him up, nursed him and fed him. And she was already moving backwards, as if she could turn and run at any moment.

"Thank you," he said.

He should at least walk her to the door, see her out to wherever she was going. He beckoned her to help him up and she did so, with a deferential obedience that startled him in someone so young. Perhaps they treated their elders differently where she was from. She could only be a teenager, or maybe in her early twenties. Perhaps she still had grandparents. Gertie had always wanted to be a nan, although she'd been careful not to mention it when Margaret was around.

They were moving through the hall now, past the side table with his letters, and the kitchen with its mugs and biscuits, the lamp still glowing from when he'd switched it on that morning. They were almost at the door now. It was her that turned the handle, and as she did he noticed the holes in her jumper and wondered where her coat was. Then she opened the door, and he was knocked breathless by the blast of cold air. The snow was falling again – flakes were caught for a moment like moths in the porch light.

She placed his hand on the radiator so he was steady, then let go. He stood there, swaying slightly. Her jumper was cable knit. Like the jumpers his mother used to make by the fire on those nights of snow.

The snow would fill her footprints, erase all traces of her, and time would do the same to his bruises.

But it was dark already, and there were holes in her clothes, and she was only a girl.

"Why don't you stay?" he said. "Just until the snow stops."

Chapter Nineteen

Suling was still scared of the old uncle, but the snow was falling again – beautiful and white and murderous – and it was night already. What use would it be to anyone if she ended up frozen in a field? So instead, she was standing awkwardly in the old uncle's kitchen while he slowly and painfully filled up the kettle and found two mugs in a cupboard. Every now and then she glanced at the phone on the wall. He could pick it up at any moment. But she sensed some sort of truce, as if the old uncle didn't want to call for help any more than she did. Anyway, he was too frail to stop her running out of the door. One night, that was all – just until the snow melted.

The old man handed her a mug. The familiar fragrance of tea knocked her – suddenly she was back with Changfa in the factory, the pattern at the bottom of the bowls growing clearer, telling them there wasn't much time left. But before she could take a sip, the man had flicked the foil cap off a glass bottle of milk and poured it into the mugs. She looked at him in mute outrage. He, on the other hand, smiled for the first time through his swollen lips. "Nah seh cah peh tee," he said.

The tea looked like mud now, but she had better smile and not provoke him. The uncle added a cube of sugar to his cup. He stirred it with a spoon, took a sip, and smiled again. "Nah seh cah peh tee," he repeated as he collapsed onto a chair.

She sipped her tea. It tasted clogged, but it was warm, and that in itself was a luxury. She smiled, which seemed to make the uncle deliriously happy. "Nah seh cah peh tee," he exclaimed. This must be some form of the polite nonsense they liked to speak to each other here, at least according to Changfa, who had read up about it. She found her dictionary and looked up the words, one by one. Tea was easy. Cup she matched with the one in his hand. The rest was guesswork.

"Nice cup of tea," she said eventually. The old uncle smiled.

The tea made her realise how cold she was. The old uncle had shown her, with a lot of pointing, that the machine that heated the house wasn't working. Now, as they sipped their tea, he picked up an envelope and began to draw. She recognised a child-like spanner. He could fix it, he just needed the tools.

"Don't worry, I'll find them," she said in her own language, before remembering he couldn't understand a word, and switching to English instead. "OK." She finished her tea, trudged back to the garage and searched for them using the torch and the last of the stove light. It was strange what a difference a day made. When she'd first entered the garage, she'd felt lucky. Now, she sensed her own desperation.

There was the toolbox, a few feet from where he fell. No doubt he'd been reaching for it. She picked it up and walked back towards the lights of the house.

She found the old uncle fiddling with the machine and humming. His bandage was slipping over his eye and his forehead was starting to turn a funny shade of yellow, but he seemed cheerful. He waved to her to put the toolbox on a stool. After that, it didn't take him long to prise off the lid and fix it.

The effect was magical. The machine rumbled into life, and although the windows were still icy to the touch, the house began to warm up. The long metal panel she'd been leaning against got hotter and hotter. She began to be aware of the heaviness of the jumpers on her, and how smoky and earthy they smelled. The old uncle disappeared into the bathroom, and she heard the splash of water.

She wandered into the living room. The white vision she had seen earlier through the big window was replaced by lunar drifts. Her mother had told her the tale of the goddess stranded on the moon. But Chang'e could look down on the lover left behind, and she had no idea how to find Changfa.

The old uncle came out of the bathroom and indicated that it was her turn.

The mirror was steamed up. The room had the sweet artificial smell of soap. Suling locked the door. Now no-one could reach her – not the old uncle, not the debt collector, not the police, no-one.

Peeling her clothes off, she wondered if she reeked. The old uncle had filled the bath full of hot water for her, which made her think she probably did. She dipped her toe in and recoiled – it was like jumping into a bowl of steaming tea. But after a few attempts, she found she could slide her whole foot in. Then, very carefully, she lowered herself into the bath.

The water made her feel weightless. She tried to stay alert for the rap on the door, or any other sign that it was time for her to hurry up and get out, but there was silence. After a while she realised there was never going to be one. The old uncle was somewhere else in this vast house, and unlike the factory, there was no queue of impatient girls outside.

Changfa would have loved a bath like this. She pictured his head against the tiles, the flash of his cheeky grin before he disappeared beneath the bubbles. But thinking about Changfa was too painful. Instead, she shut her eyes and imagined the house she would build for her mother, once she had found a proper job. It would be modern, with sparkling white tiles. The walls would be hung with the kind of prints she'd seen through art shop windows in Putian. There would be sleek, dark wood furniture and latticework on the doors. A bathroom with a marble sink and lights around the mirror. So long as she kept her eyes shut, it was real.

She was on the other side of the window now, a luxurious, beautiful place, but it was scary too, because it softened you up.

She opened her eyes and scrubbed her arms hard, until the water was black and her skin red.

Chapter Twenty

Arthur found some sheets on a shelf he didn't have to reach for, folded them in half and laid them on the spare bed. Gertie would have made it up as well, but he could barely make his own, even when his arms weren't aching. Sue would have to work it out. He laid some of Margaret's old clothes next to the sheets and was just leaving when the door of the bathroom opened, and she appeared. With her towel slung around her neck she looked like a boxer. He pointed to the door of the spare room.

"Thank you," she said. He retreated to his own bedroom and shut the door firmly behind him.

What had he done? God knows who he'd just invited into his home for the night. If Margaret knew…

Margaret. He caught a glimpse of his reflection in the mirror. Crusted blood on his forehead, his face the colour of a sunset, his fat lip. It was all the proof she needed. He couldn't cope. He was a danger to himself. She'd parcel him off to a home there and then.

A momentary miscalculation, that was all, and he'd landed face-first on the hard garage floor. If Sue hadn't been there, would he ever have managed to get up again? Margaret would have seized the house, and no doubt she'd be quick to dismantle it. The stack of magazines he'd never got round to sorting – into a black bag. The photo of Gertie above the desk – onto her wall. The books and mugs and carvings that were the flotsam of their lives together – charity shop.

She was nothing if not thorough, Margaret. She'd go through it all, like a detective, assessing every object, weighing it up against her obligations to her senile old dad. He moved slowly over to the wardrobe. His suits still hung inside – one for every promotion – next to Gertie's favourite dresses. Underneath them was the cardboard box he'd taken home from his office. It was full of things that Margaret would find meaningless. A pen he'd been given at a conference. A cheap glass award etched with the words 'Accountant of the Year 1985'.

At his retirement party, he hadn't realised a life was ending. The next day, he came into the office with a pounding hangover, collected his cardboard box and drove back from work for the last time. Gertie had met him at the door. She'd poured him a glass of sparkling wine and smiled. "Here's to my husband," she'd said, almost gleefully. They'd clinked glasses to the end of his career. And even though it had taken years of night school to get his qualifications, he hadn't mourned him, the accountant – at least not until Gertie died and he was just an old man with a picture of a woman on the wall and a cardboard box in his cupboard.

Margaret would pack him a box to go to the care home. A box of things an old man should have – soap, a book, warm knitted jumpers. Nothing that mattered to him at all.

He brushed his hand against a pin-striped suit, and it swayed as if it could hear the pianist playing in the hotel lobby. He'd always loved conference season. Maybe too much. The suit jacket was lined with silk, and it crackled when he touched the inner pocket. He felt inside and drew out a crumpled piece of paper. A bill for a dinner he couldn't remember. But he read it now – two bottles of champagne, chicken kiev, black forest gateau. One of the conference girls on the other side of the table, her laugh dancing like the candlelight.

If Margaret had found it, what would she picture? How, in that machine-like mind of hers, would she process it? Would it result in less care home visits? A tighter budget for his last years? Should he destroy it now, along with anything else that could be used against him, until there was nothing but empty space?

After he'd finished the bottle with Gertie that day, he'd put the cardboard box in the cupboard and got out a map of the fells. The next morning they'd set out in their walking boots and not stopped until they were high – high enough to see their home, nestled by the woods on the edge of the town and the shimmering bay, and almost out of sight, the rocky outcrop with the small, dark cottages where he was born.

Good or bad, virtuous or sinful, the house was the museum of his time on earth, and he its keeper. He couldn't let Margaret separate them. He just needed to find a way to manage until the bruises faded.

It was half past nine. Hardly late, but he was already weary. He checked the front door was locked and started switching off the lights. When he passed the spare room, he paused. The door was half open and a slab of light fell across the dark path of the hall.

"Hello?" he said softly. There was no reply. He pushed the door open a little and saw the girl in Margaret's old pyjamas, collapsed on the bed. The rise and fall of her shoulders told him she was already asleep.

He turned out the light and withdrew, before feeling his way along the hall to his room. The night light flickered like a guiding star. "You're fine until you trip," Gertie had said when she bought it. "That's when old age gets you." It got her another way, of course, but she was still right. The girl had helped him back onto his feet. Now he had to stay there. Margaret must never see his weakness, never see how easily he tumbled.

He closed the wardrobe door, climbed into bed, and let sleep claim him.

Chapter Twenty-One

The bed was too comfortable. She'd dreamed of Changfa. With a monumental effort, Suling rolled over to the edge of the mattress and let gravity force her out of bed.

She tried the door and it swung open silently. So she wasn't a prisoner. Still, she had to be careful. The old uncle could call the authorities any time. Or perhaps he would not. She had heard of women who ended up in the service of elderly men in this country, feeding them, pretending to love them, cutting their toenails.

She picked up the clothes she'd dropped in a heap by the bed the night before and sniffed them. They smelled of her life on the promenade. They also smelled very pungent. She looked through the pile of clothes the old uncle had left for her and found a pair of black trousers, and a pale blue polo neck. Perhaps they belonged to the girl whose portrait hung on the wall. Either way, they seemed suitable, if slightly old-fashioned. She put them on.

The corridor was lined with the same soft carpet. As she padded along it, she could hear rustling sounds, and crackly piano music from a radio. A faint burning smell jarred with this calm, clean world.

Light was pouring through a frosted glass door. The first thing she saw when she pushed it open was the bay, framed in the big window, all silvery whorls and tawny haze. Then the snow, white as incense ash, covering everything.

She heard footsteps behind her and turned to see the old uncle standing in the doorway. His face still bore the marks of the fall the day before, and the area around his left eye was swollen and purple. At the same time she noticed the phone, on a small table by the bookshelf. He could reach it in two steps if he wanted to. That was all it would take to call the police and turn her in.

Take the initiative, Changfa had always said. Don't wait. She put three sounds together she'd practised many times under her breath, but never spoken. "Good Morh Ning."

A look of confusion passed over the old uncle's face. She repeated the three syllables. Then he exclaimed: "Ahh." He'd understood. "Good morning," he repeated.

She quickly said the next phrase she'd been rehearsing. "Thank you."

He replied again, a long string of words she couldn't understand, his voice flying up at the end of each one. She shook her head, embarrassed. He opened his mouth and pretended to chew. She understood that.

"Breakfast," he said.

"Breakfast," she repeated. An offer of food was a good sign – mostly. She thought of the debt collector chewing bread by the fire and shuddered.

In the kitchen, the old uncle set a big tray on the table. It held several slices of blackened bread, the source of the burning smell. Next to them stood a brown jar with a gaudy label, a very round teapot, a glass bottle of milk, two mugs, a slab of some kind of spread, knives and forks, and one thing she was relieved to recognise – a fried egg on a plate.

The uncle took the bread. He pointed: "Toast." He began adding the spread: "Butter". Then he slipped the bread under the fried egg and handed it to her: "Egg."

"Thank you," she said. She picked up the knife and fork. She and Changfa had tried them for fun once or twice in Putian, but they'd always gone back to chopsticks. Now they lay awkwardly in her hands. She tried to cut the bread with the knife but only succeeded in pushing it up and down the plate. She stabbed the egg with the fork. The yolk oozed over the bread and formed a golden pool on the plate. A second attempt with the knife slipped.

She laughed in embarrassment, and the old uncle started to laugh too. "Here," he said, and, picking up his own cutlery, showed her how to hold the toast in place with the fork while he sawed bits away with the knife. He nodded at her. "Now you." Suling tried again and this time she managed to carve off a bite-sized piece. It tasted crisp and salty.

The old uncle took the pot and filled the mugs with the milk-clogged tea. Next he unscrewed the brown jar. Out came something black and sticky, like tar. He spread it on his toast with a knife, and then cut the whole thing in half and offered her a piece. "Good," he said.

"Good," she repeated. She bit into the toast and almost gagged – it was so rotten. The uncle cackled. She tried a word from the dictionary. "Bad." The uncle laughed even harder, and she found herself smiling, despite herself. Perhaps he's mad, she thought hopefully.

The old uncle handed her a mug. "Breakfast tea," he said.

"Breakfast tea," she repeated. And then, in a burst of inspiration, she lied: "Breakfast tea are good."

"Very good," the old uncle crowed.

Her first proper sentence. It was like turning a key and hearing the pins click into place. If words could become sentences, then sentences could be conversations, and conversations could be directions to train stations and introductions and job offers. She took another bite of toast, a bit without the black spread this time, crunchy and warm. I'm inside, she thought. I'm on the other side of the glass. And who knows where the doorways lead.

The old uncle sipped his tea. He seemed harmless enough, she thought, as she picked up the dirty plates. Not like the cockle buyers, who scowled as they barked their negotiations across the rain-swept car park. Just an elderly man. She could make herself useful, have a few more meals and then find her way to a train station. There must be maps somewhere in the house.

She picked up the bottle of washing up liquid and drooled it over a sponge. Then she turned on the tap to full blast.

Water splashed everywhere. She turned off the tap, but it was too late – the old uncle had already risen to his feet, mug still in hand. He screeched as tea slopped over the sides. Then he must have dropped it, because the mug was on the floor, the hot, brown liquid trickling between the fragments of pottery. She didn't hear the smash as much as feel it.

The old uncle was shouting like a firecracker. At her, at the mug, at the hot tea – she didn't know. The bits of his face that weren't already purple or yellow blazed red. Veins popped at his neck. His eyes were sparks of rage.

She'd broken everything. She had to go. The old uncle was still spitting venom, but her legs had taken over, and she was out in the hall, trying to wrestle her jumper off the hook. It writhed stubbornly this way and that, as if it didn't want to part from the house, but eventually she managed to slip the loop of ribbon over the brass, throw it around her shoulders, and pull the bolt from the door. She didn't need to understand the old uncle to know it was time to leave.

Chapter Twenty-Two

The wretched girl had splashed water everywhere. She'd made him break his mug. And when he asked her what the hell she was doing, she'd just stared at him like he was a strange animal, and then bolted.

"Daft foreign donnat," he shouted through the empty kitchen door. She'd no right to stare at him like that. It was his house, his country, and his bloody mug on the floor.

He looked at his feet. Shards of mug like icebergs on a brown sea. Another little bit of his life broken. Now he'd have to fetch the dustpan and brush from the cupboard under the sink, crouch down and sweep it up. Sue could have done the whole thing in a moment.

The front door slammed. "Hey, wait a minute," he called, but there was only the sound of the kitchen clock. He looked out of the window and saw Sue tearing away up the drive like she'd seen a ghost.

He took a deep breath and lowered himself slowly with one hand on the counter until he was level with the cupboard, reached for the dustpan handle, and on the third attempt managed to grip it. There was no point even trying to crouch, so he moved his hand to the drawer and settled himself carefully on his knees. As he swept, his anger turned to frustration. The tap was temperamental, that's all he'd wanted to tell her, but the hot tea had scalded his hand. How was he to know she'd spook at a few cross words?

He reached for a chair and, summoning all his strength, hauled himself upwards again. The breakfast stuff was still on the table. He'd laid out a real spread – he'd wanted to feel like a generous host. Now he felt like an eejit.

The doorbell rang.

Perhaps Sue hadn't left after all. He was shuffling towards the door when he remembered Margaret. What if she'd come back from Hull? He wouldn't put it past her. Could a hat hide the bruises? No – if it was Margaret, he had better just come up with some excuse for not seeing her. He could shout it through the letterbox. Only then she might worry more. Well, he had no choice. He would just have to say it without moving too much, because the pain would make him flinch.

He peered through the peephole. Not Sue. Not Margaret.

"You look like a bloody monster," Angela said when he opened the door, her eyebrows rising. She coughed. "I told your daughter I'd check in on you. God, I've let her down. What happened?"

So Margaret was watching him, even when she was on the other side of the country. "I tripped and fell," Arthur said. "It looks worse than it is."

"I should hope so," Angela said. "Was it the snow? I saw footprints."

There was no need to tell her about Sue. "The garage," he said hastily.

She winced. "Surprised you ever got up again."

Only with Sue's arm under his, slowly guiding him towards the light of the house. He shrugged. "I managed."

"And can you" – Angela nodded towards the depths of his house – "cope and everything?"

She'd seemed like a friend that night on the prom. But anything he told her would get back to Margaret. "Of course I can cope," he said. He could feel his patience snapping.

"Your face tells a different story," Angela said, a slight smile on her lips. "How about a cup of tea?"

"No, Goddammit," he said. Her smile disappeared. He clutched the doorframe for support, already regretting his outburst. She out of everyone knew his weaknesses.

Angela pressed a button on the arm of the electric wheelchair, and it crept forwards.

"I know what it's like to live alone," she said softly. "Apart from the last few weeks, I've done it ever since the divorce."

She glanced at her hands in her lap for a moment, as if remembering what might have been, before focusing back on him. "Look, what I'm saying is, it's nice to know someone will find you. That if anything happened, there's someone there."

But Gertie had gone, gone in the middle of the night, and there was no one else who would come and find him.

"You should have seen me when they told me about my legs," Angela said. "I was bloody furious. Would have given the doctor a good kicking if I could have."

He smiled despite himself. "And the cancer diagnosis?" he asked.

She flinched, then shrugged. "Unfortunately, it turns out you can't negotiate with your body."

A high voice shouted: "Grammy, Grammy."

"Oh, it's Kev," Angela said. She smiled. "Got to go."

"Is everything alright with the neighbour?" A woman was calling now – the Australian daughter-in-law. Arthur stepped further back into the hallway.

"Yes, he's fine," Angela shouted back. "Hold on, duck, I'm on my way." She winked at him, and then the wheelchair shot up the drive, leaving two dark tracks in the snow.

She'd covered for him. Arthur closed the door with relief. Maybe he could trust her after all. He went back into the kitchen. The damp patch on the floor had dried. The mug had just been an ordinary one, a relic from a church jumble sale, nothing to get sentimental about. Why had he been so angry? In the Navy, he had learned to master his outbursts, to channel bitterness into precision, harness energy from rage. After the war, the same discipline had taken him to night school, from the desk to the corner office. It was a surprise when they had Margaret and he held in his arms unfiltered, unadulterated fury again.

He walked carefully, step by step, to the balcony. A hand on the table there, a grip on the back of the chair, a momentary pause by the doorframe. Gertie's eyes watched him from her picture on the wall. It was a picture taken at her friend's wedding, shortly after the final miscarriage that forced them to give up on the idea of a second child. "So we'll never have a son," she'd said as they queued up for the buffet lunch, a ten-year-old Margaret huddling with the other bridesmaids. "We might have a son-in-law one day, or a lovely grandson." He'd bristled at the thought of his daughter being old enough to marry, but that was how Gertie thought – across generations, beyond blood. If she was disappointed when the son-in-law never appeared, she hid it with her web of friendships, from the grocer's lad who always slipped her an extra orange, to the young families she babysat for when they were at their wits' end.

And then she died, and the web disintegrated. Did she realise how alone he'd be? He thought again of Sue's arm, firm and steady. How she'd lifted him up when she fell. He could have opened the door and called after her. He could have let her stay, at least for a little while, until his feet were anchored on the ground again. Known someone was there.

The morning was cold and crisp. The snow dissolved time – the wheelie bins, the burglar alarms. The cars were all gone and in their place were just white drifts on the slate roofs. There were lamps in windows, and the kind of hush that used to fall every Sunday. He stayed there a while, listening to the voice of Angela's grandchild rise on the air.

Chapter Twenty-Three

The angry old uncle had been replaced by a rice-bowl world: blue sky, blue bay, and everything else a shimmering white.

The snow was crisp, like apple flesh. Suling was walking along a hill-top road heaped with it. Just a few darkened lines betrayed earlier traffic. In one of the gardens a dog barked, but she barely flinched – in this wintry world, she was just another bundled up figure. It felt good to walk down the street in daylight, even if her feet were already getting cold.

She realised with a thud that she'd left the English dictionary by the side of the bed. Well, it was too late now. A plan was already forming in her head. She would go to the supermarket bin and see what she could find. Then, while it was still daylight, she would start walking. She would follow the coast all the way around until she found the train she'd seen at night from the swimming pool. It might take days, but she could do it. She'd spent days on her feet in the factory.

Trees leaned out of gardens, their leaves brittle and pale as carved ivory. The main road continued down into the town, the houses getting closer together, the roofs clustering like birds. A ribbon of grey marked the promenade, a whisper of smoke rising from the end where the swimming pool was. She watched the smoke spiral until it became indistinguishable from the sky. Perhaps Kee Teh had made himself at home. She couldn't blame him – she would have done the same. She thought of him reaching for the tarpaulin and feeding it to the fire. Another man might have jumped up and tried to pull the debt collector off her, but perhaps he knew his limits. The debt collector was a professional, after all.

She had been careful when she arranged her journey, to put as many fake names and addresses between her mother and herself. But professionals would work it out in the end. She needed to forget about the last few days, find a job and start making things happen before they did.

The road turned onto the high street. After so many trips in the dead of night, it was a surprise to see the shops open, their steamed-up windowpanes glowing in the frozen world. She pulled her hood up further over her head and walked towards the supermarket.

The car park was dirty with tire tracks and churned up snow. A woman with bulging plastic bags on both arms was opening a car door. Suling stared at her feet as if she was waiting for someone until she heard the engine start and the car drive away. Then she crossed over to the corner. The supermarket bin was there, as always. A sandwich poked out between the bubble wrap, as if waiting for her to grab it.

"Hey!"

A woman in a purple and green uniform came rushing out of a door she'd never noticed before. "Hey," the woman repeated as she started slipping and sliding through the snow. "Stop."

Suling backed away. The woman was trying to run, but the snow and ice was making it hard. She slipped through a gap in the snow-covered hedge.

"Stop," the woman was shouting, her voice carrying on the still air.

Suling ran left, then right, until she was in the alleyway that ran behind the terraces. She glanced behind her but there was nothing, only her footsteps notching her panic into the curd-like snow. Her breath clouded the air as she slowed to a walk again.

The woman had treated her like a thief. But if it was stealing to take that sandwich, why was it in the bin? She would have to set off without food then, and hope that she could pick something up along the way.

The alleyway would take her to the end of the terraces, where a busy road led out of town. If she'd thought ahead, she might have chosen another way, but her feet had decided the route for her. They were going numb, despite her run. Thousands of tiny crystals glinted in the sun.

"That's what I'm saying. I've been driving around for hours."

She stopped. There was no one in the alleyway, but she recognised the debt collector's voice at once. He must be in the cocklers' old back yard, and he was talking loudly in Hokkien, as if he had no fear of being understood.

If she had only just entered the alleyway, she might have turned back, but she was almost halfway along it now, and he would notice the silence as much as the quiet crunch of snow under feet. From the pauses between his sentences, she guessed he was on his mobile phone.

"Don't worry. I've got people on the ground if she turns up."

The fence that separated the alleyway from the back yard was around two metres high – tall enough to hide a teenage girl, but not to stop a powerful, suspicious man from peering over and seeing her. She kept her head down.

"The landlord?" the debt collector carried on. "Some fat old ghost. I'm at his place now. Wants his rent paid." There was a pause, as if the person on the other end of the phone was saying something. He spat into the snow. "Don't worry, chief. I'll find her." Another pause. "She'll be trying to get to London. Maybe Manchester. I've got people in both."

She just had to get to the end of the alleyway. One foot after another.

The debt collector kept talking. "That old drunk said she was looking for a train." A pause. "He knows he's my eyes and ears around here. I made it very clear."

What had he done to Kee Teh? But she couldn't think about that now. Nowhere was safe. Not Manchester. Not London. Not the old swimming pool. Not the alleyway. Not Kee Teh.

"Look, chief," the debt collector said. There was a new urgency in his voice. "I will find her. Either way, she can't speak English. Sooner or later, she'll have to surface. No-one else is going to give her a job."

The corner was only a few steps away. Once she reached it, she started to run. Her feet punched holes in the snow as she accelerated, down one row of terraces, then another, until she found herself bent double, waiting for her breath to catch up with her.

"Stupid," she cursed herself. "Idiot. How the hell did you get mixed up in all this?" She kicked the snow, tears hot on her cheeks where her scarf had fallen. "You've brought yourself down, and everyone with you." She dropped to her hands and knees, hard, because she had to get used to the pain. "You've messed it all up, right from day one." She was weeping now. "He'll find you, idiot. He's looking everywhere."

Her tears left tiny hollows on the snow. As she watched the crystals disappear, her breath slowed. I can speak English, she thought. Not much, but I learned a few more words just today. And he hasn't looked everywhere. He hasn't looked on the quiet street at the top of the hill.

*

Once Suling had stood up and brushed the snow off her knees, it was only a few minutes' walk up the hill. Yet the old uncle's street felt like a different world. The snow was almost as untouched as when she left it. A bird soared overhead in the blue sky.

Suling thought of the broken china on the floor, the puddle slowly spreading to fill the kitchen. She should have stayed to sweep it up. Perhaps when she got there, the old uncle would slam the door on her, or shout. Worse still, he might call the police. Either way, she'd have to run. And then it would all be over. The debt collector would find her sooner or later, collapsed by the side of a road maybe, or picked out of a crowd of people waiting for work in London's Chinatown.

But she had to try. If he slammed the door, at least she'd know.

A soft brushing sound filled the air. She found Old Uncle in his driveway attempting to sweep away the snow. The broom slipped from his grasp and he teetered for a moment before clutching at the side of the wall. He looked at her, and she saw the regret in his eyes.

She took the broom from him and beat out a dark path to the garage before putting it away and following him through the unlocked front door.

Chapter Twenty-Four

A woman screamed. Arthur's eyes snapped open. He reached for Gertie and felt the cold, thin sheets. That girl. He should never have let her in. What the hell was happening? She was part of a gang after all. They could murder him in his bed.

He reached for the bedside table and propelled himself onto his feet. He wasn't going to wait for them, that was for sure. There were golf clubs in the cupboard. He took the heaviest one and crept to the bedroom door. The hallway was in darkness, but he could see a light through the frosted glass of the lounge door. Beyond it, voices were rising and falling. They must be in there. He could confront them. Or, if he tiptoed down the hallway and turned left towards the front door, he might be able to leave the house without anyone noticing.

The woman screamed again. He couldn't just leave her. He raised the golf club above his head and burst through the door.

"Aaaaaaaah."

"Aaaaaaaah."

He was screaming, and someone else was screaming too. Only it wasn't the woman he'd heard before. Sue had jumped up from the chair, a look of terror on her face, and beyond her was the TV blaring out a late-night horror film.

"What the hell? Goddammit!" he shouted. They stared at each other. The woman screamed again. It was the actress in the horror film, her lips pulsing as a flock of seagulls closed in on her.

He lowered the golf club. Sue's eyes followed his every movement. She was frightened. Well, how did she expect him to react when she was blaring out stuff like that? "Keep it down, you donnat," he said. When she didn't move, he reached over for the remote, almost toppling himself in the process. She jumped up and caught him. "Here," he managed to sputter. She saw where he was pointing and handed it to him, and he thumbed the off button. Finally, silence.

Rage flooded in. "Do you know what time it is? What the hell do you think you're doing, watching this rubbish late at night?" It was like Margaret as a teenager all over again, only this time the teenager opened her hands and started talking in a language he didn't understand. He jabbed at the clock. "Too late," he shouted. "Too late for TV." She picked up her dictionary. Not that thing again. He was too tired to repeat himself. "You need to be res... res." But it was no use. The word wouldn't come. He shook his head and left her still squinting at the dictionary.

*

Ousta doin? *Dustah nah*? *Nobbot lakeing*. The cocklers' language wasn't written down anywhere but was preserved mam to babby. It wove them together like ropes, at least until they went to school and were told it was all wrong. Then he'd joined the Navy and learned of pickle jar officers and snotties, Uckers and char. But it was after he made a name for himself at night school that one of his lecturers drew him aside and told him he needed to learn English. "Received pronunciation," Mr Forsyth said. "That's the trick." He'd repeated the bulletins on the radio, learned to rearrange his grammar and elongate his vowels until he hardly noticed he was doing it.

And it worked. He charmed clients with it, won promotions with it, and negotiated his salary with it.

When Margaret was a schoolgirl, she'd started to use some of the old words again. He didn't know where she'd got them from, but he'd told her to stop it. He knew the other kids thought her stuck up, but she needed to realise that your suitability for a job might be measured on the way you said "aunt" and "bath". It didn't help that there were people like Angela, who sprinkled their dinner party conversations with *bon appétits* and *ciao, darlings* – as if English could be taken for granted. The language was being muddied. Perhaps that was why when he searched for words from the language of his career, more and more they wouldn't come, and instead he was forced to resort to an old one, soft-edged but familiar, like sea glass thrown up on shore.

But Sue – he couldn't make sense of her in any language. What sort of eejit watched films like that late at night anyway? He heard footsteps padding down the corridor and a door squeak. The word he'd been searching for earlier suddenly came back to him. Respectful.

*

The next morning, Sue laid out breakfast and even made some blackened toast. "Thank you," he said awkwardly, and she replied carefully: "It is my pleasure." Then she cleared her throat. "Sorry, Uncle, to play TV so big." The way she said it made him think she had been practising. Her eyes watched him, and then flicked to the door, like she might run again at any moment.

Uncle, she'd called him. His real nieces addressed him as Arthur, when they bothered to write Christmas cards. No doubt they were too sophisticated for uncles in their fancy part of Edinburgh. He nodded stiffly. "I go to sleep early," he said. "You weren't to know." She picked up her dictionary. "Sleep?" she asked. "Sleep," he said. She wrote it carefully in her notepad. She didn't understand, not really. It was the moment in the hall that scared him, that moment when he'd forgotten about late-night TV and his houseguest and anything could be behind the frosted glass door.

Better not try to explain. He bit into the toast. Yes, it was definitely burnt. They sank into silence again.

After breakfast he left Sue drying up, pulled on a hat to hide his bruises and took the remains of the toast out for the birds. They would be hungry in the snow. The garden was still ornately white, although a few blades of grass poked through a corner where the sun had been.

Angela was in the next-door garden watching her grandson make snow angels. She raised a gloved hand. "He's never seen it before," she said, as the lad waved his arms and legs in the drifts. He nodded and continued on his way before the kid spotted the bruises. A running commentary rose on the still air: "Grammy, what happens to the worms? Are they cold? Look at the wings I've made. Grammy, have you ever made a snowman?"

The bird table was covered in snow. Arthur tore the bread into little black crumbs and scattered them like punctuation marks on its blank surface.

"Grammy, what's the man next door doing?"

"He's feeding the birds, duck."

"Grammy, I'm going to get Daddy."

A moment of silence. Arthur sat down on the bench Gertie had picked for the garden. There was a rustle in the trees above, and then a wood pigeon landed with a thump on the bird table and bent its slate-coloured neck towards the crumbs. He loved the birds. The summer was swallows, the garden full of movement as they snapped at flies in the air. Now it was just the clumsy wood pigeons.

"Grammy, are you coming sledging with us?" The lad's voice sent the wood pigeon off in a flurry of snow.

"No, duck," came Angela's voice. "They haven't made a sledge for these wheels yet."

There was no point trying to watch the birds with this racket. Arthur grasped the arm of the bench and slowly got to his feet. On the other side of the fence, the little boy seemed cross. He folded his arms. "Well, they need to make one soon. When will it snow again?"

"Next year, maybe," Angela said.

"We'll sledge together next year," the boy said, cheering up. "Bye, Grammy." He sped away, his footprints leaving tiny dents in the snow.

Angela sat still where she was. Her silver hair looked brittle against the snow. Arthur crossed over to the fence.

"Next year?" he asked.

She'd been so quick to crack a joke about the cancer, so flippant about her impending death. Now she wouldn't meet his eyes.

"Haven't you told them?" he persisted.

She jabbed a button and the wheelchair sputtered closer to the fence.

"I'm going to," she muttered. "It's just—" She looked up at him defiantly. "You know, I barely saw Kev before, with them being in Australia." She coughed, a harsh sound, like a bird's cry. "They don't prepare them for death any more," she said when she finished. "It's all sunlight and beaches and ponies."

Arthur said: "But you told me."

She shrugged her bony shoulders. "Well, that was easy. For all I know, you could have poured yourself a dram and cheered my departure."

He'd been planning to take Gertie on her favourite coastal walk, as a surprise. He'd already put their wellies in the back of the car. They stayed there for weeks after she died, her Queen-green boots resting gently against his bigger black ones.

"You should tell them," he said.

"Have you ever considered, Arthur, that I might be afraid?" Angela lowered her voice. "All I've got to go on so far is the diagnosis, and this bloody cough. When I tell them, it becomes real. I haven't found the words yet."

But it was written loud and clear in her eyes, so big and wistful, he thought, and the tremble of her lip. She'd been telling them all along. They just hadn't noticed it.

*

Sue had tidied up. Everything looked brighter somehow, like a family scrubbed up for church. Gertie's bird book lay on the coffee table, as if it had always been there, just waiting for him to find it. He felt the weight of it in his hands. Sue was attacking the glass door that led to the balcony with some old newspapers. She slid open the door, newspaper in hand, but the faint sound of a chainsaw in someone's garden sent her scuttling back inside again. Despite the hush of the snow-filled afternoon, she was jumpy, like a deer hard-wired against predators.

It was exhausting, reacting to the world like that. He'd done it himself, after Sid drowned. Just a blast of sea air was enough to make him flinch. It was a lonely kind of fear to have, but then the war came. They were drilled on how to react to sirens, commands, gunfire. And afterwards he bought a house on the hill, far enough inland to start rebuilding his life again.

He thought again of how Sue had screamed when he burst into the room. She was scared of something, or someone, and that meant something had happened to make her so. He wanted to ask her what it was, but she wouldn't understand, and he didn't know how to ask that sort of thing anyway. So after the red Volkswagen pulled out of the next-door drive, he found her a scarf, big enough to wrap round her face and be anonymous. She swept the path to the bird table. He made a flask of tea and hunted down a packet of biscuits. They sat there in the morning sun and watched the wood pigeons fight over the remains of a cheese sandwich.

He showed her the book from the coffee table.

"Bird," he said.

He quietly turned the pages until he found the right illustration.

"Pigeon."

She repeated it softly after him.

It wasn't so different from reading with Margaret, all those years ago. He'd been nervous at first when he saw all the books she brought home from school, more evidence of the classes he'd missed. Gertie was the better reader. But his daughter had placed one in his hand, and he knew she'd chosen him.

A robin landed on the edge of the bird table. Sue nudged him excitedly when she noticed its rusty breast. It hopped in between the bigger birds, nimble as a cabaret dancer on a busy stage, suddenly exotic. The wood pigeons lunged for the crumbs, but the robin was there first, and darted out before their beaks even hit the snow.

Arthur found the right page. "Robin."

Sue consulted the dictionary. "Robbing?" she said. It took her a few attempts to pronounce the R.

The wood pigeons squabbled. The robin flew to a branch of the apple tree, its black eyes watching them as it swallowed its prize.

"Rob-in," Arthur said.

"Yes," she conceded. "But robin robbing.".

A seagull swooped down, and the wood pigeons scattered.

"Scare," Sue said. "Like movie." She pointed at the flapping wood pigeon. "Like me."

Arthur pictured himself with the golf club again. How they both shrieked. He smiled despite himself. "We were flait buzzards alright."

"Flait?" Sue was searching her dictionary.

"It was something my grandad used to say." She was still turning the pages, so he tried to explain. "Not in here." He tapped his head. "In here. Like scared. But sharper, somehow. Flait."

Sue thought for a moment. "The birds are flait," she said slowly.

"Exactly," he said.

The robin bared its breast to the sky and began to sing.

Chapter Twenty-Five

The birds whirled around in the white garden. Then one morning the snow was gone, replaced by heavy rain. Suling peered through the blurry window at the pools forming on the grass, the nothingness of the bay behind. If the cocklers had still been there, how would they have coped? She wondered if Changfa, wherever he was, could hear the rain, see the puddles swelling like interest on his debts. She pushed the thought aside. You can't help him, the debt collector had said, and he was right. She had no way of finding him, and even if she did, she had nothing to offer him. She had to keep focused to survive.

Morning after morning, the clouds formed a grey fortress around the house. She attacked English with a vengeance. One afternoon, when Old Uncle was in the garden during a lull in the rain, she went through the house with her dictionary in hand and wrote down everything she wanted to know. Chair. Table. Sink. Plug. Carpet. At the end of this exercise there were only a few things that had no name, like the puffy coat Old Uncle placed on top of the teapot.

Keys jangled in the lock. Old Uncle was back. She stopped him in the hallway.

"How are you?"

He looked up from his black boots and said something she didn't understand.

"The rain is wet," she said.

He nodded. "Ayy," he said, although he should have said "yes", like it was written in the dictionary.

"Do you want a nice cup of tea?"

"Ayy."

In the kitchen she turned the tap very carefully so it wouldn't spray, and pointed. "Water."

He nodded.

She picked up a teabag. "Tea."

"That's right."

When she had finished making the tea and poured him a mug, she sat down opposite him. Will you turn me in, she wanted to ask, but instead she said a sentence she had been practising. "How old are you?"

He spluttered into his tea. She tried again: "How old are you?" He laughed harder. She looked down at her tea and felt defeated.

But then she realised he was saying something. Asking her a question, the same question.

She counted the numbers in her head. "Seventeen," she said out loud.

He looked shocked. She should have lied. "Seventeen?" he repeated.

"No," she said. "Twenty."

This was a better answer, because he seemed to relax, and now he was peppering her with questions, some of which she knew and some which he needed to mime before she got them. Did she like gardens? (Or was he talking about the rain?) Did she like the cold? Did she like tea? She answered them all as inaccurately as she could, just to be on the safe side.

*

Old Uncle had a mobile phone, but he never used it. When she found it in a drawer and brought it to him, he backed away and said "no", like she'd just tried to hand him some of her unwashed clothes. Perhaps it was broken. She pressed the buttons and the screen glowed. No charger, as far as she could see, but half a battery left. "Okay," she told Old Uncle. He shook his head. "Not for me," he said. "Books better." He put it on the shelf and pulled out a paperback before retreating to his armchair.

Most of Old Uncle's books were filled with dense writing, like bricks in an impossibly high wall. But there was one big, leather-bound book packed with photos of a younger Old Uncle and his family. She flipped through pictures of them posing with the sea behind them, Younger Old Uncle and his unnamed wife and the little girl. The woman had a straw hat, a round face, eggshell skin and a big smile. The little girl was light-haired and frowning.

She guessed the photo must have been taken a long time ago. The Old Uncle was so lonely now, it was hard to imagine him surrounded by family.

When Old Uncle got up from his armchair, he caught her staring at the photograph of the family by the sea. He tapped the image of the little girl. "My regret, my regret."

She looked it up in the dictionary. A phrase full of hard-to-pronounce sounds. It meant something very sad had happened, a ghost from the past that continued to haunt him even now.

There was a photo of the woman hanging on the wall, Suling noticed, only she was alone this time, and hatless, her hair the colour of sand. She smiled out of the frame at something only she could see.

"Name?" she asked.

"Gertie," Old Uncle said. He mumbled something else, something subdued, and she understood the woman was dead. Old Uncle gazed at the picture reverently, and then leant over and adjusted the flowers standing next to it. He did it without fuss, as if it wasn't supposed to be a big deal.

She remembered being nine years old, standing in front of the dark wooden ancestor tablet after her grandfather died, her father murmuring as the scent of incense filled the house. She wished she could describe it to him. Perhaps if he knew they had something in common, he would be less likely to betray her.

Old Uncle was speaking again now, and from the way his voice rose, he seemed to be asking a question about her family. He jabbed at the photo and pointed at her.

She tried the word she knew. "Mother," she said.

"Father?"

That day the scent of incense filled the room was the last time she saw him. She shook her head.

He must have thought she meant he was dead, because he patted her on the shoulder and gazed solemnly at the photo again. Then he pointed at the little girl.

"Sister? Brother?" he asked.

Suling would have liked a sister. She'd heard once or twice in the village that her father had a new family, in Manila, where people lived stacked on top of another and no-one asked questions about who was really married to whom. But half a sister was twice the trouble.

She shook her head again. No. She had only her mother and Changfa.

Old Uncle frowned. He opened a drawer and pulled out a

battered book. It looked far older than the ones she'd flipped through.

He sat down in an armchair and beckoned her over. These pictures were all black and brown and grey and white, and small, as if she was looking the wrong way down one of his telescopes. The pictures showed houses, not grand ones like his, but low-lying lodges with small windows and rough roofs, and people who looked like peasants, their faces roughly hewn in light and shade by the camera's shaky gaze. They looked, Suling realised with a jolt, like the people in her village.

Old Uncle turned a page. The new photos revealed they were not peasants, but fishermen, because here they were, the women and children as well, knee-deep in water, staring straight-faced at the camera.

Old Uncle pointed at a little boy. "Me," he said.

The boy looked back, frozen forever at nine or ten. It seemed impossible that he was the same flesh and blood as the old man. But it was the photograph in the bottom right of the page that really caught her attention. A family, perhaps the same one, stood on a mirror-like surface with a horse and cart, the boy bending to touch something on the ground.

"Ayy," Old Uncle said, noticing. He pointed to the grey haze outside. He made a sudden lurching movement. She knew exactly what it was. He was pushing the cockles up from the sand of the bay.

*

Changfa had believed in cockles. "Like a gold mine," he'd said, the first day she joined him on the sands. He saw every setback as temporary. When they got caught in the rain on their walks home from school, he would gesture, laughing, for her to follow him under the trees and kiss her as soon as they were out of sight. He laughed a lot in those days, even though his family was very poor and skinny – except for his fat father, who beat him. And while they waited for the sun to come out again, he'd dream up extravagant plans for their future, imagine the homes they'd build for their families, and how the doors to the bedrooms in his house would be narrow, so his fat father couldn't get in.

They often talked about the world. According to Changfa, the people of Fujian had always been adventurous. Even hundreds of years ago, young men had set out on boats across the sea. When his overseas relatives returned for a visit, he would skulk in the corner of the room, listening to everything they said and relaying it back to her. That's how she heard about the clean streets of Singapore, the riots in Jakarta and the crumbling palaces of Europe.

So at first, after Old Uncle had told her he was a cockler, Suling imagined that was how he got wealthy. She tapped the photograph in the old album.

"Me," she said.

He looked surprised, so she made the same lurching movement and raked invisible cockles from the carpet's sand.

A shadow passed over his face, but all he said was: "Ah."

She tapped the photo again. "Rich?" she asked.

The question made him laugh. "No," he said. "In fah tee."

She checked the dictionary several times to make sure she understood. "You? Factory?"

"Yes."

So she had borrowed all this money, endured so much fear and hardship, and all for something even lower than a factory job.

Perhaps the Old Uncle sensed her disappointment, because he beckoned for her to follow him into his bedroom, a place she had not entered since that first day she explored the house. He opened the wardrobe and she saw it was full of suits.

"Ah can tan," Old Uncle said. He tapped a certificate framed on the wall. She found the word in her dictionary. Accountant. A record keeper. A finance man. Old Uncle tapped his head. "Start in factory. But I learn."

He looked at the suits quietly for a moment and then shut the wardrobe.

Later, in her room, Suling remembered the tiny wooden abacus on the window ledge. She slid the beads back and forth and thought of Changfa. Every time his dreams had broken, he'd managed to find another one. He'd come up with the idea of the factory after she'd said she couldn't marry him. And then there was the conversation they had just before the new year, the last proper conversation before they met again at the bay.

He'd found her in the factory dorm. It was empty for once. The previous evening, the other girls had packed their bags and one by one set off home for the festival.

He'd bought her a ticket with his savings to go back to the village.

"How can you ask me to go back?" she'd said.

He sat down next to her on the bunk. "Don't you want to sit by the stream again? Breathe fresh air?"

She could hear the hurt in his voice, but it was the end of a long shift, and she was exhausted.

"If I go back, I need to build my mother a house," she said.

"She has a house."

His complacency stung her. "You know what I mean. She's

waited so long. And they will all be saying I ran away with a bare stick. I can't go back until I have something to show for it."

"Fine," he said, his voice hardening at the slur. "Then we'll build her a house." And he'd stalked out of the room.

After that, everything had happened very fast. He'd made a deal with a broker, taken out a loan to pay for the journey. When he told her how big it was, she'd chased him out of the dorm room, but he had recovered his good humour by then, and he laughed at her, said that where he was going, you could earn that much money in a year. The broker was arranging a job for him on the other side. He just had to get there.

She'd said goodbye to him on a busy street, where there were too many people around to cry. But she missed him instantly. Without him, her life consisted of tasteless food, monotonous factory lines, and the giggling dorm mates she had nothing in common with. She looked at the trainers she was applying soles to in the factory and imagined people in another country wearing them. A wealthy country, where you could change your future in a year.

Chapter Twenty-Six

So the lass was a cockler. The idea was absurd – no wonder she'd run away. Arthur stared out through the glass balcony door. He'd said she could stay until the snow melted, but there was a wall of rain where the bay was supposed to be. On days like this, out on the sands, you felt you could disintegrate. It wasn't the rain that would kill you, of course, but the deep water; the sudden floods, the fog. That day he'd set out with Sid, it had been sunny, so sunny they'd forgotten about the downpour a few days earlier.

It was mid-morning, but the sky was still so dark it could be dawn, the clouds closing in like thugs. The O'Briens' house glowed with yellow light. He saw a flash of movement in one of the windows – the grandson causing havoc, no doubt. He thought again of the conversation with Angela in the garden. She was so quick with words, and yet she couldn't tell her family what mattered most. If she was in pain, she'd managed to hide it. But then, it had been a surprise to almost everyone when she left the first time. How long had she known she was leaving, even as she shopped, gardened and volunteered at school fetes?

He turned on the TV. It was a classic film, one of the Ealing comedies. Sue came in half-way through and sat down on the chair next to him, her dictionary in her lap as she scribbled down words. He glanced over at her notepad – it said "jolly", "I say" and "darling". He laughed.

The phone rang and he got up to answer it. He felt Sue's eyes on him. She was always twitchy about the phone. "Hello, Arthur," Angela said. He could hear someone shouting in the background. "Kev's not used to being inside all day, so they're taking him to an indoor amusement park. Kids' Jungle or something equally dystopian. Anyway, it's a few hours' drive and they don't have a map."

Arthur glanced at his bookcase with its perfectly ordered maps. "Don't you know the way?"

Angela sighed. "Oh, I'm not going. It's a hassle getting the wheelchair into that car. And I'm very tired today."

It was the way she said "tired", a tiny crack in her voice, that betrayed the fact she hadn't told them yet.

"I'll drop the map round now," he said. He found his raincoat and a stick in case it was slippery, and was just putting his wellies on outside the back door when he saw Angela in the next-door garden. She was sitting in her chair, with no attempt at an umbrella, a lone figure in the rain.

He heard Sue behind him in the hallway and beckoned her over.

"Friend," he said. "We eat with friend?"

Her expression told him she very much did not want to eat with his friend.

"You can trust her," he said.

*

"What, tinned chicken soup for tea?" Angela said.

"You were happy to be invited," Arthur said.

"Yes, I know. I'm only being curious. Food is one of my remaining pleasures in life." Angela wheeled herself into the hallway. "And who's this?"

She'd already spotted the lass. He cleared his throat. "Sue? She's from church," he improvised. "Visiting from China. Doesn't speak much English."

The eyebrows flickered. Then, after a moment, Angela extended a papery hand. "Nice to meet you." Sue reached out gingerly and shook it, before backing away into the kitchen.

Before Arthur could follow her, Angela said: "I didn't expect you to listen to my advice."

"What do you mean?"

"Making friends."

"Oh, I'm just doing Father Mulroney a favour," Arthur said. "You know how involved Gertie was with all his projects."

Angela nodded. "Very Christian of you," she said. "But Arthur—"

She asked too many questions. He should never have invited her over.

"—what on earth are we going to eat?"

He threw up his hands. "Gertie cooked," he said as Angela steered herself into the kitchen.

"And you never learned?"

He stared at her. "She liked it."

"I'm sure she did." Angela said "It was by far the most interesting part of being a housewife. She had a fabulous recipe book."

She pointed at a yellow diary shoved on top of the fridge. It was so much a part of the kitchen that Arthur hadn't noticed it before. "That's it, there." She patted Sue on the shoulder. "Can you get it for us, duck?"

The girl might not have followed the words, but she understood the question. A few seconds later, the book was on the table.

"Well, this brings back the memories," Angela murmured, turning the pages. Arthur glimpsed his wife's handwriting. "Treacle tart – yes, she was famous for that – and quiche, and, oh, her Sunday roasts." She shut her eyes for a moment. "Those potatoes." The eyes snapped opened again. "She used to invite us round sometimes, before she realised what a bad influence I was."

Before you started writing her letters, Arthur thought. But he let it pass. He was back at that table, with the roast lamb, the crispy potatoes, the gravy boat and Yorkshire puddings, the afternoon light streaming through the window. He couldn't say when the Sunday Roast era started exactly and when it finished, but it was a time when all was right with the world, even if it was just for a few hours.

"We could make it," Angela said.

Her voice brought him back to the present. "What do you mean?"

Angela tapped the page. "All the instructions are here. I'll raid our fridge."

"I told you – I can't cook," he said.

"I'll tell you what to do," Angela said. "Anyway, you've got Sue to help. I bet she's never had a roast dinner before."

And so Arthur found himself staring at a carrot while Angela, who seemed to have regained her energy, barked directions from her chair.

"Yes, that's right, chop them into sticks. Watch what you're doing with that knife."

"Too late," Arthur snapped. This is what he got for doing women's work. The knife had nicked his skin and blood was welling up.

Margaret would have had a panic attack. But Angela said:

"Maybe you should stick to peeling instead."

"Easy for you to say," he said. She had the pot of lamb in her lap, which she was scattering with herbs. He went to find a dressing for his finger. When he came back, Sue was splintering carrots with the speed of a woodchipper.

"Slow down, duck, or you'll take your hand off," Angela said. Sue looked at her in confusion, and then carried on chopping with expert precision.

Arthur picked up a potato. That bloody tremble in his hand. How Gertie did it, he didn't know. He'd come home from work and tell her about his day, and all the time they yattered, the peeler would be flashing away. He'd always known he loved her – he hadn't realised how much he depended on her until she was gone.

Eventually, though, all the potatoes were in the oven, along with the carrots and Angela's lamb and Yorkshire puddings. Arthur found a dusty bottle of Merlot in the cupboard. It was Gertie's favourite, even if he hadn't ever managed to tell the difference.

"Cheers," Angela said, when it was poured into three glasses. She turned to Sue. "Or should we pray?"

Sue reached for her dictionary. "Pay?" she asked.

"She's not that sort of Christian," Arthur said hastily.

"Good," Angela said. "In that case, I can make a toast." She lifted her glass into the air. "To good scran, as long as I can still taste it."

"To Gertie," Arthur said.

"Gone Bay," Sue said, and tipped her glass back and downed it.

"Music," Angela said brightly. "Jazz." And then there was a rush to find a record, get plates on the table and dishes onto mats, and more wine in glasses. The lamb was juicy and the potatoes crisp. Angela's voice lost its mocking tone. Sue finally looked like she was enjoying herself.

"This is the life," Angela said. She drank her wine. "They say after chemo, everything turns to dust."

Arthur realised the music had stopped.

"I'll put on the next one," he said.

He found a record of a big band that used to play in the music hall on the prom, back in the days when big bands came, and the place was stuffed with lamps and ferns.

"Now this is what I miss," Angela said as she topped up their glasses. She winced. "Being able to dance." Then she smiled, and he saw what an effort she made. "That reminds me. What does the church say about gambling?" She reached into her handbag, which was hanging on the side of the wheelchair. "I brought cards."

Sue grinned for the first time all evening.

"I'll take that as God's blessing," Angela said. She turned to Arthur. "What about you?"

He thought he saw in her eyes a plea for the evening not to end.

"Wait here a moment," he said.

The black velvet bag was in a box next to the wine rack, along with other things he never managed to throw away. When he got back to the table, Angela was dealing out the cards.

"I know you like a flutter," he said, and emptied the bag onto the table.

Angela crowed with delight. She picked up the old coins – ha'pennies, farthings and shillings – and let them fall through her fingers. "Ridiculous," she said, but there was affection in her voice. Sue held a half crown to the light and examined it with the respectful expression of a tourist in a museum.

"Rummy?" Angela asked. "We'll take it one step at a time." She began to deal. The slap-slap of cards on the table took Arthur back to the poker evenings before Jimmy went blind and Dougie's daughter forced him to move halfway across the country – and Bob, who'd always hosted them, died. Angela gave the deck a final shuffle and started a running commentary as she demonstrated the game. "Here, you pick up a card, and see if it matches, and if not—"

"I know," Sue interrupted.

"You do?"

Sue nodded. "Like mah-jong."

"Well, in that case, let's start," Angela said. They picked up their cards. Soon Arthur was immersed in the game, the shadows of Jimmy and Dougie and Bob urging him to pick up this card, discard that. He hunted clubs, then hearts and diamonds. Sue discarded cards without a second thought. Angela poured them all another glass of wine.

"Your turn," she said.

The ace of spades. Arthur searched his cards for the best one to combine it with. In the background, the phone began to ring. "Should you get that?" Angela said.

Margaret was the only person who called him these days. But they were still at the table, and he had to decide whether to discard the ace or keep it. There was a roast dinner and wine, and a brass band on the record player.

He took a swig of wine before discarding the Seven of Diamonds. Now he had the ace, he might actually win. "Probably just a cold call," he said.

Chapter Twenty-Seven

Water. She needed water. Suling forced herself out of bed and got dressed. She was halfway along the hallway when her stomach turned upside down. She scrabbled with the bolts on the front door and got out just in time to throw up on the paving stones.

She crouched down, her head throbbing. Was it food poisoning? Looking at the watery pink sludge on the ground made her retch again. She crept back into the house and poured herself a glass of water. English words pounded in her head. Cheers. Cheers. Cheers. She fixed her eyes on the window over the sink and sipped slowly until the glass was empty.

After what seemed like a long time swaying, she felt strong enough to turn around. The kitchen table was strewn with evidence. Two wine bottles, both empty. A wine glass still half full. Three plates – what remained of the meal they cooked. The auntie's handbag, forgotten. The pack of cards, untidily stacked. She picked up the Three of Hearts off the floor.

There was no sign of Old Uncle. She turned the tap on and very slowly started to clean up. She had never really drunk before. In the village it was the men who drank and in the city, it was the rich. One of the dorm girl's boyfriend had worked in a club, and he used to make them laugh with his stories of the little emperors who would spend as much as their year's salary on a bottle. She held her nose as she emptied the wine glass in the sink.

A door clicked – Old Uncle was alive, at least. What had she done? Had she made a fool of herself? She poured herself another glass of water. No doubt the factory girls would laugh at her too. But the evening had been fun, the most fun she'd had for a very long time. She had even won some games. The heaps of coins they'd played for were piled on the side of the kitchen table, the yellow recipe book beside them. She picked it up and put it carefully back on top of the fridge.

"God-bah-luh-day-dam-hell," Old Uncle shouted from somewhere far away.

She rushed into the corridor and saw the front door was open. Old Uncle was standing outside in the pool of vomit. His slippers were a nasty shade of pink.

"Fah-keh-bug-gah-cah-lee-nah-up-sick." Old Uncle's face was a nasty shade of pink now too.

He was quivering with rage. She could run away, she could leave now, only her legs were wobbly and the pain in her head relentless. She reached for the first polite word she could think of. "Please," she said. "No, sorry."

Old Uncle kept bellowing. Across the road, a window opened. She ducked back inside the doorway.

"God-dam-dee-vee," Old Uncle shouted.

He was interrupted by a peal of laughter. The auntie was sitting in her electric wheelchair on the driveway, her head thrown back as she chuckled.

Old Uncle kept shouting, but he was starting to wheeze between curses. Electric Auntie barked something at him and nodded to Suling. "Here," she said, as she reached into the bag hooked to her chair. "Catch."

A newspaper came crashing onto the mat. Electric Auntie pointed at Old Uncle's slippers. "There," she said, and made a smoothing motion with her hand. Suling staggered to her feet. She managed to wrench the newspaper apart and lay down the pages like a bridge over the vomit.

By this stage, Old Uncle was calm enough to shuffle out of his slippers and walk barefoot over the paper into the house, although he was still cursing under his breath. Electric Auntie said something. But it didn't seem to placate Old Uncle, who burst into another stream of words.

It was the broken tap all over again. The kitchen filled with Old Uncle's fury. Suling sat down at the table and cradled her head in her hands. She was too stupid to ever be a success. All she could do was try not to be sick again, and she might even fail at that.

Someone prodded her, but her head felt too heavy to ever lift. She knew she couldn't sit like this forever, but she was too sick and tired to run.

They prodded again. "Su." It was Electric Auntie. With a huge effort, she lifted her head. Electric Auntie placed a mug of steaming tea next to her. "Drink."

The mug was solid and warm. Old Uncle was sitting on the other side of the table, his face gnarled in a frown, his hands also clamped around a mug of tea.

"Eggs," Electric Auntie said firmly, a frying pan in her hand. "You need eggs." A few sips of tea later, something began to sizzle.

*

Suling was not convinced that what she needed was a greasy combination of fried eggs, pork and toast, but somehow it worked. Even Old Uncle's plate gradually emptied, even if his lips stayed firmly pressed together in an unhappy line. Electric

Auntie ate her own, smaller, portion. After the last crumbs had disappeared, she told Suling: "Go outside."

Once again, she was right. The fresh air did make Suling feel better. At least until she saw the slippers, still half submerged in vomit, proof of her crime.

She fled to the garden. Although the wind and rain had stripped it bare, it was still beautiful in the watery sunlight. Suling followed the overgrown path past the vegetable patch right down to the hedge, her nausea gradually replaced by shame. She sat down on a tree stump and let her head fall into her hands. The slippers. Old Uncle's glowering face at breakfast. How could she stay here any longer? And yet, where could she go?

Something soft was tangled in her hair. She pulled out a purple feather and stared at it. At some point, after the second wine bottle, they'd all put on silly hats. Old Uncle had donned a baseball cap and refilled their glasses with a sweet liquor. She let the wind take the feather and watched an earthworm disappear into the black soil. He'd led them all in a song about a sailor – she could barely remember the tune now, but last night, somehow, she'd mastered all the words. Electric Auntie had been keeping time on the table with her cigarette case. Then Old Uncle had shouted "Shun" and they had all saluted. It felt like they'd all understood each other extremely well, despite the language barrier, and everything was alright.

Then she woke up and was sick on the slippers.

She walked back through the garden and forced herself to look at them. They were a faded brown tartan, worn inside, and now splashed with pink vomit. If she left now, they would stamp after her forever. *You almost seized your future*, they'd say with a relentless rhythm, *only you threw up on us instead and ruined it.*

When it was clear her father wasn't coming back, the girls in the village began to follow her around and whisper. At least, they did until she turned round and shoved the ringleader straight into a ditch.

She marched down to the garden, turned on the hose and blasted the paving stones clean. Then she picked up the sodden slippers and sniffed them. They still had the sour smell of vomit, so she lathered them with soap she found in the garage until the soap was black and the tartan revealed in its original blue.

The house was quiet – Electric Auntie must have left while she was in the garden. Old Uncle was slumped in his armchair. Suling dried the slippers with a hair dryer and entered the lounge.

Old Uncle opened one eye and glared at her.

She placed the slippers by his feet. He did not move.

"Clean," she said.

He clutched his head.

"Okay?" she asked.

"Ha go weh," he spat. She leafed through the dictionary. Ham. Hand. Hangover. He had drunk too much as well. That explained his foul mood. She felt a sudden relief.

"Head bad," Old Uncle said. He raised his fingers feebly to his mouth.

He wanted painkillers, she realised. After a hunt through the bathroom cupboards, she found his pill collection in an old biscuit tin. She brought it to him with a glass of water and opened the door to the balcony while he swallowed one and sipped.

"Out?" she asked.

He shook his head.

"Better," she urged him.

"So bad."

"Here." She took his hand and very gently pulled him to his feet, before walking him to the door. They leaned over the balcony, drinking mouthfuls of air like medicine. Old Uncle sighed. She wondered if he was regretting the adventures of the night before. He didn't seem as angry any more, but he could still blame her – she had a vague memory of climbing on a chair and conducting them all with a fork.

Out in the bay, the sea was slowly swallowing the sand. A tune came to her, and after humming it for a moment, she realised it was the sailor song. She glanced at Old Uncle in case he was irritated by the reminder, but he'd closed his eyes.

"Sid," he muttered.

She consulted the dictionary. "Sad?"

He shook his head. She stared out at the bay. The alcohol made her act like a child. Today she felt about a hundred years old. Still, for a few hours, she'd been free.

Old Uncle frowned. Then quietly, under his breath, he began to sing.

Chapter Twenty-Eight

Sid usually whistled. But he'd learned one song off an uncle, and he liked to sing it because the words were good craic, at least if you knew what they really meant. He'd sing it under his breath when they were pulling on their boots and at the top of his voice when they were out there on the sands, where even his mam and her sharp ears were no match for the wind. Arthur taught it to some lads in the Navy, but afterwards he'd met Gertie, and it wasn't the kind of song a husband should sing to his wife. He thought he'd forgotten it, and then out of nowhere it came hurtling out of a bottle and into his head. Now he couldn't get rid of it, and yet Gertie's bird book had gone missing again.

"Food's ready," Angela shouted through the open door. Arthur turned away from the window. They'd fallen into a sort of routine, these last few days, of Gertie's meals. That's how Arthur had started thinking about the recipes they'd tried from the battered yellow book. But tonight Angela had told him to lay the table in the lounge and stay out of the way – she wanted it to be a surprise. He poured white wine into the glasses, as she'd asked.

"I'm bracing myself," he retorted. In a book packed full of decent, traditional recipes, Angela always wanted to try the experimental ones.

Sue came through the door with a big bowl of spaghetti, dotted with greyish blobs.

"Cockles," Angela said with some satisfaction, as she rolled in behind her. "I bought them from a stall on the prom." She drew herself up to the table and began to ladle it out. "Wasn't that a good surprise?"

"Caught me out," Arthur said. He felt a sudden fury at Angela, even though he knew she couldn't possibly know that he never ate cockles, hadn't for the good part of seventy years.

"This is local," Angela told Sue. She took a bite. "Needs more seasoning," she muttered and reversed back into the kitchen.

Arthur was left alone with the sound of Sue eating. After a moment, she looked up anxiously.

"There's nothing wrong with it," Arthur said. "I just don't eat them any more." He took a swig of wine and looked past her, out of the window which was almost in darkness. That bloody song was back in his head.

"Sid and I – we wanted to prove ourselves." Sue glanced up from her meal to watch him. "We worked like hell all day. Stayed out later than we should have, but we knew the tides. We would have been fine, but—"

He let the spaghetti slither off his fork.

"You learn to read the sands like the back of your hand. But things can shift, and maybe we weren't as good as we thought we were. Or maybe it was just that we were lads and thought we were immortal. We stepped in quicksand."

Sue was watching him. Angela was still in the kitchen. He speared a cockle with his fork and deposited it on the side of his plate.

"It was warm, actually. Once you stopped struggling."

He added another cockle and nudged the plate towards her.

"Want them?"

She nodded. He tilted his plate and scraped the cockles onto hers. The wine glass was cold in his hand.

"We yelled and hollered and screeched alright. But the bay's a big place. Easy to vanish in it. I heard later they realised something was wrong, and they sent a horse. But they couldn't have helped us, not really."

Something clattered in the kitchen. He should get up and help Angela find whatever she was looking for. But his feet seemed glued to the floor.

Sue scooped up a cockle and ate it. "Sid?" she prompted.

He looked at her in surprise. The words had flowed out of him for once, but he hadn't expected her to understand.

"The tide," he said. "The tide came in. And I thought that was it. Sid shouted, 'Stay strong, lad.'"

He paused, the words echoing in his ears. They'd both wept for their mothers. He could still hear the rasp in Sid's newly broken voice.

"And then – I don't know. Somehow, the tide churned up the sand, and I kicked and the next thing I knew I was afloat. I was free. The water was icy cold. I looked for Sid… I tried to find him."

He trailed off.

Sue put down her knife and fork. She paused for a moment, as if putting her words in order. "You find Sid?"

A jawbone, in the sand, ten years later. A leather boot. "No," he said. "I never did."

He saw himself and Sid like an equation – a bit of accountancy work, one life minus another. That was the difference between living and dying. Sixty-five years where he went to war, started a career, married, had arguments with his teenage daughter, retired, grew old. But in the first few days, he just thought: *Isn't it strange that I'm here and Sid is not?*

In the Navy he'd met city lads he would have scoffed at a few years earlier. One got him the factory job. Another told him about accountancy. He built a life around the solidity of numbers. He wanted memories of mowed lawns, tea on the table and camping holidays. "I'm right here," Gertie had whispered into his ear, as the letter burned.

But that song was stuck in his head. And he could never forget Sid.

"Pepper," Angela shouted from the door. "I found it. Hiding with the bloody shoe polish."

Sue glanced at Arthur. Then she slid her plate over, and he scraped the remaining cockles onto it, and when Angela returned to the table, she didn't appear to suspect a thing.

*

They were playing blackjack on the table in the lounge, the dishes safely cleaned and stacked on the kitchen sink, when they heard a jolt. It was the sound of a key turning in the lock. Angela paused, card in hand. "Who could it be?" she asked.

There was only one person it could be. Arthur realised with sudden dread that it was a Saturday. "Margaret," he said.

The name had hardly come out of his mouth when she was there, framed in the doorway. Her bag landed on the floor with a thump. "I thought you were dead," she said. "Never picking up the phone, not a word when I left all those messages."

Arthur felt a stab of guilt, followed by an even bigger rush of panic. He'd seen the red light flashing on the answer machine, but he'd been too busy, what with practising English with Sue, all the meals and getting his winnings back.

"God, Dad, do you know how much I worried?"

"There's no need to be so dramatic," Arthur said. "You can see I'm alive." He should have paid more attention to the flashing light. But deep down, he knew he'd taken a perverse pleasure in ignoring it.

Margaret shook her head. "*No need to be dramatic.* I came to this house not knowing what I was going to find." She sat down heavily on an empty chair.

Arthur wanted to ask how she would like it if he barged into her flat whenever he damned pleased. But as he opened his mouth, he felt the tender spot on his cheek and remembered the bruise. It was on the right side of his face, the side in shadow. If Margaret spotted it, there would be all kinds of questions. She'd never understand.

He kept his face rigid. "Well, now you can see I'm fine," he said.

Margaret let out a great sigh, like a tyre deflating. Her eyes flicked from one person to another, as if she'd only just noticed they had company. She turned to Angela. "Mrs O'Brien?"

"Hello, Margaret," Angela said.

Now she was speaking to Sue. "And your name?"

Sue pushed her chair backwards. "Hello, nice-to-meet-you," she rattled off, her expression suggesting there couldn't be anything worse. Margaret stared at her.

"Sue's from Arthur's church," Angela said.

"You said I should get more involved," Arthur said. "It's a befriending scheme."

He watched Margaret carefully. She seemed to be struggling with the idea that he had, for once, obeyed her. If she didn't believe him, there would be more questions. If she did, it would embolden her. Still, anything better than her noticing the bruise on the side of his face. He kept very still.

Margaret picked up the pepper pot and held it between her hands. "Dad," she said. "I've been calling all week. Panicking. I don't understand why you couldn't just pick up the phone." Her voice broke a little on the final word.

"Here," Angela said. "Let's make Margaret a cup of tea." She patted Sue's arm. "Would you mind?"

Margaret croaked: "Decaf."

Sue, who had got up, looked confused.

"Mint'll do," Angela said, waving at the kitchen. Sue got up. Through the open door, Arthur watched her put the kettle on. She flicked the switch and turned to stare out of the darkened window. Was she thinking of running away? But if she did that, Margaret would ask why she'd disappeared, and then there would be endless questions, risk assessments, and strangers dropping round to check up on him. *Stay,* he willed her. *Just a little longer. Just pretend everything is okay.*

Suling turned away from the window and stared at the floor. Then, after a moment of hesitation, she emptied his jar of Horlicks into a mug and picked up the kettle.

Once she had a drink in her hand, Margaret's shoulders became firm again. "Look, Dad, I really have tried, but you push me to the limit. You really do. That incident with the builder, and now not even answering my calls? You're my father."

She was his, not the other way round. He'd held her when she howled in the night, tied her shoelaces. It was up to him if he answered her calls. But he felt Sue's dark eyes on him and bit back his words. Let Margaret finish her drink and go without noticing the bruise. He'd deal with everything else later.

Margaret took a sip of Horlicks, and grimaced. She turned to Sue. "So, tell me – how did you get involved in the befriending scheme?"

"Don't understand," Sue said. Arthur wished she'd smile, instead of watching Margaret like she was a dog that might bite.

Margaret persisted. "Have you recently moved here?" This time, Sue only shook her head. Her knuckles were white, Arthur noticed, as if she might spring from the table at any moment.

"There's something familiar about you."

"You must have met at church," Angela said.

"Maybe." Margaret peered into her mug then put it down on the table.

Angela picked up her cards. "Would you like to join us for a game, Margaret?"

Arthur could have cursed her. To his relief, Margaret shook her head. "I've got to pack for another work trip. Dortmund this time."

Arthur wasn't sure where Dortmund was, but it sounded reassuringly far away. "That sounds nice," he said.

"I'll be back next Saturday night," Margaret said.

"Well, you don't have to worry about me."

"But I do, Dad." Margaret stood up. "I wish you'd understand."

In the low light of the lounge, he could see something of Gertie in the arched eyebrows and the big grey eyes. He wanted suddenly to take her hand, to tell her some little fact about her mother, but as he hadn't the words. He just said: "Bye, Margie."

She paused where she was in the doorway, bag still in hand. "Dad, what's that on your face?"

"What? Nothing." He'd turned, just a little, to watch her go.

"It's a bruise," she said. She was already crouching by his side. "Did you fall?"

She should be in the car by now, should be turning the key and finding the bite while he emptied the mug in the sink.

"Just a little knock," he said. "Nothing serious."

"When did this happen, Dad?"

"I told you, it's nothing."

"Why didn't you tell me?" Now it was Angela whom Margaret was questioning. She turned to Sue. "Or you? You're supposed to be his befriender."

Sue pushed her chair back. Any moment now, she might bolt for the door.

"Enough," Arthur said. "They're not your spies." The lamplight was deceptive. This was the real Margaret, the one who wanted power. "I don't have to tell you about every little incident."

Margaret lowered her voice. "Dad, the befriender is supposed to be checking up on you. That's the whole point of these schemes." She shook her head. "What actually happened with the bruise, Dad?"

"I told you," he said.

"You should see a doctor."

He'd avoided doctors since Dr Thomas retired, and a stream of cool-headed women in their thirties took over the GP surgery. "It's only a bruise."

"But how did you get it, Dad?"

Would she never leave? "None of your business." The words slipped from his mouth before he could stop them.

Margaret's voice hardened. "When I'm back, I think it would be best if I stayed a few nights. Saw how you're managing. I can stay in the spare room."

Watched in his own home. Sue would have nowhere to go. But he couldn't say that. "I'm happy on my own," he said.

"You're only half an hour's drive away."

"Forty-five minutes," Margaret corrected him. "Anyway, that's not the point. Sometimes it feels like you're on another planet." She nodded at Sue and Angela. "Goodbye. Dad – call the doctor. I'm back in a week. I'll see you at church on Sunday. Then we can discuss how to keep you safe"

"We'll do nothing of the sort," Arthur said.

Margaret shook her head. "I'm coming to stay, whatever you think about it." She cleared her throat. "I owe it to Mum."

Dragging Gertie's name into it, when the good woman would never have asked her to do anything of the sort. But before he could respond, his daughter was already walking through the door, and a few seconds later, he heard the click as she let herself out.

Chapter Twenty-Nine

There was something obscene about the way My Regret had shouted at her father. She had been so loud, so angry, like a malfunctioning machine. Then some spark had finally died, and her anger turned to suspicion. Suling felt it on her, like the spotlight on the dark street outside the factory walls.

Now she had gone, there was an uneasy silence. Electric Auntie had started asking Old Uncle questions, and then the two of them had gone into the kitchen — Suling could hear them muttering through the half-closed door. She was not sure what Old Uncle had said to My Regret, but she was certain his daughter didn't like her. If they asked her to leave, she would have to go. She had no choice. They could phone the police within seconds.

The cards were still scattered on the table, a snapshot of her last carefree moments. They had been playing a funny version of Ban Luck, and before My Regret stormed in, Suling had been winning. She collected the cards in a pack and shuffled them. Luck and danger grazing past each other in her hands.

Old Uncle and Electric Auntie returned to the table.

"Game?" she asked. Perhaps if they started playing again, they could forget the interruption.

But Old Uncle cleared his throat.

"Why you here, Sue?" he asked.

She put down the cards. There was a right and a wrong answer to his question, but she didn't know the rules.

"You got passport?" Electric Auntie asked. It seemed like a clue.

She thought for a moment. If she said no, they would think she was breaking the law, and if she said yes, they wouldn't need to shelter her any more.

"Passport lost," she said.

They looked confused, and for once she was glad. Confusion meant they couldn't make a decision.

"How?" Old Uncle asked.

She didn't want to lie to them, but the truth could be long or short. The debt collector's hands gripping her. The fire. The dog starting to bark. All this had happened.

"Man chase me," she said.

Old Uncle opened his mouth again and then Electric Auntie hissed something at him and he shut it. He glanced at the phone on the wall.

She could read his thoughts far easier than she could understand his words. He was thinking that if he just called the police, they would take her away and he could forget about the whole thing before his daughter returned.

She held her breath.

Electric Auntie picked up the cards and dealt them.

Old Uncle looked at his hand. "Passport lost," he repeated slowly. "Police could help."

She looked at her own. A three and a two. She needed more to have a chance of winning. But if she went higher than thirteen, she'd lose.

"No police," she said as calmly as she could. "Hit me."

Electric Auntie dealt again. A five. Now she had ten. She fanned the cards against her chest and watched Old Uncle. The lines on his face betrayed how deeply My Regret had scared him.

She wanted to explain everything. She wanted to tell him how her mother spent every day bent double in the fields, and still lay awake worrying about food at night. She wanted to tell him about the bus she caught to the city, how it was like going forward in time, to a place where money sparkled, just out of reach. She wanted to tell him the reasons why, once you went forward, it was impossible to go back.

Old Uncle's eyes flicked to the phone again, then back to the cards in his hand. His forehead crinkled. He wanted her to stay, she realised, but he didn't know how. She needed to make it easier for him.

"A job," she said in English. "A job could help."

Electric Auntie shuffled the pack of cards and murmured something.

Old Uncle nodded to show he'd understood. "Hit me," he said.

*

Later, after the card game was over and she was tidying up the lounge, Electric Auntie's question came back to Suling. "You got passport?" she'd said. But Suling had vanished when she got her passport. In it she had a different name, and a different identity. She was Li Meihua, from Xiamen, a big city on the coast, and at twenty she gained three years of age overnight.

She got her passport from a broker with a tiny office near a temple, just a short walk from the fortune tellers and lantern sellers, and other such vendors of luck. She'd already tried a few more official-looking places near the factory, but they all expected her to raise the funds for the journey elsewhere. Changfa had persuaded his cousins and uncles to take out loans to invest in him, but she didn't have that kind of family network. So there she was at the broker by the temple.

"Not so long ago, you could just turn up and say you were in trouble with the Government," the broker said. He was a middle-aged man with glasses and a white shirt stained with sweat. "They liked that. They didn't care if your belly rumbles, but if you picked a fight with the authorities – welcome in!"

"So I should pretend I'm in trouble with the Government?"

The broker shook his head. "They've changed the rules." He picked up a pen and started filling in a form in front of him.

"There's another thing." She reached for the strap of her bag. This was the time in the conversation with a broker that it usually became clear there was no point in her staying any longer. "I need the full loan."

He put the pen down.

She picked up her bag. "I guess it's just not possible," she said.

The broker jumped up behind his desk as though he'd been stung. "Of course it's possible. That's my job." He named his price. It was far more than her savings.

She sat in the chair in the poky office with Meihua's passport in her hands, and thought as fast as she could. The sum of money was so vast, she had no idea whether she was getting a good deal. But once she had completed the journey, she'd be earning more too. In just a few years, she'd be able to build a home for her mother in the village, maybe even start a business. She could pay the money back in instalments.

There were other countries she could try, countries that were closer, easier to slip into. But Changfa had gone to England.

"It's a deal," she said.

At first Meihua just seemed part of this crazy wager, but later, when she realised what she had got herself into, it was comforting to have her passport in her hand.

It was Meihua who arrived at the airport in some unpronounceable European country. It was Meihua who climbed into the van driven by men whose only words were "shut up" and "no". It was Meihua who huddled in the dark for hours and hours with other invisible people as they crossed borders they could not see, and Meihua who was forced to agree to an even bigger loan to get into the next truck, the one that would take her to England. It was Meihua who felt like she was about to suffocate in the hot, tomb-like container, before finally, the door opened and she fell out into the fresh, damp air.

Now, Meihua too was gone. "Sue," Old Uncle had written in his crooked handwriting on the jar with her winnings.

The table was still strewn with cards and coins. She had relaxed too much in this house. If she didn't reinvent herself quickly, sooner or later, the debt collector would come to the end of the trail of false names and find her. Or worse still, My Regret would tell the police, and Meihua's whole, terrible journey would be in vain.

She gathered the cards and gave them one last shuffle. All the broker's false reassurances would be worth it if she could just get a proper job. And she was so close now, just a promise away. If only she could explain to Old Uncle how much she needed it.

She paused by the kitchen door, but Old Uncle was talking to Electric Auntie again, and the words still would not come.

"Good night," she said.

"Good night," they said.

She kept walking down the darkened hall.

Chapter Thirty

Sue had gone to bed. Angela was searching for her bag. "Stay for a dram," Arthur said. He still felt shaken from Margaret's visit earlier.

"Are you sure?"

Once in the lounge, he found the whisky in the sideboard and poured the golden liquid into two crystal glasses.

"Sorry about the whole church thing," he said awkwardly.

Angela laughed. "I'm more relieved. I worried I was leading Sue into sin."

Arthur sat down at the table. Sue had cleared it of the glasses and the wine bottles. Just a neat stack of cards remained. He picked one up and played with it as he thought over the evening's events again. What was Margaret doing storming in here and telling him what to do? His anger flared as he thought of how she'd questioned Sue. She could be his befriender, for all his daughter knew. Only she wasn't, and if Margaret came to stay in a week's time, she would soon find out the truth. He'd be shipped to sheltered housing by teatime.

He cleared his throat. It was hard to force the words out, but it had to be done. "I'll call the police tomorrow," he said.

Angela spluttered into her drink. "What?"

"Well, who else can I call?"

Angela's eyes narrowed. "Sue asked us to help her, Arthur."

"I've helped her enough," he said. His bruises were fading. He'd make damn sure not to fall again. The house was all he

158

had left, and Margaret was not going to separate him from it.

Angela set her glass down. "A friend got me my first job after I left Reggie," she said. "I hadn't worked since the war. Well, I had raised a family, but suddenly none of that counted." She leaned back. "The day I got the phone call was the best of my life. I could heat my flat."

Arthur remembered how Gertie used to invite Reggie round for tea. "The poor man," she'd say, as they waved him goodbye.

"A situation, we used to call it," Angela said. She picked up her glass again and rolled her whisky round. "Sue's suggestion isn't bad. Her new boss can sort the paperwork and she'll be able to look after herself."

Arthur thought of the shuttered-up shops on the high street. "There's no jobs round here for anyone."

Angela downed her whisky. "I know a man who hires a lot of people from abroad. Maybe he can sort it out."

"This is daft," Arthur said.

"If Gertie was here with us, what would she say?"

The question made him bristle, but Angela's steady gaze was on him. For once, she looked serious. He glanced over at Gertie's empty chair. His wife had been no soft touch. For all her printed dresses, she was a pub landlord's daughter. When they were alone, she'd make him laugh with the stories of the gattered gadgees she'd ejected from the doorway on her father's orders. But she also knew how to comfort a man when he was down, to welcome almost anyone, and she never quite understood the point of locking the front door.

He tipped the whisky into his mouth. It burned. "Alright," he said.

"Good," Angela said. She looked at her watch. "I'd better

go. Tomorrow morning for the care home?"

Her words caught him off guard. "What are you on about?"

Angela laughed.

"I don't see what's funny," he said.

"No, it's just – I meant the man I know," Angela looked far too merry. "The one who hires people. He works at Reggie's care home."

*

The care home towered over the town. It was a grand red brick building on a hill, and from a distance a stranger might mistake it for a hotel. Its doors were painted a glossy green, and the panes glowed deceptively, as if there were girls inside trailing silk dresses along the tiles, and ferns and a piano playing.

Arthur hated thinking about it. The place was a halfway house to death, the guests suffocated by fluffy carpets and padded slippers and thick glass windows that never opened. Those green doors had shut behind friends and neighbours, and he'd never seen them again. This in turn reminded him he had promised to visit and had found an excuse every time. He was grieving. He had a cold. They wouldn't remember him anyway.

But now he was here, and he couldn't turn back because, after the initial battle of getting her from the car to the wheelchair, Angela was gliding along beside him. "I came last week, you just sign the visitor's book. It's very lax," she was saying. Arthur imagined Margaret leaving him in a cell-like room, Gertie's picture tacked to the wall in a gesture of consolation. Never, he thought to himself. I will never let her do it to me.

And now Angela was jabbing at the button that opened the doors, and they were in a large reception room, light streaking across the old, wooden floor. A visitor's book lay on a table next to a bottle of hand sanitiser. He stooped to sign it. When he straightened up again, Angela had motored off somewhere. He squeezed the bottle and wiped his hands until the liquid had disappeared.

"Got the code," Angela said cheerily.

"What code?" he said.

"The code to get out, of course," she said. "They keep the doors of the ward locked. The lifts are over here."

In the lift, Angela squinted in the mirror. She'd put on lipstick, he noticed.

"Bit strange, isn't it, visiting your ex-husband?" he said.

She coughed. "I stopped worrying about being strange a long time ago."

The doors opened and he found himself face to face with a woman, her grey hair straggly, her nails childishly painted. "Freddy," she said.

"I'm not Freddy," Arthur said.

"Freddy." The woman swayed towards him, grasped at him. He felt a deep panic, as if her touch would drag him into her world.

"Freddy's over there," Angela said. She accelerated out of the lift and patted the woman's arm. "We'll find him in the TV room, I think."

"Freddy," the woman moaned. Arthur waited for his horror to subside.

He was standing in a brightly lit central corridor. It was humid and smelled of nappies and custard creams. All around him were confused sounds. An insistent thump, as if someone

161

was stamping their foot again and again. A low murmur. And from an open door, above the crackle of a TV, still, that plaintive note: "Freddy."

Arthur hoped Angela really did know the code.

The door with 'O'Brien' on it opened into a small room with a single bed, a chest of drawers and some photographs on the wall. In the middle of it, a man was sitting in an armchair with a book in his hands. His skin was crumpled, like greaseproof paper, and he was almost completely bald but for a fringe of white hair above each ear. In front of him was a small table with a plate of biscuits, untouched.

The man sat so still he could have been a mannequin. But then he spoke one word. "Picnic."

"He's reading," Angela said behind him. "Hello, old comrade."

The man looked up and gazed at them benignly. "Hello," he said, and then his eyes slid back to the book. "Hermitage," he read.

Arthur sat down on the bed. "Hello, Reggie," he said. The man's watery eyes looked at him with more curiosity this time. He opened his mouth and said again: "Picnic."

Angela waved a hand at Arthur. "Help yourself to biscuits."

"He might want them himself."

"Oh, Reggie had many flaws, but he's always believed in redistribution. And he isn't eating them, is he?"

Her flippancy annoyed Arthur. "No doubt you've got the same rule for the house," he said.

"That's the kids' business, not mine," Angela said. "I'm just dropping in. Anyway, it's the practical thing to do. They kept him there as long as they could."

"I'll bet they did," he said grimly.

"Hmm." Angela picked up a book and flipped a page. "How well do you think you would have looked after Gertie, do you think? If she had lived?"

Her question almost winded Arthur, it made him so angry.

"What kind of man do you think I am?"

"It was just a question."

"In sickness and in health," Arthur said. "That's what we promised. At least I did. Maybe you said something else."

"Okay." Angela held her hands up. "I'm sorry. I shouldn't have asked."

"Picnic," murmured Reggie.

Arthur would have cared for Gertie, of course he would have cared for her. Still, it felt obscene to imagine pushing her in a wheelchair, spooning food into her mouth.

"Where's this man you were mentioning anyway?" he said. "I want to get out of this place."

*

Mr Taylor – "call me Adam" – was a middle-aged man in a bulging shirt. His brown hair was greying. "Chocolate?" he asked when they squeezed into his office at the end of the downstairs ward. "The families are always giving us them."

"No thanks," Arthur said. Angela dug her hand in.

"So, what can I do you for?" Mr Taylor said jovially. Angela looked at Arthur and began to peel off a purple shiny wrapper.

"I have a friend," he began, realising how ludicrous his story was going to sound. "A friend overseas. She's looking for work. She's young, strong and polite – and respectful. She'd be very good for you here."

"I'm sure she would, I'm sure she would," Mr Taylor said, unwrapping a Bounty and popping the chocolate in his mouth. "Problem is" – he chewed – "we only take overseas workers with nursing qualifications. Does she have those?"

"I didn't know you needed nursing qualifications to help someone get dressed," Arthur said. "Don't you just need them to be kind?"

Mr Taylor waved his hand. "Competitive market, competitive market. And this is a good nursing home, you know." He nodded deferentially to Angela. "Unless she has already got a visa because of relatives, or something like that."

Arthur thought of Sue on that first day in the garage, in the jumper with the holes. "No, she doesn't have any family here."

"Very independent," Mr Taylor said. He bit into a chocolate caramel and fought with it a moment before continuing. "Well, mmm – look, we'd love to have her, but as you can see there are these tiddly problems with the visa and qualifications and all that."

They sat there in silence. Arthur realised how much he'd been banking on this donnat taking Sue off his hands.

"Another chocolate?" the man said.

"Is there anywhere else we could try?" Angela asked.

Mr Taylor tapped his fingers on the desk for a moment. "Hmm, ahh, well... Have you tried the agencies?"

"What agencies?" Arthur asked.

"We very rarely use them – I mean, we are a good care home," the man said. "But occasionally when we're short-staffed." He scribbled an address on a post-it note and handed it to Arthur. "They've got an office in town. Helpful when you're in a tight spot. Mostly warehouse jobs and agriculture. As I say, I really don't know very much about them."

Arthur noticed he had chocolate in his teeth.

"Thank you," Angela said. "I knew you'd help us. You were such a duck when I turned up on my own last week."

"Well, er, your friend might want to look into it a bit before signing anything," Mr Taylor said, as they stood up to go. "They're a bit cagey there. Might be worth asking a few questions before you tell them why you're there, if you see what I mean."

Arthur didn't, but the heat was starting to itch at him, and he could smell something sickly sweet, as if someone was trying to disguise the realities of being ninety and not able to use a toilet by yourself. Anyway, there was no need to stay any longer. He felt the piece of paper in his pocket. They had the address of the agency. Margaret could worry all she liked. He was going to take care of everything.

"Goodbye," Mr Taylor said, shaking their hands and pressing a chocolate into each one. "As I say, we are a good care home. We'd much rather have nothing to do with them at all."

Chapter Thirty-One

Suling thought she'd struck a deal with Old Uncle, but then he'd disappeared after breakfast and still wasn't back. When he'd left the house, she'd assumed he was going to the garden. But a few moments later, she heard an engine, and when she looked out of the kitchen window, his car was pulling out of the drive. It felt like an omen.

The mobile phone was still on the shelf, but its battery had died, and she still hadn't found the charger. She went into the garage, unhooked a rucksack that looked like it had hung there for at least ten years, and began to fill it with anything she thought might not be missed. A rusty knife under a chest of drawers that Old Uncle could never stoop to retrieve. A tangle of wire that would take hours to ease into one, perfect coil. A jumper drowned in dust. Some big round coins, not like any she'd ever seen before, but then she hadn't seen much money in this country. A pair of boots – too small for Old Uncle – that fitted her perfectly. She wondered who they belonged to as she slipped her feet in. A jacket too, that looked smart and felt surprisingly snug. She dug her hand in the pocket and found two small woollen gloves.

Now she was ready.

She went back into the house, unlocked the back door and waited, rucksack by her side, for the police to arrive.

But no-one came. She looked at the clock. Old Uncle had been away for two hours. If he had gone straight to the police, they should be here by now. She made herself a pot of tea and tried to concentrate on her English dictionary.

The doorbell rang. She thought of Changfa and the blue lights. At least she had her bags packed. It rang again. A shrill blast, like a policeman's whistle. But nothing else happened. She crept towards the door and peered through the tiny glass eye.

A girl about her own age was standing there. She was dressed smartly, in a shirt that showed off her cleavage and a short black pencil skirt, but her hair was striped brown and gold like a tiger. She had a big white cardboard box in her hands.

Old Uncle never opened the door to strangers. Suling kept her eye pressed to the glass. The girl tucked her hair behind her ears and rang again. She seemed determined. Was she a policewoman? Someone sent by the debt collector?

She tried not to make any sound. The girl's eyebrows furrowed, and then she hoisted up the white box and walked away.

Suling stayed at the glass eye, watching her. The girl clip-clopped up the driveway. A policewoman would wear flats. The debt collector would send someone more intimidating. The girl disappeared from view. Suling put on her coat, pulled the hood over her eyes and let herself out.

From the bushes she could get a good view of the street without revealing herself. The woman was now at Electric Auntie's door. Maybe she was a friend of My Regret's, sent to gather information after the scene last night. The door opened and Electric Auntie's blonde, stringy daughter-in-law appeared. They spoke on the steps for a few minutes, and then the daughter-in-law waved her away dismissively.

Suling had seen that gesture before. It was the same dismissive wave her mother made when the tofu seller came round. Miss Tiger Stripe was not looking for anything. She was a saleswoman.

The girl picked up her box again and marched up the driveway towards the next house. She would go all the way down the road, no doubt, and try the houses on the opposite side. Suling wished she had opened the door now. She would have liked to know what was in those boxes, how much money the woman made.

She went back to her studies.

She was learning about giants, gin and giraffes when the doorbell rang again. It was the girl with tiger striped hair.

This time, she didn't hesitate. She opened the door. If Old Uncle came back, she would act stupid.

Miss Tiger Stripe stood on the doorstep. She blinked nervously. "Hello, want health?" she said.

"Wait," Suling said, and opened her dictionary.

Miss Tiger Stripe's eyes widened, but then she forced a smile and said again: "Want health?"

With a lot of page-turning, Suling learned that Miss Tiger Stripe had a "health secret" that would "purify" and "cleanse" her, and it was all contained inside her cardboard box. A cold wind was blowing, and despite all her talk of health, Miss Tiger Stripe was shivering.

"Come in," Suling said. She was interested in this girl, who looked like she could only be a few years older than her.

A few minutes later, Miss Tiger Stripe was sitting at the kitchen table and Suling was making her a cup of tea. Miss Tiger Stripe's silver lacquered nails crept round the mug and her white hands began to glow pink again. As she warmed up, she talked. Suling learned that, thanks to the health secret, Miss Tiger Stripe was purifying her life and getting a new flat. The pills would make her rich.

Suling thought of Changfa's cockling dreams. "Really?" she asked.

Miss Tiger Stripe flicked her hair and drew herself up. "Really," she said.

She reached into her handbag, all white leather and silver clasps, and pulled out a handful of glossy leaflets. They showed a happy family; a tall, tanned man and his blonde-haired wife, and two gold-and-white children. The wife wore a crisp pink summer shirt, and her head was thrown back in laughter. "Health secret," Miss Tiger Stripe said, tapping the picture.

It was more fun practising English with Miss Tiger Stripe than Old Uncle.

"How much money?" Suling asked.

Miss Tiger Stripe sat up straight. "A lot."

"How old are you?"

"Nineteen."

"Where are you from?"

"Preston."

"Why no coat?"

"No coat, better sales."

"Husband? Boyfriend?"

Miss Tiger Stripe looked down at the picture of the happy family. "No," she said.

"Family?"

Miss Tiger Stripe pointed at the child. "Daughter."

"One daughter, no husband?" Suling wanted to make sure she understood.

Miss Tiger Stripe looked annoyed. She flipped the page of the leaflet, and the family vanished.

"No husband," she said sharply. "I have health secret. I am my own boss." She looked at her watch. "I have to go."

She picked up her box and grimaced with the weight of it.

"Need help?" Suling asked.

"No, thank you," Miss Tiger Stripe said.

Suling felt like she had offended her, although she didn't know how. She noticed a few coins lying on the table by the door. "Wait," she said, picking them up. "How much?"

Miss Tiger Stripe hesitated. Then she opened her box and looked at the bottles. "You can have one," she said eventually.

Suling paid for it. She thought Old Uncle wouldn't mind. He could certainly do with a health secret. She decided she liked Miss Tiger Stripe, with her dream of being her own boss.

After the transaction, a bit of colour returned to Miss Tiger Stripe's cheeks. She flicked her hair again and smiled. "Thank you," she said. She reached for the box again.

"Need help," Suling said, and this time it wasn't a question.

"I'm fine," Miss Tiger Stripe said again with the same determination, but when Suling helped her adjust it she didn't resist. Instead, she fumbled in her pocket, box balanced on one arm, and pulled out a card. "Here," she said.

It had a name on it, and a phone number.

"What's your name?" Miss Tiger Stripe asked.

Just taking the card felt like being connected to something electric. Suling held it carefully between her fingers, scared she might crush it. She remembered a name she used to try out by the old swimming pool. "Jenny," she said.

"Well, Jenny, if you want to be your own boss, give me a call."

And then she was gone. Through the glass eye, Suling saw her teeter back to a shiny black car, put the boxes in the boot and drive away.

She went back to the kitchen, put the pills on the table, and placed the card under her pillow. Old Uncle was still not back. She leafed through his map books until she found the place Miss Tiger Stripe had mentioned – Preston. It was an orange mass on green fields, a town if not a city. Two thin black lines twisted through the centre. When she found the map key and checked it against her dictionary, her heart thudded. She had Miss Tiger Stripe's number. And Preston had a railway station.

Chapter Thirty-Two

"Look for the hairdresser," Angela said. "Quick – I'm desperate for a fag." The tone of her voice told Arthur she hadn't quite forgiven him for banning cigarettes in the car. She seemed weary, but when Arthur asked, she just said she hadn't slept well. Now they were trying to find the agency Mr Taylor had told them about.

"What does the piece of paper say?" Arthur asked.

Angela squinted as she tried to read the care home manager's handwriting. "Tarn Road. Small office – between a letting agent and a hairdresser. No name."

"That's helpful," Arthur said.

"Carol's Curls," Angela said suddenly. "That's the hairdresser. It must be somewhere near here."

Arthur parked. "I'll wait for you here," Angela said, opening the car door and lighting her cigarette.

Tarn Road had once been a street full of hardware shops, but now half of the windows were boarded up and the pavements were strewn with rubbish. It still took a bit of wandering up and down before Arthur noticed a small sign in a doorway stating: "Maloney Recruitment: first floor."

"Are you going to manage all those stairs?" Angela shouted.

Arthur ignored her. He was damned if he was going to show any signs of weakness. He gripped the handrail and pulled himself up, step by step. With each ascent, he ran the words again through his head. Friend from overseas. Young, strong, polite. The stairwell was dark and damp. At the top he teetered for a second, managed to balance himself and knocked on the door.

"Hello?" came a suspicious-sounding voice.

"Can I come in?" Arthur asked.

The door opened a crack and Arthur, who had been resting his arm against it, wobbled in mid-air before he found a radiator to clutch onto. He looked up and saw two men behind a desk, both middle-aged and bald, with faces that reminded him of potatoes. They were dressed in suits which would look smart, if not for the smear of mustard on the more potatoey one's collar, and the hair poking out of the other's loosely buttoned shirt.

Arthur wouldn't trust them with a safety pin. In an instant, he revised entirely what he was going to say.

"I've come to see about hiring a carer," he said.

Both potatoes opened their mouths, but before they could speak, he added: "Is it possible to get a chair?"

Hairy Chest got up awkwardly and dragged a chair out from the corner of the room. Arthur sat down. He thought of Angela puffing away on the street below and hoped she was keeping an eye on the time. There was something about these men he didn't like.

"So you're looking for a carer," Mustard Smear said. "And you came to us."

The two men exchanged glances. "We don't usually deal with individuals," he added.

"Or carers," said Hairy Chest.

Arthur cleared his throat. He wasn't a very good liar. But he could tell the truth.

"My daughter is hell-bent on sending me to a care home," he said. "But I want to stay in my own house." He leaned forward. "One of my mates said that you knew how to get a worker for pretty much any job."

Mustard Smear smiled in a self-satisfied way. Arthur realised with a thrill that his story had worked. "I hear you can do it cheap as well," he said encouragingly.

The smile broadened. "You're right about that," Hairy Chest said. "Look, I'm not saying we can help or anything, but tell us what you're looking for. Do you mind if they're foreign?"

"You want cheap, you need foreign," Mustard Smear said. "The locals, they just complain. They want – what's it called?"

"Minimum wage," Hairy Chest supplied.

"That's it, they're always going on about pay, and time off and stuff. The foreign ones, they don't complain."

Margaret always huffed and puffed about pay. "Sometimes young people don't realise how lucky they've got it," Arthur said.

Hairy Chest rolled his eyes. "Amen."

"He has a teenager," Mustard Smear explained.

"And you can't even smack them any more," Hairy Chest grumbled.

"It's the silly bikes they ride around on that gets me," said Mustard Smear.

"Take it from me – it was better before," Arthur said.

"Well, you've come to the right place," Mustard Smear said. "Those foreign girls, they'll take you back in time." Both potatoes started laughing.

Mustard Smear glanced at the door, as if to check it was closed. He wiped something from his eye. "They know how to be discreet," he said. "Want a bit of a cuddle, bit of a tweak, they won't say a word."

"But we'll have to charge a bit extra," Hairy Chest said. "Just to make sure it's a nice one."

They were still chuckling away. Arthur thought of Sue, in Margaret's old clothes that were too big for her. He felt like shaking them by their collars, but he forced a smile. "You mean they really don't complain?"

"Believe me, these girls don't want to draw attention to themselves," Hairy Chest said. "One look at their paperwork, and—" He stopped suddenly, as if Mustard Smear had just kicked him, which Arthur thought he probably had.

"Well, thank you for all your advice," Arthur said.

"Our pleasure," Hairy Chest said with a wink. Mustard Smear grunted.

Going down the stairs was almost as treacherous as going up them. Angela was still sitting in the car seat, making eyes at a small Jack Russell tied to the lamp post.

"Reggie said dogs were too noisy," she said, looking up. "But they love us for what we are. Well, what do you think? Should we send Sue to them?"

Arthur thought of how he'd left her that morning, curled up in the chair, mouthing English words she could catch on TV. "Certainly not," he snapped.

"They wouldn't take her?"

"The opposite."

"Then what's the problem?" Angela said, blowing a final kiss to the dog. "It sounds like they're not fussy."

"That's exactly the problem," Arthur said. He sat down in the driver's seat and put his foot down on the accelerator. They were the kind of men he hadn't seen since he was young, but he knew them. The landlord who always spent a bit too long talking to his sister when he turned up to collect the overdue rent. The overseer at the factory. The kind of small, pudgy, ordinary man who lived like a king off other people's bad luck. He had sworn to have nothing to do with that kind of man, and he wasn't about to start now.

The radio in the car was some politician spouting buzzwords about "progress". He turned it off.

But what was he to do about Sue?

"That dog was quite something," Angela said, looking out of the window.

Chapter Thirty-Three

Old Uncle seemed troubled. He'd disappeared for hours again. Now they were eating breakfast, and he had dark circles under his eyes. He was smearing more and more horrible black paste on his bread. Suling glanced at the calendar behind him, at the 'M' he had scrawled to mark My Regret's return. There were only three squares remaining.

She wanted to ask him what he'd do when his daughter got back, but she couldn't find the words. Or maybe she didn't want to know the answer.

So instead, she said: "You tired?"

Old Uncle looked up from his black paste.

"No," he said, so crossly that she knew he was. She waited until he finished and took his plate.

"I'll wash up," she said.

She turned on the tap, just a tiny adjustment at a time so it wouldn't spray. The water was hot and soapy. Three squares. Three days. She thought of My Regret's furious face. Of course, if she came home and found her mother surrounded by strangers, maybe she'd be furious too. But it was the thought of her mother alone that gnawed at her. She scrubbed the black paste off the rim of the plate.

Old Uncle appeared with a tea towel. He dried each object carefully and shuffled around the room, putting them back in their rightful place. She saw how slowly he moved, how he hesitated in front of the cupboards, as if he was a stranger in

177

his own home. She looked back down at the sink before he realised her eyes were on him.

Old Uncle put away the last plate. He gave her a nod and went to his room. When she passed the door on the way to the bathroom, she heard loud snoring.

She went back into the kitchen, pulled the card out of her pocket, and dialled the number on it.

"Hello?" Miss Tiger Stripe said.

"It's Jenny," she said.

*

Miss Tiger Stripe wanted to be her own boss, but she had strict rules for everyone else. When she pulled up, she handed Suling a tailored blouse, a short skirt and high heels and made her put them on in the back seat of the car. Then she opened her white leather handbag and brandished a mascara wand.

"Don't move," she said.

Suling stayed as still as she could while Miss Tiger Stripe applied the make-up. With her ointments and creams and pencils, she was half artist, half chemist. Finally, after what felt like hours, Miss Tiger Stripe said: "Open your eyes."

A sparkly eyelash trembled in the compact mirror. Suling leaned backwards until she could see her whole face. The girl in the mirror had glossy lips, blushing cheeks and big, dark eyes. Her hair even had highlights, although they were not as noticeable as Miss Tiger Stripe's. Suling hardly recognised herself, which was just as well because the debt collector wouldn't either. There was more than one way of hiding from him.

"That's better," Miss Tiger Stripe said with some satisfaction.

She drove them to a street Suling remembered from her days looking for food, with old stone houses and trees smouldering with the last of the autumn leaves.

They got out of the car. Miss Tiger Stripe handed Suling the boxes.

"Don't speak," she said. "Just smile."

The first door was an old woman, who took one look at the two of them and shut the door. But the next was a middle-aged man. When he saw them, he smiled, and Suling followed Miss Tiger Stripe's instructions and smiled back. She tried not to show how much her feet were already aching in Miss Tiger Stripe's high heels.

Miss Tiger Stripe explained about the health secret, and Suling, as instructed, pulled out the bottle.

"Your friend?" the man asked. He smiled a bit too much.

"Health expert," Miss Tiger Stripe corrected him.

The man's smile widened. "Go on," he said. "Give me two."

Suling's feet hurt. "Four," she said.

Miss Tiger Stripe shot her an angry glance, and she forced her glossy lips into a smile.

But the man laughed. "Okay, three then."

He disappeared into his house and came back with a crisp note, more than a cockler would earn in a day. Miss Tiger Stripe tucked it carefully away in her white handbag.

"Tarrah," the man said.

Once the door was shut, Miss Tiger Stripe turned to her. "Don't speak," she said with added emphasis. But she looked pleased all the same. They tried the next door, but no one was home, and there was no answer at the following house either, although Suling thought she saw a curtain tremble after they left.

The trees bowed in the wind. Her feet were really aching now. Maybe this job was not so different from cockling after all, scraping and scraping away until suddenly something emerged. Another door slammed in their faces. Miss Tiger Stripe flinched, and Suling saw how much it hurt her.

Suling wanted to tell her she was brave, the bravest person she'd met in this country, but she didn't have the words. So she just waited by the wall with the boxes while Miss Tiger Stripe smoked a cigarette, stubbed it out with her high heel, and then held up her head and said: "Next."

The last house on the street had a green door, with a little handwritten sign on it, and when it first opened, the harassed-looking woman jabbed her finger and said shouted "No God" before starting a coughing fit.

"No, no, no," Miss Tiger Stripe said, as if she was talking to someone very young. "No God. Health secret."

And she spoke to the coughing woman quite tenderly, too fast for Suling to understand, but she seemed to be asking her lots of questions. After a while, the woman stopped coughing and started to answer them. Her eyes flicked enviously over Miss Tiger Stripe's immaculate face as she pointed to her spots, her hair. Suling smiled and nodded. And at the end of it, the woman sighed and bought a whole box.

Once the door had closed, Miss Tiger Stripe hugged Suling, so quickly it took her by surprise. She was as happy as a little girl.

"Jenny, you are good luck," she said. She separated one of the notes. "Here," she said.

It was a £20 note, so valuable and delicate the wind could snatch it away at any moment. The skirt didn't have any pockets, so Suling tucked it into her bra.

Miss Tiger Stripe's phone rang. "Okay," she said, a slight frown skimming her forehead. "Okay, okay." She ended the phone call. "I have to go."

"I wait," Suling said. She wanted to keep going, to see how much money they could make, but Miss Tiger Stripe shook her head.

"Not today. Daughter's sick."

They got in the car. Suling glanced at herself in the wing mirror. She looked like a boss lady now, the kind who smiled down from Putian's billboards. She could swagger past the debt collector and he would never know. She wondered how long the drive was to Preston. What if she asked Miss Tiger Stripe to take her?

"Can you—" she began. But Miss Tiger Stripe's phone was ringing again. "Sorry," she said as she held it to her ear with her right hand, her left still steering the car as they drove through the terraces. "Yes, yes," she said into it. "Okay." Suling stared at the windows with their dirty blinds. If only she'd thought to bring her bag with her.

But Miss Tiger Stripe was already turning up the hill and a few minutes later, phone now clamped between her ear and shoulder, and she parked the car at the end of the Old Uncle's road. Suling glanced down at the shirt she'd borrowed, but Miss Tiger Stripe broke off from her phone conversation to wave her hand.

"Next time."

She said the words so casually, and yet they were like flicking a switch. Next time. More cash. A lift to Preston. A train ticket. The future.

Suling got out of the car. "Next time," she said. Still, she thought about grabbing her bag and planting herself back in the seat again. But before she had even reached the other side of the road, Miss Tiger Stripe had revved the engine, and the car was disappearing around the corner.

Chapter Thirty-Four

Margaret called on Saturday night. "I'm back," she said. "Did you see that doctor?"

"Don't patronise me."

"Right. Look, I'll come to church and we can discuss it afterwards. Do you need a lift?"

"I'll walk," Arthur said.

"But Dad—"

"I like it," he said. The wind whined under the door, as if calling out his lie.

The next morning, he put on his sheepskin hat with the earflaps and set out with an hour to spare. He edged down the hill, his gloved hand gripping the rail, each step threatening to wipe out his freedom. Still, it was better than waiting for Margaret in the kitchen with Sue. He'd forgotten how trusting the young were. Every time he'd come in the door, she'd look at him so expectantly. Her hopefulness weighed him down like a sodden coat.

The truth was, he'd tried a few places after the agency, places where they knew him as a customer, and they'd all said no. "We're closing at the end of the year as it is," Linda said, as she weighed the apples on the scales. "My back's gone and the kids are in Manchester." He'd had a pint with Mick from the Queen's Head, the sun showing up the shabbiness of the empty pub. The shop where Gertie bought her shoes for years was closed, with no indication of when it would reopen again.

He reached the church. Margaret was already there, but any chance he had to speak to her before the service was sabotaged by Amelia Clancy. "Are you coming to the social afterwards?" she cooed as she lowered herself into the pew beside them. "It would be lovely to see you there."

Arthur could think of nothing worse than sitting in the draughty church hall eating Mrs Clancy's limp cheese sandwiches.

"We're looking forward to it," Margaret said brightly, and when Arthur nudged her in protest, she hissed: "We talked about it on the phone." The congregation began to squawk the first hymn. Their dissonance made Arthur feel even more like he was falling apart.

So it was that he found himself sitting at a fold-out table in the church hall, a polystyrene cup of tea in his hands, while his daughter laughed at Father Mulroney's tales of weddings gone wrong. He watched her coldly. He saw her plan. She thought she could order him up some friends, the same way she rang suppliers for this part or that. He thought of the moment playing cards with Angela and Sue before she burst in. He already had friends. She just didn't like them.

"It was so sad, wasn't it, about Gertie?" Mrs Clancy said. She bit into a custard cream. "You must have been devastated."

Across the table, Margaret laughed as Father Mulroney croaked: "The rings, the rings."

"I'm fine," Arthur said shortly.

"But to be left all alone so suddenly—" Mrs Clancy pushed the plate towards him.

"I like my own company," he said. He thought of Mr Clancy, confined to a single, stuffy room. "You get a chance to visit your husband often?"

The lip-sticked mouth thinned. "Whenever I can," Mrs Clancy said. She tugged the plate back again and carefully picked up another biscuit. "I suppose you visit Gertie," she said. "Her grave, I mean. Is she buried in the churchyard here?"

"Up in the cemetery on the hill." Margaret broke off her conversation to interrupt. She cast a glance at Arthur. "Dad insisted on it."

"What a long way to walk," Mrs Clancy murmured. "I would so like to pay my respects, you know."

"I can give you a lift," Margaret said. "That okay, Dad?"

Mrs Clancy smiled. It wasn't a question at all, Arthur realised. "Of course," he said.

"Have a custard cream," Mrs Clancy said. "Well, Arthur, if you ever want to join the church social committee, we meet once a week, and we plan all kinds of events. Knitting, tea dances, introductions to computers." She began to list activities that Arthur never wanted to do. Across the table, Father Mulroney drank his tea and he heard Margaret say "befriending scheme".

"Tombola, bingo nights, flower arranging."

Margaret was now deep in conversation with Father Mulroney, and there was a red spot on her cheeks that Arthur didn't like.

"Choir – everyone welcome." Mrs Clancy's trembling hand hovered over a Jammy Dodger.

"What a shame," Margaret said loudly.

Father Mulroney murmured: "Well, the door's always open, my dear."

Margaret looked at Arthur and he knew straight away she was furious.

They were the only people left in the car park. Margaret helped Mrs Clancy into the car and shut the door. "There is no befriending scheme," she said, her brown hair crackling in the wind. "Father Mulroney said they haven't run one since 1999."

"I never said it was a formal—"

"Dad, why are you lying to me?"

Because it was all that stood between him and the care home. Because he felt closer to Sue than his own daughter.

"You burst in on me when I had guests round," he said.

Margaret shook her head. "No, Dad. Not guests. I realised why that girl looked so familiar. She was wearing my clothes."

It was unfair, his daughter's memory. She had the advantage, and she used it.

"She was borrowing them," he said.

"Yeah right, Dad." Margaret rolled her eyes.

"What's that supposed to mean?"

Margaret's hands were on her hips. "Linda at the grocer's told me you were trying to persuade her to take on a teenager, cash in hand. One of the Chinese lot from the sands."

He never should have trusted Linda. Always sneaking bruised fruit into the bag. "She's talking rubbish," he said.

Margaret ignored him. "How long has she been staying with you?" She sighed. "Actually, I don't want to know. You realise you're breaking the law, Dad? You're sheltering an illegal immigrant?"

A gust of wind nearly toppled him. "She's not illegal," he said. "She just had nowhere to go."

It was a mistake. Margaret seized on it.

"She is staying with you," she said. "Wearing my clothes. Putting you in danger."

Sue's steady hand, guiding him through the snow. "That's ridiculous," he said.

Margaret's eyes narrowed. "What's ridiculous is you don't like your daughter checking up on you, but you'll let a complete stranger into your house. What's ridiculous is—"

There was a knock on the car window. Mrs Clancy's watery eyes peered up at them through the dim glass. "We'll get this over and done with," Margaret hissed. "Then I'm coming home. We're going to sort this out."

*

Margaret drove. Arthur sat in the back seat and quietly fumed. If only he could warn Sue, tell her to scram for a couple of hours, leave the garage door on the latch so she could slip in at night. All those things Margaret said might be true, but they weren't fair. She'd flattened Sue just like she'd flattened him.

Instead, he was on his way to the wretched cemetery trapped in the back of Margaret's car with Mrs Clancy. Gertie was not that fond of Amelia in life, so why should she have to put up with her in death? But Margaret was talking away to her now, desecrating every bit of the day. What if one day he didn't remember anything, and all he had was Margaret talking about it? The idea gave him the shudders.

He'd chosen the cemetery on the hill because it was near where Gertie and he liked to walk in the early days, when they had just bought the house and their evenings were long and carefree. Margaret pulled up outside the stone arch, and they walked through the dark, brittle tunnel of yews, past the oldest stones, with their memorials to the mother and son who

186

drowned in the bay, a merchant's little slave boy. Mrs Clancy, her arm tucked in Margaret's, was playing an annoying game of guess-the-stone. "It's that one, isn't it?" she demanded behind Arthur. "Not quite," Margaret said. Somehow she'd managed to disguise her anger with the kind of false brightness you might use with a child.

Sorry, Arthur willed to the simple slate stone in the far corner. When he got there, the other two were still making their way through the rows, and he had time to look squarely at it: the curved grey headstone, the green grass where a queue of elderly relatives had sprinkled dirt into a deep pit, the epitaph, Gertrude Cleary, and then the blank space below it, where one day his name would be carved. If he was alone and steadier on his feet, he would have dropped to his knees and lain there, heart as close to the earth as possible. But Mrs Clancy was only two headstones away.

"Oh, isn't it nice and plain," Mrs Clancy declared. "Very thrifty of you, Arthur." Somehow, she had hooked herself onto his arm now. Margaret, freed from this chore, stepped closer to the grave. She began to cry in great, booming sobs. Arthur wished his daughter did not have these sudden, unselfconscious, expressions of grief. They made everyone uncomfortable. Even Mrs Clancy, a notorious weeper herself, fidgeted on his arm. "The flowers, dear," she said. "Don't forget the flowers."

Sniffing, Margaret laid down the bouquet she had picked up on the way – a large bunch of hothouse flowers.

"Lovely colours," Mrs Clancy said, as she clutched Arthur's arm. "What are those orange and pink ones again?"

The two women stood there chattering. Arthur stared at the stone. If it was the other way around, Gertie would have handled the day so much more deftly, he thought. She never lied, because she knew how to deliver the truth. She had a knack for cheerfully ending conversations. Perhaps that was why she was never afraid of starting them in the first place. He remembered what she'd snapped at him that day he'd complained about Angela coming round. "You're just flait. I like to think for myself."

He shut his eyes. He had wasted so much time being afraid. A gust of wind sent Mrs Clancy swaying. He felt the earth beneath his feet, the earth that was Gertie, holding him firm.

Chapter Thirty-Five

It was the day of the square with the M on it. After Old Uncle left for church, Suling called Miss Tiger Stripe.

"Hello?" Miss Tiger Stripe sounded confused.

"It's Jenny." Suling repeated the question she had rehearsed. "Are you working today?"

"It's Sunday," Miss Tiger Stripe said, as if this was an answer in itself.

Suling tried again. "Are you working Sunday?"

Miss Tiger Stripe laughed. "No," she said. "Look – I'll call you next week. Bye for now."

"Bye," Suling said. The phone clicked. She put the receiver down and stood there for a minute listening to the clock ticking. My Regret could kick her out of the house at any moment. She found the map showing the area around the bay. The main road ran along the coast, all the way around the curve of the bay before it finally reached a town with a railway station. That was the one she'd planned to walk along, and that was where the debt collector was most likely to check. But there were other roads, smaller ones that she could string together to get to the same place. Then a train to Preston, and a call to Miss Tiger Stripe. She tucked the business card into the map and put both in the rucksack.

She found a can of soup in Old Uncle's cupboard. Behind it was a black plastic cable, and when she tugged at it, she saw it was the charger. While the soup was heating on the stove, she plugged it into the mobile phone and watched the screen light up. There was only one number saved in the address book, and when she pressed on it, the house phone rang. She ate the soup with her eyes fixed on the window, the darkening sky, and the bay.

Old Uncle had left his telescope by the chair, so she put her eye to it and tried to find the trains across the bay. But there was nothing – it was too hard to pick them out in daylight. So instead, her eye wandered down the familiar streets of the town. There was the supermarket, easy to spot by its candy-coloured glow. There was the promenade, and that huddle of people might signify the tavern, what Old Uncle called a "pub". There were the walls of the swimming pool, where Kee Teh was no doubt finishing off her careful stores of food.

And there was the bay. It was hard to work out how big or small anything was here, because there was nothing to measure it against, only a bird that set off as soon as she came across it, as if it could sense that, far away, someone was watching. She drifted into nothingness. And then she stopped.

Something was moving.

She edged the telescope and saw black dots on the sand. They trembled with a rhythm that was too decisive to be birds. Cocklers. She knew enough about raking and pounding to recognise them. She edged along further. Yes, there were more – the cocklers were back. Of course, they could be red heads, but the red heads had tractors, and this was just a huddle of figures, alone in the sand.

Her heart thumped. Changfa. Maybe, just maybe, they had let him out. In her excitement, she nudged the telescope too far, and when she tried to find them again, she couldn't. Still, they must have somewhere to sleep at night. It was a long time since she checked the terraces.

Old Uncle would have found them with the telescope again. But he was still not home. Perhaps the church service was a special one. She didn't want to think about the other reasons he was still not here.

To distract herself, she put on a record, the one with the brass band. The sun was setting. Usually they would be in the kitchen, Electric Auntie leafing through the yellow cookbook while Old Uncle made them drinks. Those moments were the only times she felt warm in England, both inside and out. Like she'd arrived at her destination.

Old Uncle's whisky bottle stood on the table by the window. She poured herself a glass, turned off the sitting room light, pulled on a coat and slid open the window to the balcony. The evening was warmer than usual, and the fresh air cleared her head.

She wanted to keep her eyes fixed on the bay. The whisky was painful to drink. She sat curled up by the railings, surrounded by withered pot plants, listening to the sounds of the evening. The garden vanished into the dark. The lights of houses flickered across the bay. She poured herself another glass and shut her eyes, and with each sip she thought of Changfa. The first time she'd crept out to meet him in the fields at night. Sip. How he'd thrown himself onto the earth, humming "the moon represents my heart". Sip. His hand brushing hers. Sip. Their pulses colliding. Sip. The universe sparkling above them.

There was fire on her lips. She heard a car door slam and pushed the sliding window open a crack to listen. A few moments later she heard Old Uncle talking, muffled through the walls of the house. He had finally returned.

Then she heard another voice, one that instantly made her open her eyes. It was My Regret.

She sat up and winced with pain. She needed to get off the balcony and put the whisky bottle back before Old Uncle noticed. But just then, the light in the lounge came on, and My Regret entered.

Chapter Thirty-Six

"Here's what I think we'll do, Dad," Margaret said, as she pulled off her gloves. "I'll stay the night. Then tomorrow, first thing, we can all go to the police station."

The lounge, for once, was empty. Sue must have already gone to bed. Margaret collapsed in a chair. "I'll help you get what's-her-name into the car. We'll say you found her in a mess and took pity on her, and I was away on a work trip so you didn't have anyone to ask for advice. Just play the confused old man. And then we can go home and have some tea."

Arthur thought of Sue inhaling the black tea she liked to make. "Where would they take her?" he asked.

"Oh, somewhere safe," Margaret said. "It'll be like a hotel. Probably."

"Like a hotel." Arthur thought of the nursing home and shuddered. He thought of the woman clawing at him, asking for Freddy, and the care home manager popping another chocolate in his mouth.

"You don't know, do you?" he said. The house was silent. On any other evening, Angela would be arriving now, and Sue would be shuffling the cards in preparation for the game after tea while he poured them all drinks. They might be a bunch of misfits, but it was the closest he'd felt in a long time to having company. He lowered his voice. "What if I don't want to take Sue to the police right now?" he said.

Margaret leaned forward in the chair. "It's not a case of want, Dad. It's a case of—"

"I think she could tell us a lot," Arthur said. He thought of the potatoes in the agency, laughing. "A lot about how rotten this town is. I've made enquiries."

"Dad, you're being ridiculous." Margaret said.

"If she was in my garage, it wasn't an accident, Margaret." He felt Gertie's eyes gazing down on him from the picture on the wall. "This town runs on people like her. The care homes run on people like her. The farms. The cockling beds. There are people who would take her off my hands, I've met them. Do they care that she doesn't speak English? That she doesn't have any paperwork? That makes her more attractive."

"Dad, you're avoiding the question," Margaret said.

Her smirk infuriated Arthur. He was sick of her self-righteousness. "No, you're avoiding the question. Why aren't you poking your nose into that, eh? If you're so bloody capable, why aren't you down at those agencies, asking proper questions, instead of trying to run my life?"

"What did you just say?" Margaret's smirk disappeared. He could see the hurt on her face. "Do you have any idea…?"

But it was too late. He could feel years of pent-up rage rushing up to his vocal cords, rage he didn't know he had, rage about being patronised, about losing his wife, about his joints aching and his friends disappearing, about his town changing, rage that he didn't love his daughter as he should. It was all colliding into one great roar, like the sound of a tide, long banished, coming in.

Chapter Thirty-Seven

Suling stared at My Regret and Old Uncle through the glass. She had not been able to follow every word, but she was clear about one thing – it was not going well. They were both furious with each other, and now My Regret stood up, her face purple, and stormed out of the room. A moment later Old Uncle followed her, pale but twitching with anger.

There could only be one thing making My Regret so angry. The room was empty, but in a few minutes she would be back, and in a few more she would call the police. She needed to leave, now, and she only had seconds to do so. She pushed open the glass door and crept across the carpeted floor. The argument seemed to have temporarily relocated to the kitchen – she could hear shouting, and the banging of pans.

She was about to leave the room when she noticed Old Uncle's mobile phone lying by the plug socket. She turned the silver case over in her hand, unsure.

My Regret already thought she was a good-for-nothing. But what about Old Uncle? Still, he didn't even want it, and it would have been useless if she hadn't found the charger. She took the glass jar from the shelf that held her winnings and placed it on the table before stuffing the phone in her pocket. She hoped he would understand.

Then she opened the living room door a crack. Old Uncle and his daughter were still arguing in the kitchen. The hall was dark. She crept down it and into the room she had been sleeping in – it was not her bedroom any more. She stuffed all her clothes into her bag, pulled on her coat, and then, as she had practised in her head many times, she opened the window, hoisted herself onto the ledge and climbed out.

From the garden, she could see the kitchen windows mottled with steam and hear the shouting and tears. She had some time at least, before they knew she was gone. She began to walk along the darkened street. Alone and untethered, she felt a low thrill of excitement. What was next for her? The night, so drowsy before, had turned bitterly cold.

Chapter Thirty-Eight

In the kitchen, Arthur shouted at his shouting daughter until he started to feel his chest tighten and had to sit down. She kept bellowing for some time. A lot of nonsense about love, and family, and absent fathers.

"What do you mean?" Arthur demanded. "I was there all the time."

Finally, though, she too was overcome. Her eyes spurted tears and her mouth wobbled like a rubber band, and she half-fell onto the other chair, her place at the table when she was a child.

They sat like that for some time – Arthur silent, Margaret gasping, but more quietly now. Eventually, Arthur said: "Let's go out on the balcony."

It was a cold night, and Margaret shivered. Above them the sky swelled with stars. It was as if they had the front-row seats in a vast auditorium.

"What am I to do with you, Dad?" Margaret said. "Mum always said you were someone who needed a helping hand. Left to his own devices, she said, he's the kind of man who'll jump in as soon as he sees the Do Not Swim sign. He's too stubborn to be alone. That's what she said."

Arthur bridled at her words. He remembered, unwillingly, arguing with Gertie. They used to have these petty fights. Over what tie was suitable for a funeral. What time to go for lunch.

But she understood him too, perhaps better than he did himself. A touch on the arm, a smile. A reminder of how trivial this was, that she still loved him underneath it all.

"Well, what about you?" he said. "Are you going to help me?" Suddenly the words came out. "You've no idea how boring it is, Margaret, waking up every morning alone, finding ways to spend the day, and then the long evening, and yet the type of people you meet are donnats and eejits. You've no idea what it's like to spend days without speaking a single word out loud."

"Don't I?" Margaret said, and her voice broke a little. "Don't I?"

Arthur put his arm round her and felt her hot wet tears against the side of his neck. His heart ached for her – his beautiful daughter, so keen to grow up, for whom adulthood had turned out to be so monotonous and stale. Gertie had worried, but he had preferred to assume she was happy with her routines, her one-bed flat, her holiday cruises.

Margaret pulled away and straightened up. She leaned against the railing of balcony, not looking at him but out at the great dark night. She sniffed. "Okay," she said. "I'll help. What do you need me to do?"

Arthur squeezed her shoulders. "Stay here tonight," he said. "We can talk about it with everyone in the morning. Look, can you see Orion?"

"And the Frying Pan, and the Bear, and the North Star," Margaret said. She laughed. "See, forty years on, and I still haven't forgotten what you told me."

Chapter Thirty-Nine

The road came to a crossroads. Standing there, Suling could see over the whole of the town and the dark absence of the bay beyond it. Here everything was spread out before her – the terraces where she found Changfa again, the bay where she'd last seen him, the streets where she'd learnt to rely on herself.

She pulled out the map she had taken from Old Uncle's house and checked it. The road on her left was the one that led up through the dark wood and onto the hills. The one on her right would take her back into town, towards the old swimming pool and the terraces. But if she kept on going, eventually she would reach a back road that ran parallel with the coast, and if she followed that all night, she would come to the town with a train station. She would catch the first train of the morning and ride it south. She would reach Preston with Miss Tiger Stripe's card in her pocket, and as the dawn broke, vanish into the crowd.

She folded the map up again, stuffed it in her bag and took a last look around her. The bay was full tonight, the lights from the land on the other side reflected in the water.

She remembered the black dots in the circle of the telescope. The cocklers would go out in a few hours' time. What if one of them was Changfa? Or someone who knew where he was? What if there was a way to get a message to him?

The thought swallowed her up, like quicksand, and the more she tried to put it out of her mind, the more it pulled her in.

She remembered her first day in the factory. Her mother had always kept her busy with chores, but the factory was a windowless room that thudded with noise, and the task was the same, again and again and again. She felt like an extension of the machine. No one spoke to her, and her feet ached. She didn't try to find Changfa at the end of the twelve-hour shift – his night watch would have already started. But as she was descending the stairs, a security guard slipped her a note. "Hey," he said. "Your classmate says hello." And just like that, she found herself reading Changfa's untidy characters. "Hope you survived," he wrote. "I will survive by receiving your message tomorrow."

If she made it back to the village, she would never be able to forget that, no matter how many houses she built. Old Uncle had left a friend behind, and it had haunted him all his life.

You can only help yourself, the debt collector had said. But she was near him, so near. And this might be her last chance to find him.

"Goddammit," she swore like Old Uncle to the night sky.

Then she picked up her bag and took the road towards the terraces.

Chapter Forty

Whoof, whoof, whoof – Arthur tried not to get irritated by the sound of Margaret pumping up the air mattress in the lounge.

"I'll get sheets," he excused himself. The hallway was dark and quiet, and for the first time he wondered where Sue was. Could she be asleep? He hadn't seen her all evening. She was probably hunched over a book. He felt too tired to try to explain what they had been discussing. He'd do it in the morning.

He knocked at the door of her room and waited. No reply. Perhaps she was asleep. But it was only just after six, and all the linen was in the room. He knocked again, louder. Give her time to wake up. "Come on, Sue," he muttered under his breath. He knocked a third time and opened the door a crack. He saw there was light inside and opened it fully.

The first thing he noticed was how cold it was. Then the flapping curtains alerted him to the open window. A newspaper lay on the table and its pages had blown onto the floor, where they rustled like dead leaves in the draught. The bed was unmade.

"Sue?" he called into the hall. But he knew instantly that she was gone. The window was a gaping hole into the night.

"Margaret?" he called instead, sinking onto the bed. "Margaret?"

When his daughter arrived, she didn't say anything, but shut the window, drew the curtains, and tidied up the newspaper. The room started to return to its normal state. For all the mess she might have made, Sue had come with little, and left little behind.

He wondered why she'd gone. She didn't like Margaret, he had worked out that much. But if only she'd waited a little longer, he could have explained. And to hurl herself into the middle of a dark winter's night! The lass was a bloody eejit.

Margaret put the newspapers in a pile and sat down next to him. "Look, Dad, it's for the best. She solved your problem for you."

It was true – he had been worrying about it all week. Margaret was talking comfortingly, in such a soothing voice it was hard to remember that they'd been shouting at each other earlier in the evening, shouting over Sue, who wasn't even here. She had vanished as quickly as she came.

"Don't worry about making the bed," Margaret was saying. "I'll do that. I'll sleep in it after all." He took it as his cue to get up and by the time he reached the door she was stripping the bedsheets.

"Wait," he almost said. "What if Sue comes back?" But the words never reached his lips. Instead, as Margaret wrestled with the pillows, he went to every room of the house and drew the curtains, their heavy fabric a shield between the books and lamps and picture frames, and the uncertainties of the night outside.

Chapter Forty-One

The buildings known as terraces were crammed together, one apartment stacked on top of each other, like the walls of a fortress. Each apartment had one large window made of three panes, draped with curtains. In the dark, they glowed like giant lanterns. For a moment, as she descended from the hill, Suling saw the grand streets of Old Uncle's memory, where hotels overflowed with laughter and wine. Perhaps she would find Changfa this night, and they would walk through them together, like they were still living in that time. She would be drunk on the touch of him.

But when she reached the terraces, the illusion faded. The street was silent, and the gaps in the curtain revealed cracked ceilings, a woman smoking. The few windows that still belonged to guest houses looked shabby. A bike frame was chained to a fence – someone had plundered the wheels.

The sight made Suling hesitate. The last time she'd been here, she'd overheard the debt collector promising to find her. Even if his attention had shifted to the big cities, she should be careful. But then she thought of Miss Tiger Stripe marching up the garden path with her box in her arms. She had her mission. Changfa could be just a few metres away. Or someone who knew where he was. If there was any sign of the debt collector, she would retreat at once. If it felt safe, on the other hand, she would stay just long enough to find out what the cocklers knew about Changfa, and then, as she had planned, she would follow the map to a station and catch a train to Preston. If she did find out where he was being held, perhaps Miss Tiger Stripe could help her get a message to him. A number for him to call.

She walked round the corner to the alleyway, opened the back gate to the cocklers' yard and stepped inside.

She'd stood here so many times before, but now it was utterly different. Although the front of the house still looked uninhabited, there was light here, spilling from a window onto the broken paving stones. A cloth hid the inside of the house from view, but she could see the shadows of figures moving this way and that.

Next to the window was the door. She took a deep breath and knocked.

At first, no one answered. Then she heard scuffling in the hallway. The door opened a crack. "Hello?" said a voice unused to speaking English.

Suling answered in Mandarin. "Have I come to the right house? The boss just dropped me off and told me to come here."

The door opened a little wider.

"I'm a late hire," Suling said in Hokkien.

"Okay, okay, don't stand around, then," the voice said in the same language. The door opened to reveal a woman, who hustled her inside. Suling felt the door slam deep inside her. She could be walking towards a train station right now, but instead she was following the woman down a narrow corridor. She could hear chatter through the walls. The voices were so familiar, the way they rose and fell. Her legs trembled.

The woman turned. "I'm Caixia," she said. Her tea-stained skin suggested a life outdoors. She looked middle-aged, although Suling knew that in these kinds of jobs, workers aged early. "You'll have to sleep in the front. We're full up back here."

"How many are there here?" Suling asked.

Caixia made an attempt to count, and then gave up. "Around twenty," she said. "You'll see in a minute. Through here."

She pushed through a door in the darkened corridor, and Suling stepped into a sudden blare of light, and a room full of people. They were all staring at her, just like the day she'd arrived in England and entered the house the first time. It had been overwhelming, but then she'd seen a familiar face, a face that made it all worth it.

Now, she searched them all, just in case. None of them were the debt collector. None of them were Changfa.

Caixia pushed her forward.

"Hey, look," she said to the dozens of eyes. "We've got an apprentice."

"I'm Meiyi," Suling invented.

A young man stepped closer. "They told me we had all twenty-two," he said. The others stopped talking. He had a manner of speaking that demanded attention. General Cockle won't like that, she thought, before she remembered the blue lights. How replaceable General Cockle turned out to be.

The youth was waiting. Miss Tiger Stripe had won over the angry woman at the door with kindness. Out loud, she said: "The boss said you were such a good leader that you could handle another one." She gazed up at him with as much respect as she could muster.

It worked. The man seemed to relax. "Okay, well you should have turned up earlier," he said. He looked around. "Sort her out with a rake," he told Caixia. "She can prove herself tomorrow."

He left the room, and they heard his stomp on the stairs. "Number One Cockler gets his own bed," Caixia said when the chatter began again. The room they were standing in, which contained nothing except some mattresses resting against the wall, was about the size of Old Uncle's kitchen, but while the kitchen could just about contain one angry Old Uncle, the cocklers curled themselves up to create as much space as possible. It was a dance Suling had done her whole life without realising it, but now, after so long in Old Uncle's spacious house, she felt out of practice.

She settled herself on the floor next to Caixia.

"So why are you really here?" a man cradling a flask of tea asked.

Because she was connected to Changfa in ways that were too deep to forget. Because he'd once sent her a note, and she needed to write one back. But she couldn't explain without revealing everything. Suling tried to look embarrassed. "I have a debt."

The man laughed. "Don't we all?" he said. "Well, good luck paying it back. I thought I'd be done in six months."

"They love you so much, they won't let you go," joked a woman wrapped in a hat and scarf. She turned to Suling. "How much did you get in your old job?"

"They always paid late," she said honestly, remembering the factory. "What about here?"

The man with the flask laughed again. "They say it's £5 a bag, but the bags weigh 25kg and that money only exists on Number One Cockler's balance sheet."

"I heard of one guy who paid his dues in months and left," Caixia said.

"Yeah, he's in the ground now," the man with the flask said.

The others *shh*-d him.

"I thought I'd be doing field work," the woman with the hat said. She was skinny, with shadows under her eyes, and introduced herself as Yue. "Picking strawberries, the broker said. I didn't realise it was winter."

Suling remembered Old Uncle's stories, the way he watched the tide come in. "The sands make me nervous," she said.

"Can't afford to get scared, can we?" the man with the flask said. "Your debt says you're going out there. Otherwise your family pays the price."

Changfa's family must be paying now, even his father, who scared them so much as kids. "What happens if you get caught?" Suling asked. "By the authorities, I mean?"

The man with the flask opened his mouth, but before he could speak, Caixia said: "Number One Cockler wouldn't let that happen." It was hard to tell whether she really believed her own words, or just wanted to change the conversation.

"I owe them a thousand," another man said. "My wife gets strange phone calls night and day. I just got to get out there and back enough times to pay it off, and then I'm out of here. I've got a cousin up north, where the oil fields are. He'll sort me out with something better than this."

"Maybe one day you'll be able to pay your flight home too," Caixia said as she stood up. She left the room for a moment and came back with a bowl of tea, which she handed to Suling. "Here, you missed food. Drink this."

"Thanks," Suling said. She sipped her tea and lapsed into silence, while the others grumbled and joked, and for once she could understand every word. The last month felt like a dream. Here she was, back in the room with peeling paper and cocklers' patter, sustained by dried food brought to life with a kettle. The same conversations – jokes and heart sickness knocking around in the same steamboat dish, each of them taking a slurp and a nibble of each other's stories. Like the man with the cousin, they imagined this was a stop gap, their time as an ugly grub in a chrysalis before their transformation.

To mention the cocklers who disappeared would break the spell. She would ask about Changfa tomorrow.

Chapter Forty-Two

Arthur set his alarm clock for six thirty. If he had a quick bite to eat, he could be in the garden by the time Margaret woke and they wouldn't have to say more than a brief goodbye. He'd dig the vegetable patch. It was hard work, but straightforward. It was what he needed. A reason to avoid Margaret and a distraction from fretting about Sue. No more of this emotional nonsense. Just planting his vegetables, ready for spring.

But when he dragged himself out of bed and stumbled into the kitchen, Margaret was sitting in Sue's chair, and she had already made breakfast – two boiled eggs with tea and buttered toast.

"I have to get to work, Dad," she said between bites of toast, "How far can you walk these days?"

Not this again. Sue was gone – what more did she want? "I'm always going for walks," Arthur said. "I go everywhere on foot." Except that he preferred to drive, of course, but she didn't need to know that. She'd probably start worrying about his reflexes.

"Good," Margaret said, her teaspoon breaking the eggshell with military precision. "I've still got two hours. There's something I wanted to show you."

*

The clouds were stained red by the dawn. Margaret seemed to have forgotten about Arthur's frailty. She marched up the hill, and if she noticed her father struggling to keep up with her, she didn't show it. All Arthur's efforts were concentrated on watching his feet, but he didn't want to complain, not now. They were passing through the wood where, in summers long past, he and his daughter had built dens among the shimmering green leaves. But it was grey as a prison yard on this winter's day, its bare trees like sentries to the fell beyond.

They came to a stile, one he'd once helped little legs over, but now each stone was a potential hospital trip, and he dug his hands into the mossy cracks of the wall to keep his balance. Sue would have extended an arm, but Margaret was already setting off up the muddy path that led across the fields and up to the fell.

His feet landed with a thump on the soft mud. The path got steeper. Each breath came sharp and raw – it was like listening to the bellows over a failing fire. He wanted to think about things – where Sue had gone, what happened last night – but all he could think about was oxygen. He was just a pair of old lungs, nothing else. Then finally Margaret stopped, and turned and said like it was an order: "The view."

He paused, relieved, and looked out beneath him. They were high now, high above the wood and the town and the bay, which was a sulky pink under the last of the sunrise. He felt alive, wobbling a bit, but alive all the same. He wanted to squeeze his daughter to his side, like he had when she was young, and point out the landmarks to her. "That was where your dad was born, that was where your parents met, that's the famous pleasure beach, can't you see?"

But Margaret had started walking again. Her brown leather hiking boots beat out a rhythm on the fell like his mother on laundry day – thud, thud, thud. A sheep baah-ed and ran to join the rest of the flock. They kept going.

Finally, the hospice came into view. Why it was called that, Arthur didn't know. It wasn't a hospital, just a small, square stone building built in olden times for the travellers who once crossed the fells. A good marker for a walk with the family. He remembered a much smaller Margaret running towards it on a summer's day, Gertie laughing as she tried to keep up. But it was a weekday in winter and there was no one else around.

Margaret stopped and waited for him to catch up.

"I used to come here when I was a teenager," she said. "When we had our fights."

Our Fights, she said, as if it was a big historical event, instead of her being stroppy and unreasonable. Arthur would have said as much if he wasn't so out of breath.

"I'd pack a bag like I was really leaving," Margaret continued as he wheezed. "One time I even took a sleeping bag. Sometimes I'd go to the woods. Other times I'd come up here and light a fire while I figured out what to do next."

So that was what she meant when she said she wanted to show him something. Well, she could have just told him while they were sitting comfortably in the kitchen, rather than dragging him up this fell.

They reached the hospice. Margaret walked straight in and sat down on one of the stone benches.

Arthur collapsed on the opposite bench. The stone was cold, but at least he was starting to breathe normally again. He leaned his head against the wall and concentrated on the poem on the other side of the room, painted in gold letters on a black board. No doubt put there by some Victorian romantic who wanted to inject meaning into everything.

Where you are from we do not know, a traveller may come and go.

"I wanted to be independent," Margaret said. "Turn up in a city I knew nothing about, where no-one knew me. Where no-one expected anything of me."

We merely share our open door, a like to welcome rich and poor.

"Mum always found me," she said, with a choke in her voice. "She always persuaded me to come home."

A shard of memory came to Arthur – a summer evening sitting by himself on the balcony. Gertie must have gone after Margaret. An evening of insects buzzing, the sun glowing through the trees as it fell, and his faint annoyance that the ice was melting in her drink. She had come back eventually, smiled at him and apologised for being late, and he'd forgiven her.

He was like the people on the shore that day that Sid drowned, the ones who told him later at the funeral that they'd looked out at the bay and seen nothing. Just the sand and the tide coming in.

"She knew I was lost," Margaret said. "And that's something, isn't it?"

"That's something," he said.

Margaret fell silent. He could suggest they walk back to the house, and she'd probably say yes. The conversation could end there. He might forget they ever had it. But he had seen something now, a stirring on the empty plain of sand.

"What did we argue about?" he asked.

There was a pause. He waited. For accusations. For judgement.

Margaret said: "I don't remember."

She got up slowly. "I remember more the feeling of it." Her eyes collided with his and then she immediately glanced away again. "Like you were disappointed in me for growing up. You were away so much for work. I think it took you by surprise."

She gazed at the gold writing on the wall. "I saw how much you wanted the perfect home," she said. "How hard you worked for it. Of course you wanted the perfect child to go along with it. And then I spoiled it. I wasn't smart, or pretty, or even funny. I didn't go to war, like you did. I couldn't bake cakes and play housewife, like Mum did. I didn't better myself. I was just awkward. A dud."

But it wasn't just Margaret, it was everything – the marriage, the house, the office with your own telephone and secretary, the garden with its fruit trees and bird table and bench. You built something so solid you fooled yourself into believing it would last forever. And then, just like that, it started to ebb away, and you were left with your own flawed self, the thing you were trying to hide from all along.

He grasped the old stone fireplace and very slowly hauled himself up. "I'm sorry," he said. "It was a daft thing to want. Gertie was the perfect wife, it's true. But I was never the perfect husband."

Margaret turned to look at him.

He thought of Angela at all those stuffy dinner parties, so desperate for someone to confide in, how she'd disguised it with jokes and lipstick and laughter.

"I know," Margaret said.

Gertie was different from Angela, he realised with a chill. She did have someone to confide in. It just wasn't him.

His daughter was staring at him steadily now. It was the kind of look he imagined she'd give a supplier who had just sold her substandard parts. Like she was sifting through the boxes and working out what the damage was.

He could tell her she was a smart-arse. That she didn't know anything. And then she'd snap back, and the whole thing would begin again. Or he could stop being so flait and let her make her mind up for herself.

"We had a wonderful marriage," he said. "I wonder if it would have survived if Gertie hadn't had you."

Margaret's eyes softened.

"Mum knew what mattered to her and what didn't," she said.

The relief made him shaky. "For what it's worth," he said, as he teetered on the stone-flagged floor. "I think you'd be good in a war. You get things done. I'd just have to hope we were on the same side."

A little smile tugged the side of his daughter's mouth.

"Look," she said. "The tide's going out." She held out her arm, and he clung onto it.

Chapter Forty-Three

"Hey, wake up. The tide's going out."

Suling opened her eyes and saw two eyes staring into hers. A hand shook her shoulder gently.

"The driver's coming any minute," a skinny girl said.

Suling sat up. She'd planned to ask about Changfa in the morning. But all around her was commotion. Some cocklers were clearing away their mattresses while others wandered past, hoisting up their waterproofs.

"Here, take this. You won't have time for breakfast," the skinny girl who had woken her said. She handed Suling a bun. "I'm Weiying, from Yongchun County."

At Old Uncle's, she had eaten eggs for breakfast almost every day. Now she held the bun like it was a precious object. "Thanks," she said.

Weiying grinned. She seemed kind, Suling thought. "Yongchun County, eh? How long have you been here?" she asked as she pulled on her waterproofs.

"Here? Or in this country?" Weiying said, her thin frame disappearing beneath an oversized rain jacket.

"Here," Suling said.

"Oh, this just started a week ago." Weiying's voice was muffled under the rain jacket.

"So there weren't any cocklers here before?" Suling tried to keep her question casual.

Weiying's face appeared again. "Huh?" she asked. "Maybe. I only heard about it when Caixia called. And someone had

just called her. I was a nanny, but it really wasn't working out."
Her hands popped out of the rain jacket arms. "You know,"
she said, twisting them this way and that as she grimaced.
"The usual. My boss's husband never could let me alone."

Before Suling could ask any more questions, there was a
shout from the hallway – the minivan driver had arrived. He
was a young man who spoke Hokkien but hardly glanced at
the passengers as they squashed themselves in the back. He
looked familiar, and she wondered if he'd driven the last batch
of cocklers. Someone had to remember them. Surely when
the men and women crammed around her in the minivan lay
down at night, they must wonder who slept on the mattresses
before them.

She kept her face down. "Move up," one of men she was
crushed between told her. There was hardly any space, but she
obliged as much as she could. Stay invisible.

The minivan sputtered through the streets of the terraces
and then turned sharply onto the country road. They drove
through the hills – further than Suling remembered, but
perhaps they were being more cautious these days – until they
turned down a road that ended in rubble. The minivan passed
a warning sign and drove onto the marsh grass.

Suddenly it was quieter. A kind of sludgy sound, mixed
with mournful bird cries, filled the van. On either side Suling
could see the glimmer of water, where the sandbank ended. It
was grey and rough today. She remembered the sound of the
tide and shivered.

The minivan stopped. "Everyone out," Cockler Number
One cried. They began unloading the luminous orange bags
that would hold the cockles, the jumbos, the rakes. Cockler
Number One set off onto the sand.

Old Uncle had almost been swallowed by the sand. "Does he know a safe path?" Suling asked Caixia.

Caixia shrugged. "He's the one that speaks to the bosses."

That wasn't an answer, but it would be hard to argue without drawing attention to herself. From the stomp of their boots, few of the other cocklers feared getting sucked in. She tried to follow Cockler Number One. At least if he got stuck, she'd see where to avoid.

But they reached the cockling beds safely. Cockler Number One gave his orders cheerfully enough – there was no need to shout when everyone had their debt.

Even her, Suling thought – the girl who had disappeared. The fear was already creeping back. Had they found the factory? Had someone there blurted out the broker she used? Would he remember her, and if so, would he give them the right name? After that, even with all the steps she had taken, it would not take long to work out her lineage, and which village she came from.

As a supposed newcomer, she was careful not to look too familiar with the rake, but in the end she didn't need to, because the work was hard. The strongest men stood on the jumbos and moved them until the sand quaked. Her muscles had strength-ened during her time at the old swimming pool, but still, her arms and back ached with the pull and thrust of the rake, her hands even through the gloves were getting blisters, and all the time around her, the wind wailed in her ears. Sometimes it pushed them this way and that, and the whole line of rakers seemed to slant like a dance troupe. The scarves around their faces showed only their eyes.

She wondered who they were raking for. Children, wives, parents. Some, like Changfa, wanted to be great men. They all longed to return home.

She fell into a reverie, one where she and Changfa were older, but reunited, and back home. While before her imagination had sparkled with luxuries, now she found herself lingering on smaller things. Sipping tea on the balcony with Changfa. Dropping round to see her mother. Opening a bottle of soybean milk, still ice-cold from the fridge. The day wore on. As the sun dropped lower in the sky, the glimmer of the water intensified. It lurked there, a reminder of how quickly everything could change.

Finally, someone shouted that the minivan had arrived, a speck on the faraway land. She'd only managed to fill one bag, and even though she would be leaving soon, she felt the familiar wave of dread.

"Here," Caixia said, throwing her a net of cockles. She heaved it over her shoulder and started following the others back to shore. At the minivan, Cockler Number One counted the bags and handed them over to a redhead with a truck, who passed over a wad of cash. It disappeared quickly into Cockler Number One's pocket.

The cocklers crammed themselves into the minivan. Their faces were lined around the eyes – tanned, ordinary. The man with the flask, so chatty the previous evening, was fast asleep. Suling's resolution began to waver. She felt exhausted. How would she ever have the energy to find Changfa? Even if one of the cocklers did know where he was, she would still have to work out how to get a message to him. The debt collector had compared the place he was being held to a prison.

One day, she thought, as she collapsed on one of the mats crammed into the living room. One day is all it takes to be reduced to this. There was one shower, and she hadn't managed to get in it, so her hair still smelt of the sea. Her arms felt heavy, and her back ached. She knew she would be sore tomorrow.

She checked her mobile phone under the blanket. No messages. Miss Tiger Stripe must still be busy. As for Old Uncle, he was probably relieved to be free of her. Now she was just a dot in the circle of his telescope.

Chapter Forty-Four

After Margaret left, Arthur tried calling Angela to break the news about Sue, but he only got Reggie's answer phone message. Even after the light began to fade, the house remained in darkness. Its blank windows added to his unease. First Sue, then Angela. Had the Australians really left? He was certain she'd try to say goodbye. But so much had happened in the last day. What if she'd tried to send him a message and he'd missed it?

He was washing up and fretting when the red car appeared on the road. He left the plates to soak and put his hat and coat on.

The Australian daughter-in-law answered the door in a blast of hot air, her blonde hair scraped back into a ponytail. She was wearing leggings so tight she might as well have been barelegged, and a strappy top that showed off her cleavage.

"Hello?" she said.

Arthur looked at her feet, bare and wedged into furry slippers, each toenail painted bright purple. "Is Angela here?"

The daughter-in-law shouted something over her shoulder into the gloom of the hall.

"She's in the living room," she said. Arthur stepped over the threshold for the first time in years and followed her into the house. He found Angela in the lounge, a cardboard box in her lap, illuminated only by the lamplight and the old gas fire.

"Just helping them sort through stuff," she said with a smile. He noticed how thin she looked, as if she was being hollowed out from the inside.

He closed the door so the Australian couldn't hear.

"Sue's gone," he said.

"What?" Angela stopped rummaging.

Arthur sat down on the sofa and told her about the argument, how he'd discovered the window open.

"Bloody stupid," he said. "When we were trying to fix things for her."

Angela sighed.

"It was a difficult situation for everyone." She picked up a necklace from the box and let the beads run through her fingers. "We couldn't have protected her, not really."

Her resigned tone annoyed him.

"Don't you want to know where she's gone?" he asked.

Angela looked surprised. "I already have a good guess. Don't you? She only knows how to pick cockles."

Arthur remembered the dark night, the rain, the blue flashing lights.

"The police shut that down," he said. "I was there."

"Well, they're back," Angela said. "I could see them when we drove round the bay this morning."

Arthur thought of Sue, a grin on her face as she laid her full hand of cards on the table. "She wouldn't be that daft," he said.

Angela shrugged. "Desperate people do daft things," she said. She looked down at the beads in her hands. "We've been at the hospital."

He thought of the Australian in her furry slippers. "You told them, then."

The hands played with the beads.

"I said I'd do chemo," she said.

"But I thought—" Arthur stopped himself.

"That there was no point?" Angela finished for him. She sighed. "I wanted to die with a full head of hair and a cigarette in my hand. But you know, that's just clinging to past glories."

She cleared her throat, or at least she tried to, but her voice was still raspy. "I've been talking a lot to my grandson. I keep thinking of more things I want to say." She nodded at the door. "They're going to stay for a while."

"Here?" Arthur asked.

Angela laughed. "No. Back at home in Oxford."

"Of course," Arthur said, feeling daft. So she would be gone soon. Part of him was relieved at being spared the slow deterioration, the sick room with the stench of antiseptic and the Australian's slippers in the hall. The feeling of relief was almost immediately replaced by one of abandonment.

"Do you want me to come and visit?" he said.

"I'm not sure," Angela said, looking at the beads again. "I think I might prefer you remembering me how I was. But call me. On the phone, we're just voices anyway."

She smiled and closed the box. "What are you doing for tea? I know we don't have the guest of honour, but I've still got a lot of meals to get through before they start tasting like cardboard."

"Actually, Margaret's picking me up," Arthur said. "We're going to some sort of show." His daughter had suggested it on her way out of the door, and it had felt wise to say yes.

"Oh, well it was just a thought," Angela said hastily.

Arthur looked at the woman who, sometime in the early 1960s, had somehow seemed such a threat.

"Do you want to come?" he said.

If Margaret objected to the extra guest, she kept her

thoughts to herself. She turned up at five minutes to seven, put down a seat to fit the wheelchair in, carefully lifted Angela into the car, and then waited by the door while Arthur rushed around and fumbled with his coat. Then she drove them down to the prom and parked near an old music hall that Arthur remembered shutting many years ago. The paved area around it was strewn with rubbish and the ashes of bonfires. But the windows were blazing with light.

"It's owned by one of the trusts Mum was always involved with," Margaret said. "They open it up for special occasions."

"The Belvedere," Angela crowed, as Margaret helped her back into her wheelchair. "That's what they used to call it."

She zoomed off up the wheelchair ramp while Margaret linked arms with Arthur and marched up the steps at such a furious pace that he felt like his shoulder was being pulled out of its socket. Once inside though, she slowed, and he was able to take in the splendour of the hall. The ceiling was painted red and gold, although in some places this had faded to a salmon and yellow. Dusty red curtains fell at either side of an old wooden stage.

Arthur couldn't remember Gertie ever mentioning it. "When did your mother take you here?" he asked, once they had taken their seats among the small crowd. He felt like he might have been talking about a stranger.

"Oh, ever since I was a teenager," Margaret said. "And always for the cabaret."

The cabaret – since when did Gertie like cabaret? But he couldn't ask her without revealing how ignorant he was. "This group still do some of the original songs and dances," Margaret was telling Angela. "They're amateurs mostly, but they tour around, and they always draw a crowd."

The lights dimmed, and a spotlight appeared on stage. The audience started to clap. A woman appeared in a dress that to Arthur's eyes seemed to mostly be made of feathers, and a trilby hat. She tipped the hat and began to sing.

It was a song he hadn't heard for decades, but it was as clear and real as a light in the dark. And even though the woman was wearing the most outlandish costume, he could feel the yearning in her voice. It was the kind of song he might have sung once himself, after a few pints, arms linked with his Navy pals as they careered down the promenade. The kind of song Sid would have liked. She could only be half his age, but she sang it like it was her song, with a lot of swagger, and he found he didn't mind at all.

He glanced round at the others. Angela's eyes were shut and she had a slight smile, as if she was in a different world. Margaret was watching with full concentration, as if she was a student at a lecture taking notes. But then she blinked, and he saw her eyes were wet.

He thought of Gertie, taking her daughter to this year on year without ever mentioning it to him. What had she felt, when she sat here on this hard seat, in her respectable skirt and jumper? For a long time, he had thought of himself as the one who kept the family together – the one who kept them warm, well fed, who kept a roof over their heads. But those things were replaceable. She was the family's life blood, the heart that pumped oxygen into every crevice of them. He hadn't realised until she'd gone, and everything fell apart.

He reached out for Margaret's hand, and felt her plump fingers squeeze his. The singer closed her lips and bowed, and the great hall was filled for a moment with the storm of applause.

Chapter Forty-Five

The cocklers were only ten days old. Before that they were nannies, like Weiying, or waiters, or onion pickers, or production workers in factories that didn't officially exist. None of them seemed to know about the previous cocklers. It was like they had vanished into the sand.

Maybe that was why no-one wanted to know either. "Who lived here before?" Shijun said amiably on the second evening. "People who went on to better things. That's what I'm hoping." He lowered his voice. "But don't go asking things like this in front of Cockler Number One. He doesn't like questions."

Suling searched the back of the cupboards, the corners of the room, for some trace of Changfa. Something to remind her that he was real. But there was nothing.

Her last hope was the drivers. General Cockle had been in the minivan that day, but there were other drivers, maybe even the same ones. The next few days brought more of them, young men who didn't say a word but were the subject of the cocklers' whispers.

The original driver they nicknamed Little Cockle Emperor. He came from Fujian and listened in on their conversations, even if he never said a word. If anyone knew what happened to a previous group of cocklers, it was him, but the whispers claimed he had a direct line to the snakeheads. She took care not to meet his eyes.

Then there was the one they called Precious Curd, who had milk-white skin and blonde hair, and was said to be from the far edge of Europe, somewhere near Russia. The whisperers said the other drivers made fun of him. Their least favourite was Splinter, a skinny local youth who she remembered from before. He had a swagger and often muttered under his breath.

When she got into the minivan on the second morning, Splinter's eye flashed up, as if he recognised something about her, and she looked quickly at her jolting lap. The debt collector had warned her she would never escape him. He had his eyes and ears everywhere. She was relieved the next day when it was Precious Curd in the driving seat. He had a distant look, as if he too was longing for home.

On the way back, when the cocklers heaved themselves into the minivan, she planted herself in the seat closest to him. She could see his neck, the dark spots on it, the light blonde hairs on the even paler skin.

When the other cocklers got out in the now-dark street, she hung back to make sure she was the last to leave, and as she opened the minivan door, she said: "Good night."

He turned in surprise, and she wondered if she had misjudged him. His eyes flickered over her. But then he said good night in return. She jumped out and he drove away.

She watched the lights of the minivan disappear. She had revealed too much. Cocklers were supposed to be deaf and dumb, imprisoned in their language. But she had put down her first card now. She should see the game to the end. So the next day, when he came again, she volunteered to haul the bags of cockles into the minivan. He stood watching her with the same sort of smile as the man who had bought the health secrets.

Under the cover of the wind, she said: "Where are you from?"

He said something incomprehensible. She nodded, as if she understood, and told him the name of her village. His face wrinkled in confusion.

"You know Changfa?" she said.

He shook his head. She tried again. "My friend. Police take him."

At the mention of police, his pale eyes blinked. He knew. But he shook his head again.

"Where is he now?" she asked, as he turned away and hurried back to the car.

The next day it poured with rain, and when Little Cockle Emperor came to pick them up they were soaked through, and Caixia sat clenched by the rain-streamed window, muttering to herself, and the bowl of hot noodles in the evening scarcely seemed enough to ward off the ever-present icy damp. The steam of the noodles mixed with the clouds of their breath.

Suling cradled her bowl and wished she'd never seen the cocklers through the telescope. She kept the phone beside her, and willed Miss Tiger Stripe to call.

But the following morning, there was brilliant sunshine, and Precious Curd was their driver again. He screwed up his pale lashes to look at the sky. As they were getting out of the minivan, he tapped her on the shoulder. "Stonehouse," he said in a low voice.

"What?"

"Where your friend is. Stonehouse."

"Prison?"

"Like prison."

"Is he okay?"

His eyes rested on her. "Better you forget about your friend."

Stonehouse. Suling repeated the name as she raked until it was carved into her memory. She wanted to believe that Changfa was strong enough to do what he'd always done before – find the next bit of the future to focus on. But what if he couldn't? The debt collector said people went crazy in there.

And she had her own future to think about. Her questions were attracting attention. She had already revealed too much to Precious Curd. The debt collector could turn up at any time.

The skirt and blouse Miss Tiger Stripe lent her were still in her rucksack. Now she knew where Changfa was being held, there was no need to stay another minute. She would start walking this very night. When she got to Preston, she would call Miss Tiger Stripe and ask for more work. It would be harder for her to say no to her face. Maybe she could even help her get a message into Stonehouse.

Rake, rake, rake – it was only this motion keeping her nervousness away. She could slip out after the cocklers went to sleep. They were so exhausted, they were unlikely to hear her go.

She was so preoccupied that she did not notice the sun falling down the sky, and only became aware slowly that the others were complaining. "Why hasn't the minivan come?" Caixia said. She had big circles under her eyes.

"They just want more and more out of us," Shijun, one of the jumbo operators, said. "Those fancy cars aren't going to pay for themselves."

Suling looked around. Their shadows were like slender giants on the sands. Old Uncle had shown her through the telescope how the tide times changed every day by an hour or so. Yesterday, at this time, they were already back at the terraces.

"Caixia's right," she said, trying to keep her voice steady. "The minivan should be here by now. The tide'll come in soon."

Her words had an immediate effect on the others – they shivered and glanced at the distant shore.

Caixia straightened up. "I don't mind getting a bit wet," she said. "But if the others get my share of noodles…"

They all laughed. "I mean it," Suling said. She remembered Old Uncle's stories at the dinner table. "The tides are very fast."

"Maybe we should walk back to shore," Weiying, the skinny girl from Yongchun County, said.

"Do you know where you're going?" Suling asked.

Weiying shook her head. "Cockler Number One knows the way."

They stood where they were, no-one raking now, just looking at the dimming sky.

"They can't be that stupid," Caixia murmured. She pointed at a car on the shoreline, revealed by a flash of evening sun. "Look, isn't that them now?"

But the car drove on and disappeared. Weiying dropped her rake and sat down on the sand. The sunlight glittered on the streams that criss-crossed the bay. They looked so harmless and pretty.

The sound of raspy breathing. Weiying was having a panic attack.

Suling remembered the phone in her pocket. Old Uncle knew what it was like to be out in the bay. "I've got an idea," she said.

But just then, Cockler Number One shouted: "Oi, why have you stopped?"

"We're looking for the minivan," Caixia said. "It should have arrived by now."

He shook his head. "Not today. They're coming as late as possible because we're behind on our quota. Here, get up and start raking again."

He was young enough that his face was still smooth, despite the wind and sun. Suling wanted to shake him. She was so close to getting out of this place, and this idiot could ruin everything.

"Are you mad?" she said. "We can't stay out here any later. Don't you know about the tide?"

It was clear no-one had spoken to Cockler Number One like that for a long time. As soon as the words had come out of her mouth, she braced herself for his reaction. But he forced a smile. "Don't you know anything about work?" he rebuked her. "The cockles won't pick themselves. And the bosses have a contract to deliver on."

He smiled again. "Come on, get back to work, and I won't mention this to anyone."

Suling stared at him. He really did think that this was all a ploy to cover up not doing work. And what he said became the truth. At least, it did once. Not so long ago, she would have felt ashamed of her own laziness. But now, she realised, he just didn't understand the tides.

Seconds – that's how long Old Uncle said it could take to drown.

"That's it, I'm calling my friend," she said. She pulled out her phone, dialled Old Uncle's number and waited for him to pick up. But there was a long ringing and then she heard the crackling of an answer machine.

"Uncle," she said impatiently in English. "I'm in the bay.

Please come. The water will rise." And she was going to say more, say how urgent it was, but Cockler Number One grabbed the phone from her hand.

Chapter Forty-Six

Arthur was rummaging for a glass in the cabinet when the phone rang. "Can you get it?" he asked Margaret, still on his knees. The damn glass would be here somewhere. What was this daft pottery figurine getting in his way?

"Dad." His daughter's voice came from somewhere outside the stuffy cabinet. "It's gone to answer phone. You need to listen to this."

A toast to Mum, Margaret had said when she suggested the visit, but here she was, already bossing him around. It would take him ages to get to his feet, and he still hadn't found the glass.

"Dad?" Margaret's voice sounded shaky now. Perhaps it was something to do with her work. That afternoon, when they'd been burning leaves in the garden, she'd confessed how stressed she was. He'd had no idea about the pressure she was under. The redundancy rounds, the constant reviews, the threat of relocation. He'd found himself talking about fresh starts, like he was some kind of self-help book.

But then why would the call be for him? He stood up slowly. Margaret had the phone receiver clamped to her ear, and a worried expression on her face. He took it off her.

At first, he only heard a faint crackling. "Bloody cold callers," he cursed, and was about to put it down again, when he heard a familiar voice. Sue.

"Uncle," she said. A cold shock went through his body. "I'm in the bay. Please come. The water will rise." And then, unexpectedly, she shrieked. He heard shouting in a foreign tongue, another shriek, and then – silence.

He looked around the living room, still and peaceful in the last of the afternoon sun, the silly china shepherdess lying by the open drinks cabinet. The bay looked so calm from here.

He pressed the button again. Suddenly his ear was filled with the crackling of the wind. "Uncle," said Sue, somewhere in time and space. "I'm in the bay."

He looked at the clock. Three-thirty. The water will rise. It always did. It would swallow up the sand, first rushing through the gullies, but then rising, until it was too deep to stand. And it would be so cold too, at this time of year, like being clouted with ice. The walkers in the hills would remark how pretty it was and congratulate themselves on finding such a shimmering view.

Everything in his life drifted now, one day differentiated from another only by the weather and the ringing of the church bells. But your life could be squeezed into an hour on the sands. Less. He thought of Sid's breathless recitation of his prayers.

"We need to call the police," he said, and told Margaret what happened. She hadn't been pleased with Sue after she realised that mobile whatsit was missing. But now she pulled out her own one and dialled 999. "Cocklers… Yes, cocklers. They're in the bay," she said.

Arthur thought of the two policemen down by the shore that night, and found his coat and hat.

"What are you doing?" Margaret asked when she put down the phone.

He wasn't going to let her stop him. If he drove there now, he might be in time. "I'm not leaving this up to that lot of eejits," he said.

His eye fell on the phone on the table. "Can I borrow your phone thingammy? Maybe I can call them if I learn more."

Margaret hesitated.

She was so bloody precious about a bit of plastic. "Please, Margaret."

Nothing, Goddammit.

"I'll pay for a new one if I break it," he said.

"You won't need to," she said.

"What do you mean?"

She pulled on her coat. "I'm coming with you."

Chapter Forty-Seven

The phone had fallen into one of the little streams. Suling shoved Cockler Number One away and plunged her hand in after it, but when she pulled it out, the screen was blank.

"I was calling for help," she told Cockler Number One, trying to keep her voice even. "You just broke the phone."

"You were drawing attention to us," Cockler Number One said.

"Soon there won't be an us," Suling said. She couldn't believe how stupid he was being. "Don't you understand? The tide will come in, just like that, and no one will see us—"

"Do you want to be locked up?" Cockler Number One interrupted. "Do you want to end up in jail? Who were you speaking to in English, anyway? I knew I should have asked you more questions when you turned up."

Suling pressed the phone's buttons. It was as useless as a toy. Each pointless jab of a button made her angrier.

"If the police lock us up, at least Old Uncle will know we're locked up," she said. "If the tide comes to get us, at least he'll know the tide got us. We should draw attention to ourselves. That's all we can do."

But Cockler Number One was furious too. He spat on the ground. "Right. I'm telling the boss. Just as soon as we're back on dry land. You're putting us all at risk. He's going to deal with you."

Once she would have been scared. Now she was just impatient. "As soon as we're back?" She looked out at the empty sands, the distant shore. "Where is the minivan? Who is the boss, anyway? That ghost making money out of us. Where is he?"

Cockler Number One started to reply, but just then Weiying began to mutter.

"She's scared of water," Caixia said.

"Then why did she pick this job?" asked Shijun. "There are other ways to die."

He was still joking, but Caixia didn't laugh. Suling realised she was scared too.

She looked out at the sand, great pillows of it. They should have walked to the shore by now, the minivan should have picked them up by now, they should be leaving.

"Cockler Number One, do you have the bosses' numbers?" Caixia asked.

There was silence. Cockler Number One kicked the sand. He looked younger than ever, young enough to be a schoolboy. "They don't give me their numbers," he muttered. Up above them, the gulls squawked and cried.

Chapter Forty-Eight

Arthur was driving at such a speed that he nearly missed the track. Sid, yelling for help. Sid interrupted mid-prayer by the tide. The smooth tarmac road curved right, and the adjoining track, made of gravel and dirt, was an abrupt left. "Careful," Margaret protested as he swerved.

Now they were rattling down towards the coast between green fields, until the track ended, somewhere in the marsh grass and the rivulets, and sand. No doubt many drivers had realised their mistake at this point, and hastily turned round. But Arthur drove on. The car slowed and began to jolt.

"Dad, stop," Margaret said.

Arthur stopped. Through the windscreen, he could see the bay stretching out in front of him, yellow like the pages of an old, unreadable book. Soon, the tide would rush in and cover it. He thought again of the eerie crackling, how much time had passed since he heard Sue's muffled calls on the phone, and where she might be now. Perhaps it was hopeless – her scream suggested she was already being punished in some way. The light was thinning. All he could hear was the birds crying, and the wind, and Margaret muttering under her breath.

He needed to get out of the car. He unfastened his seatbelt and opened the door. The afternoon smelled of salt, with splashes of vinegar. Three sheep stared at him from the field, then bolted. He watched them run. It was then he saw the tractor. An old Massey Ferguson parked on the verge of the lane, just before it disappeared into the marsh grass.

He began to make his way across the green islands between the rivulets. "Dad," he heard Margaret shout behind him.

The tractor's paint was flaking and some animal had tried to make a nest out of the seat. The wooden trailer was rotten in one corner. If not abandoned, it looked at least forgotten. Its one remaining mirror framed the sinking sun.

Margaret was following. "We'll take this," he told her.

"What do you mean?"

"They always leave the key in the ignition round here."

"Yes, but, Dad—"

It was a long time since he'd driven a tractor. He might not even remember. He gripped a bar at the side of the seat and tried to hoist himself in, but felt his muscles collapse like paper.

"Dad, please—"

He could keep trying, and sooner or later, he'd hoist himself in or fall off and hurt himself. If he took a tumble, he'd never be able to get out there in time. He looked at his daughter. "Can you drive?"

"Yes, but not a tractor—"

They'd argued so much when she was a teenager that she'd paid for her own driving lessons. Still, she was a good driver, and time was running out. "Sit down, make sure the pedal is level, and turn the key. I'll stand behind and direct you."

"Dad—" Margaret was still objecting.

"Just try," he said. He clambered slowly onto the wagon and clutched the back of the tractor frame. Margaret sighed, but she climbed onto the seat. A moment later, the wagon shook beneath him and he almost fell over. The tractor was rumbling into life.

"Which way, Dad?" Margaret asked.

"Straight ahead onto the marsh grass."

"And after that?"

"Just keep your foot down. I'll tell you when to turn."

He longed for his youthful expertise. He had known the names not just of the three rivers that flowed into the bay, but the dykes and the treacherous streams that riddled the sand, which he knew he must avoid at all costs. And then there were the springs that bubbled up from deep under the sand, and the old spots, the water that had lain there collecting, like a trap.

They were in the bay now, the wheels of the tractor disturbing the polish of the wet sand, the vibrations making his bones rattle. The fells rose on either side, as if to remind them of how small they were. Doubt crept in. All he could see was sand and the darkening afternoon sky, and the wind that was feeding off them, creating an almighty racket as it tugged at their jackets and turned their hoods into sails.

Perhaps he had misunderstood. Perhaps she was somewhere else. Or, worse still, perhaps they had done something to her. He thought of the shriek he heard on the phone and felt his whole being sag. All that time he'd wasted fussing about visas and passports, legal and illegal. In the garage, her hands had come out of nowhere and bandaged him, she had built a fire and brought him noodles. And now it was her turn to fall.

Chapter Forty-Nine

It was hard for anyone to make jokes now. They walked across the sand as fast as they could, dragging the bags of cockles behind them. The streams were slowly swelling, although this, Suling knew, was only the warning – the real tide would sweep in before they knew what had hit them.

"Should we head there?" Cockler Number One said, pointing to a cluster of rocks before the shore. "We could leave the nets there come and back for them later." He seemed childish now – the fight had gone out of him. Suling almost wished he was angry again.

"There must have been a traffic jam," Caixia murmured, and they all made noises of agreement, even though they knew that the roads were quiet and clear.

"Where are the others?" Suling asked Cockler Number One. She'd been so distracted by the thought of Changfa, she'd barely noticed where they had been dropped off, but now Cockler Number One pointed and she saw the little dots of people further out in the bay.

"We should warn them," she said.

"They'll see the cars soon," Cockler Number One said, with newfound confidence. "They'll know to start walking. Anyway, it'll be dark soon. They'll have to."

Suling remembered watching the sunset from Old Uncle's window, how the water spangled gold, then black. She waved her arms at the distant figures and shouted. One of them waved back.

"I took this job for my siblings," Cockler Number One said. He was following Suling meekly now, the others huddled behind. The last of the evening sun swept their faces. "My parents both died when I was young. Bad luck, eh? Of course, when I first got here, I realised I wasn't going to have much left over to send home. But I'm playing the long game. They're only kids still. By the time they need a proper education, I'll be ready."

Perhaps he was being cheerful to make up for his earlier outburst, but Suling found it unbearable. Her stomach jumped, as if she was waiting at the start line of a race. She thought of her mother, alone in the village. Changfa, behind barbed wire. Her lungs filling with salty water.

She turned round again. The cocklers were still there. She waved again. This time the figures fell still, as if they had understood. Then once again, someone – it could have been Yue – waved back.

"They don't get it," she said. "Someone needs to go back and tell them." She pushed the thought of her mother away. She was young – she could run. "I'll go."

Number One Cockler shook his head. "No. I'll go. I'm in charge."

He turned on his heel. She could go after him, argue with him, but now she was thinking of her mother again, and Weiying's eyes were on her.

"Keep walking towards the shore," she said. "If we walk fast, we should be fine."

At least there was a rhythm to walking, the soft sound of boots on sand confirming they had not given up, even if the sand clung to their soles, and each step ate away at their energy. In Putian, Changfa once confided in her that he still dreamed of his father, dreams in which he tried to run, but couldn't.

She looked over her shoulder. The other group were moving now. Cockler Number One must have reached them.

"Walk faster," she urged Weiying, who was dragging her feet.

But however fast they marched, the hazy line of marsh grass didn't seem to get any closer, and the sun was low now. She realised with a heavy certainty that they would not reach the shore in time.

No doubt the message she had left on Old Uncle's answer machine was still flashing, just a tiny red dot in that big house, the last of her that would exist after everything else was swept away. And yet she wanted to believe Old Uncle heard it, that he was somehow on his way, that he had stepped away from the telescope and into real life.

Weiying screamed. "The water – it's coming."

And she saw it, a white blade severing the sand from the sky as it swung towards them.

The dead mobile phone was still in her hands. There was no point pressing buttons. But its silver case flashed in the sun and it gave her an idea. She tilted it to the light. Weiying didn't seem to notice – she was still babbling.

She tilted it this way and that, to reflect the last of the sun's rays, to make them visible.

Chapter Fifty

"There," Margaret said. "What's that?"

Arthur squinted.

"A flash," Margaret said. "I think they're trying to get our attention."

She turned the steering wheel, and the tractor sputtered forward. Arthur could barely see, but Margaret kept up a running commentary.

"The water's rising."

"Should I go left?"

"There's someone there."

"Someone on the sandbank."

"I think we need to go further right."

"They're shouting."

"Uncle!"

And it was Sue, standing on the other side of a stream, waving and shouting, and there were other people behind her, and he heard the roar of the tide at the same time.

"Quick," he said. "Get on – quick."

The next moment she was beside him, grasping his hand, and he squeezed it for a moment, because it was simpler and faster than saying how glad he was to see her out loud.

"The others," she gasped.

They were jumping over the stream, and then they were in the trailer, which made the tractor buck and churn sand, but he gripped the tractor frame and shouted directions to Margaret as confidently as he could. He tried to cling to the old tides of memory. But the traps in the sand were laid deeper than even memory could reach. He had to trust his instincts – the shade of the grains, the shimmer of a stream, the engine's mutter.

Behind him, he heard the cocklers in the trailer exclaim. The waves must be coming. They would canter down the channel, dragging the tide behind them. Someone tapped him on the shoulder, but he brushed them off – he couldn't talk now, not until he was closer to the shore. He needed every ounce of concentration. Soon the water would lasso the remaining sandbanks, and they'd be driving through the sea.

But they kept tapping, and then the tap became a hand shaking his shoulder. He turned around, and saw one of the cocklers gesturing to Sue, who was pushing her way through the crowd on the trailer towards him.

She had to shout against the wind several times before he got what she was saying.

"The others."

But the others were in the trailer with her. "What others?" he asked.

They were cutting a splashing path across the marsh grass, just in time, because he could see the water moving and rising, but instead of relief, he felt dread tolling deep within him. "What others?" he said again.

This time it was Margaret who answered – Margaret, who of all people had managed to understand what was going on and who had halted the tractor so she could shout in his ear.

"She's saying we only saw one group, Dad. The others are still all out there."

Even then, he didn't understand, because they had barely been in time to rescue them, so how could the others be further out, when there wasn't any sand left to stand on? And he'd rescued so many. How could there be more?

"The tide—" he said. "We can't—"

"Tell the police," Margaret said. "They're coming."

And sure enough, as they pulled up on the shore, the sirens came down the hill to meet them.

Chapter Fifty-One

There were so many blue lights, they could have been underwater. Weiying froze when she saw the uniforms, and Caixia clung to My Regret. The darkening sky thudded. Before Suling could make sense of it all, a spotty young redhead wearing a policeman's uniform grabbed her arm.

"The others," she said, trying to shake herself out of his grasp, but his fingers only tightened. "The others."

He said something that she didn't understand and steered her towards a car. Another uniform opened the door and pushed her into the back seat. And then there were only the blue lights, flashing in and out of focus as they drove away in the dark.

She slumped against the leather seat. Scooped up like a cockle in a rake. Just as Cockler Number One had warned her. Is this what happened to Changfa? At least now they might be reunited. She was too tired to struggle any more.

But the uniforms didn't take her to a prison – not yet, anyway. They parked in the town outside a large, old building and led her through a room with all kinds of people in it – teenage boys, and untidy, wild-looking men like Kee Teh, and young, anxious-looking women. None of them gave her a second glance. To her relief, the uniforms took her to a quieter room, and the spotty one asked her if she wanted water.

"Cup of tea," she said, and the uniform left the room, the door clicking behind him.

She wondered what they wanted to talk to her about. How she got to this country, no doubt, and where she lived in this town, and what they were doing on those sands. Well, her answer would be simple: "I don't know." It could have been any town, any sands. Whatever suited the brokers and their debt collectors. The country she'd wanted to reach – that country could only be glimpsed through a lighted window, or after a late-night card game, or over a cup of tea. No broker could get her there.

Or maybe they would ask her about this afternoon. She thought of the dots on the horizon, the other cocklers. Had Cockler Number One managed to warn them? But this was a rich country – the hills had been full of flashing blue lights. They must have got there in time.

It seemed like hours since the uniform had gone to get her cup of tea. Then the door opened, and there he was, with a white mug.

Standing next to him was a woman who looked Chinese. She was not in uniform, but a pale pink blouse with a little silver necklace and a black skirt.

"Hello," the woman said in Hokkien. It was the same greeting that she'd heard a thousand times, from Changfa in the schoolyard, to the cocklers when she arrived at the house. She never expected to hear it in a police station. She grasped the mug and began to feel more hopeful.

The two of them sat down, and the uniform said something in English, too fast for her to understand.

The Hokkien-speaking woman smiled. "Tell us about the cocklers," she said.

So Suling did, taking care to muddle up their identities, forget their names. She described the long hours they worked, and the food they ate, and what they were paid for the cockles. When they asked about the bosses, she played dumb, which wasn't hard because it was the truth.

She talked for a long time, and the Hokkien-speaking woman translated with the same smile, and the uniform listened without any expression on his face at all. Then, when she finished describing the drivers, he stood up, said something to the translator, and left.

"You're from Fujian?" Suling asked the woman when they were alone.

"I'm from here. I studied languages," the translator said. "I learned this dialect because my grandmother spoke it."

She fiddled with her necklace and glanced at the door, as if she wanted the uniform to come back.

Suling knew she didn't have long to ask, but she needed to, for Changfa. "Tell me one thing," she said. "Do you know about Stonehouse?"

"The detention centre?" The translator almost whispered. "Yes, I work there, sometimes."

Suling's heart jumped. "Have you ever met someone called Changfa?"

"There are so many people there," the translator said. "Hundreds and hundreds."

The door opened again, and the spotty uniform was back. He did not have a mug of tea this time, and he didn't sit down. Instead, he threw his shoulders back, cleared his throat and barked out a string of words.

The translator sat up straight. "Meiyi, or Suling, or whatever your name is," she said. "You are a suspect in manslaughter. You are under arrest."

Chapter Fifty-Two

It was chaos. Arthur was exhausted. There were police all around him, swarming in the dark, and for a moment he wondered if he was being arrested, but Margaret was speaking to them, keeping them at bay. He leaned against the empty trailer.

The wood creaked under his weight. He felt a new sense of panic – where was Sue? He'd seen her shouting on the trailer. Then, when they reached land, everyone had jumped off, and at the same time, the doors of the police cars opened and uniformed officers had spilled onto the marsh grass. She'd begged him not to call the police. But it was different now. Surely she'd see that.

The waves slapped the edge of the trailer. What the hell was she doing out there so late, anyway? Hadn't he told her about the tides? But it wasn't just Sue. There was panic in her voice when she shouted: "The others."

Margaret came over just then and, without asking, offered her arm. Once he was standing upright – trying not to sway – he managed to ask her: "Do they know about the others?" And she said, in a voice that mirrored his own: "I don't know. They've taken everyone we saved away."

The word "saved" should have made him proud, but instead it set off the tolling in his stomach, the way it was in hospital that awful night, when a lad in scrubs said the doctor would just be a minute, that she had something to tell him.

"But what about the rest?" he asked. A policeman was blowing his nose. He lurched towards him. "Aren't you doing anything about the others out there?" he demanded. He tightened his grip on Margaret. "I can go out there again, if you need me to show you the way." Even as he said the words, he knew it was too late for a tractor – but still, they had boats, didn't they?

The policeman shook his head. He was another young one – he could only be in his mid-twenties, Arthur thought.

"Don't just stand there," he said. "Why aren't you out there, in the bay? Or don't you know anything about it? Where's Sue?" But he couldn't speak any more, because there was a whirring in the air.

"That's the helicopter," someone shouted.

Arthur couldn't see the helicopter yet, but the night seemed to be churning, as if the shape of its final form was about to appear. Like everyone else, he kept his eyes on the black clouds, the rain appearing like pinheads in the artificial light. Then the wind from the helicopter ripped through the crowd, and he felt his jacket flapping, and even Margaret next to him shaking. The police ducked as if some great power was upon them.

The young policeman opened his mouth, and perhaps it was the youthfulness of his voice, broken but still high, that cut through above the sound.

"It's too late. I'm sorry. You should step back. The bodies are coming in."

Chapter Fifty-Three

The uniform wouldn't answer Suling's questions.

"What is manslaughter?" she asked.

"What role did you play in the gang?" came the response, through the thin-lipped translator.

"Is someone – is someone dead?"

"Did they value you for your English?"

It was when she stood up and shouted in panic, "Are they okay?" and he replied asking: "How many cocklers were there?" that she knew for sure something terrible had happened. She thought of the cocklers, black and small on the sand like scattered seeds. She tasted cold salt water and knew she'd never cough it out.

"Tell us what role you played in the gang," the translator said. Her face was stony now.

She was submerged in a brackish pond of grief, but when she opened her eyes, they were still waiting. It was just them and her in this windowless room. They had not hit her, they had not threatened her, not yet. They were like the sand – so still, and they could swallow her up at any moment. She tried to make sense of what they were saying.

"I am not in any gang," she said slowly. "I am just a girl lost in this country, trying to find my way out."

The uniform said something to the translator. The fixed smile returned. "Tell us what role you played in the gang," she said.

Suling thought of the last of the sun on the sand, and Cockler Number One babbling about his siblings, and how he insisted on going back to warn the others. The rakes would be bobbing on the water now.

"I am not in any gang," she repeated. "We were just cocklers."

The questions went on and on, until she was exhausted and she began to fear she would never get out of the room. The translator repeated them all in Hokkien in a brisk, business-like way, and as she spoke Suling began to think that language was not so important after all, that they had nothing in common, this translator and her.

"How did you know about the tide, when the others didn't?"

Old Uncle in his living room, at the window, pointing at the silvery horizon. Crouching down to put her eye to the telescope. That day they leaned over the balcony and nursed their hangovers.

"A friend told me," she said wearily. The uniform and the translator exchanged a glance, as if they didn't believe her.

Then they both got up and left the room again. The door clicked behind them. She didn't bother to check if it was locked. Even if she managed to leave, she would be followed by the faces of the cocklers, pale and motionless and slithering into one another like noodles in cold soup.

She put her head in her hands. If only she had taken the other road, she would be in Preston by now. Knocking on doors with Miss Tiger Stripe. A second job washing dishes in a back kitchen. At some point, the news about the cocklers would be dropped off along with the cabbages, and she would have been glad she'd never seen the sands again.

But the bosses would have still wanted the profits. Cockler Number One would still have asked the minivan driver to come late. The cocklers would still have stayed out on the sands and found themselves stranded. And here she was, in the middle of it.

The door opened. She didn't bother to lift her head. She'd had enough of their questions.

The translator cleared her throat. She said: "You have a very good friend."

Suling looked up slowly. Had Old Uncle found her? The thought was a tiny reflection on the sea of her pain. But she didn't recognise the thin, dark, balding man in a suit next to the uniform.

"That's your lawyer," the woman said.

The lawyer handed her a sheaf of papers.

"For you," he said in English.

"It means you can go," the translator said.

The lawyer spoke again.

"The papers are your application to stay," the translator said. "Use your real name." She arched her eyebrows. "Your friend's certainly a very determined woman."

She? Did she mean Electric Auntie? Suling didn't dare ask any questions. The translator sat down next to her and began to explain the form, and then finally she was allowed out of the room, into a bigger one, and there was another flurry of papers to be signed. And then, just like that, the uniform left. The translator turned to follow him down the corridor.

"Wait," Suling said. "What happened out there?"

The translator pulled at her necklace. "We don't know yet," she said. "People died. I'm sorry."

So it was true. Suling wished she was anywhere other than this room, with its strip lights and bare walls.

The translator hesitated.

"Changfa," she said. "I think I do recognise that name from Stonehouse after all." She gave a tiny smile. "I translate for the troublemakers, you see."

And then she turned and walked down the corridor, leaving Suling alone in the waiting room with the silent lawyer, watched by the uniformed attendant behind a glass. She looked at the papers in her hand. It was as if she was suddenly naked. So long as she had been invisible, she was relieved of certain duties. Now she needed to write to her mother. But how would she explain? What did she have to say for herself? How many thousands of times had her mind wandered back to that small house and hovered on the threshold, dreaming of being invited in?

"Sue," a voice said.

It was Old Uncle, looking frail under the yellow glare of the waiting room lights. "We can go now."

She felt a hand on her shoulder. "Come on," My Regret said. She nodded to the balding lawyer, and Suling realised this was the determined woman the translator had been talking about.

As she left, she saw for the first time the other surviving cocklers, huddled together. Weiying's face was buried in Caixia's shoulder. Shijun looked scared. She longed to go to them. But Old Uncle was waiting outside in the car, and My Regret was helping her in.

Old Uncle put his hand on her shoulder and opened his mouth.

"I know," she said. "They told me."

She stared back at the windows of the police station.

"What will happen to them?" she asked, stringing the foreign words together as calmly as she could.

"I don't know," Old Uncle said.

"What will happen to me?" she said.

My Regret tapped the letter in her hand. "Right now, you stay," she said.

The car window was streaked with rain and the tar of the night.

"How long?" she asked.

"No-one knows."

Chapter Fifty-Four

In the days after thirteen people died in the bay, Margaret and the lawyer she'd found helped Suling with her application, and Arthur remained glued to the TV. The stories were grim, but he couldn't help it. By day two, the facts of the matter were this: the cocklers, most of whom didn't speak English, lived in crowded accommodation, rented from a local landlord, who now seemed to have gone into hiding.

"But how did they get to the sands?" Angela asked over the phone, her voice slurry with painkillers. She was back in her home on the other side of the country now, but they had talked several times since the tragedy.

Arthur picked up the remote with his free hand and turned down the TV volume.

"Minivan drivers."

"So why couldn't they just call them?"

On the TV, a news reporter was flinching in the wind.

"The drivers only answered to their boss," Arthur said. "And he's gone to ground."

Angela sighed. "I just don't understand why, Arthur. What could have been so important to risk so many lives?"

According to the news reports, money from the big European seafood companies. On that beautiful evening, the order had come down the chain that they wanted more. No one seemed to have checked the tides. The drivers had just been setting off when one of them received the first call of distress, and then they scarpered. A man with an Eastern European accent had called police to raise the alarm, but that was the last anyone heard of them.

The cocklers spent their final minutes using up their remaining mobile phone credit to leave anguished messages on their relatives' phones.

By day three, someone had translated them.

By day five, there was a full-blown investigation, and the first of the relatives was spotted staring dumbly out to the horizon.

On day six, there was a ring at the door, and Arthur opened it to find a reporter with a notebook, who managed to blurt out: "Were you the hero tractor driver?" before he slammed the door in his face.

On day seven, he climbed into his car and went to visit Reggie.

*

The nursing home still gave him the heebie jeebies, but he was glad to get out of the house, where every little thing he did reminded him of what he hadn't managed to do. It was still weeks till Christmas, but they'd erected a huge pine tree in the foyer and decorated it with twinkly lights. He had a nurse write down the code to get out, just in case.

He found Reggie in his armchair, pushing a digestive biscuit around his dinner tray like a toddler. "Here you go," he said, and placed a bottle of whisky on top of the chest of drawers. Reggie brightened visibly. He hoped the nurses wouldn't confiscate it. Or maybe they would help themselves to it. He hadn't made up his mind about them yet.

"Biscuit," Reggie said.

"Angela sends her love," Arthur said. He emptied Reggie's mug, refilled it with whisky and took a swig from the bottle before sitting down on the bed. Reggie's books were not bad, he had to admit. He might stay and read one for a while, at least until the nurse noticed him and kicked him out. "The state of this town. You wouldn't believe everything that's happened in the last few months." He raised the bottle. "Anyway. Season's greetings."

His old neighbour blinked.

"Biscuit," he repeated.

Arthur felt a surge of irritation. "Come on, Reggie, can't you see it's Christmas?" Reggie's gentle eyes looked at him with confusion. Arthur noticed that his jaw was clean shaven. His brain was shrinking and dying. Yet every day, his chin still grew stubble and every day, someone came in like clockwork with a razor, and removed it.

Reggie's hands enclosed around the digestive. "Biscuit," he said. There was something desperate about the way his fingers scrabbled at it for a second, as if he sensed the meaning in what he was saying, but then his fingers relaxed, and he fell back again.

"You tried, Reggie," Arthur said. "You really tried, ol' fella." He knew he was really speaking to himself. Reggie wasn't a toddler trying to piece together the world. He was an old man disintegrating.

The sickly-sweet smell of air freshener was overpowering. Arthur put his head in his hands and shut his eyes. He had a feeling suddenly of not being the centre of everything any more. He saw an old man bent over on a bed and another in an armchair, one hand pushing around a biscuit on a tray. He saw a long-married couple asleep in bed, and then the woman's body jolt, as the stroke took her. He saw two hungry lads scrabbling for cockles on an endless stretch of sand. He saw—

A hand on his shoulder. He opened his eyes and saw Reggie looking at him with concern. The hand patted him gently.

"Biscuit," Reggie whispered.

Arthur's old neighbour sat down on the bed next to him. In his garden fence days, Reggie was always chattering, but now he sat quietly, so quietly Arthur could hear him breathing. Air into his lungs and out again. They sat like that for some time, how long Arthur didn't know. It didn't really matter any more, anyway.

When he eventually got up and looked out of the window, the light was fading. A car pulled out of the car park, its lights glowing in the half-dark. A carer going home. He wondered if they had a child to collect from nursery, or maybe their family was waiting in a different time zone for them to call.

"I know it's pointless," Angela had said to him over the crackling phone line. "I'm only prolonging the pain. And I am bloody furious about losing my hair. But I do love my grandson. And we've only just started talking."

Beyond the car park he could see a last silver gleam – the bay before it disappeared into the dark. Suling would be back at the house by now. He wasn't a hero. He might soon be nothing. But he could put the kettle on and make her a cup of tea. They could sit at the kitchen table together and watch the steam rise.

He stepped back from the window and pulled on his coat. "Tarrah, Reggie," he said. "See you soon."

Chapter Fifty-Five

Suling had been scared of My Regret, but now she saw there was something in this woman to admire. She might be too loud and a bit overweight, but once she had decided to pursue a goal, she was forceful – she was like the iron rail of the promenade in a gale.

And she needed the rail to hold on to. In the days after she left the police station, she felt herself tossed this way and that. Sometimes she woke up and lay in bed replaying every hour in her head. If she had realised the time sooner, spoken up sooner, raised the alarm sooner, thought about the other cocklers sooner, waved to them sooner. She knew the cocklers' fate was steaming relentlessly towards them, and yet there were so many ways she could have derailed it. On those days, she didn't dare get out of bed.

Other days she tried to swim through, but they were charged with forces she couldn't control. Boiling the kettle for tea, she found herself collapsed in a heap on the floor. A glance at the telescope reduced her to uncontrollable tears. Even sitting in silence with Old Uncle was hard. She often hid in the garden.

And then there was the paperwork. The lawyer, Mr Khan, had worked hard to explain to the police she was a victim, not a snakehead, but now they wanted her to give evidence in court. If she agreed to do so, Mr Khan said, it would be a reason to let her stay. That meant My Regret driving her to the lawyer's tiny office, to fill in forms so dense and enigmatic she felt like she was making the deal with the broker all over again.

Mr Khan asked a lot of questions. He didn't understand the cocklers. "But why didn't they just leave?" he asked, for the third time, one afternoon, through the tired-looking translator, a man who only spoke Mandarin. My Regret's face asked the same question. Piecing together the words to reply seemed impossible.

"If you were in a foreign country, wouldn't you stick with the people you knew?" she asked in Hokkien. How to describe Changfa's face on that first night in the cocklers' house, how his eyes sparkled when he saw her? She had seized his arm in that crammed, damp room.

The translator shook his head at the unfamiliar words. The lawyer put down his pen and sighed.

"I wish to go to Stonehouse," she said slowly in English. "I wish to see Changfa."

My Regret and Mr Khan exchanged a glance.

"Then why don't you?" asked My Regret.

*

Stonehouse seemed to be in the middle of nowhere. It didn't appear on any map. Even after Mr Khan had managed to text Margaret an address, Old Uncle got lost at least twice on the way there. Suling looked out of the window, hoping to see something of the cities she'd heard about, but there were only hills, then farmland, and then, suddenly, this small town and entrance with barbed wire.

The translator had called it a detention centre, but the debt collector was right. It was a prison.

The visitor's entrance was a hut the size of a shipping container in the car park. When they went in, it was crowded.

An African lady in an intensely patterned print dress was rocking a baby. But for the most part, although they looked like they came from all over the world, the visitors dressed like they wanted to blend in. Perhaps it was the bare bulbs or the guard lurking at the door, but Suling got the sense that they, like the centre itself, didn't want to be noticed.

My Regret spoke to a man in a booth while Suling and Old Uncle waited. He was separated from them by a thick pane of glass, and My Regret had to speak through a microphone, so it took a lot of shouting. After a long discussion My Regret came back to them and gave Suling a ticket with the number twenty-three on it. "You wait here," she said. "They call you."

It was a cold afternoon, and the wind rattled the door of the hut. The baby in the woman's arms grizzled. Everyone avoided each other's eyes. Every now and then, a number flashed up on an electronic screen and two or three of the people would get up and quietly disappear.

Twenty-three – Suling's number flashed up on screen. She was nervous now – nervous about seeing Changfa, and nervous for herself, walking straight into this prison. She realised with a panic that all her paperwork was in the car. What if they wouldn't let her leave? How long would they wait for her? My Regret was not a patient woman.

"This way," the guard said. He was a middle-aged man, porridge white, with grey stubble and a belly that flopped over his belt. "Bye," she said to My Regret and Old Uncle, trying to keep the fear out of her voice. She followed him down a narrow path through the grounds, although a high fence separated her from them on both sides. Then up some steps and into another room where she was searched, and her bag put through an x-ray machine and finally into a canteen-style hall with strip lights and plastic chairs.

The guard pointed to a table. "Sit," he said.

A man was already sitting there. He was thin and wary, with close-cropped hair, and he was staring at the wall blankly. But she recognised him all the same.

"Changfa," she said. He looked up, and a smile ripped across his face, and she was in his arms.

The guard cleared his throat, and she worried he would break them apart, but he didn't.

They sat down at the table because there was nowhere else to go, with nothing to eat because neither of them had any change for the vending machine in the corner, and they talked.

"I thought General Cockle had taken you somewhere," Suling said.

Changfa made a face. "He was caught like the rest of us. Actually, I was worried about him. He kept shouting at the guards. But now he just sits in a corner and barely opens his mouth."

He spoke so gently about General Cockle, it was hard to imagine they were talking about the same person. "What actually happened that night?" she asked.

"All I was thinking about was dropping off the nets and seeing you," Changfa said. "But the police came when the cockles were being counted." They had been arrested right there in the car park. "We never got a chance to go back to the house."

"I waited outside it in the rain," Suling said.

"We were treated like criminals," Changfa said. "But there was no trial." They were moved from prison to prison, until only a few of them remained together. Their hopes grew smaller and more trivial. They stopped talking about getting let out, only whether they'd get something edible for dinner. Sometimes, in the canteen, they struck up friendships in broken English with the inmates sitting next to them, only to find the chair empty the next day. Those inmates were never mentioned again. No-one wanted to think about the moment their future died.

"I heard people finish their life in here," Suling said.

Changfa lowered his voice, even though they were the only ones talking in Hokkien, and began to speak fast.

"I thought about it too," he muttered. "Many times. You do go mad. Never knowing where you are, what's next. But if they think you're going to do it, they watch you. They won't even let you leave in that way."

She listened, appalled. The laughing boy she'd walked home from school with was gone. The man in front of her had dark circles under his eyes and a nervous twitch.

"You would have left me too," she said. "Where did you think I was, all that time?"

Changfa shook his head. "I don't know. I hoped you hadn't been caught." He cleared his throat. "I thought you'd found a new job. When I was feeling jealous, I figured you'd found someone else as well."

He paused. "But I liked to imagine you the way you talked about being – you know, when we were still in the factory. I pictured you in the house we were going to build."

"Well, I thought you were after Huimei," Suling said.

Changfa laughed, and then stopped. "Poor Huimei," he said. "They moved her after just a few days. I hope her daughter isn't worried." He cleared his throat. "Anyway, what happened to you?"

She told him about her time in the old swimming pool, how she'd learned to find food and clothes, how she'd escaped the debt collector.

"So you know how to look after yourself," Changfa said, admiringly. And she explained about Old Uncle and the house on the hill, and learning English, and going back to the terraces and all the time picking up information wherever she could, like cockles glistening on the sand.

Then she took a deep breath, and slowly began to explain what happened that day on the sands. Changfa's face sagged as she talked. He reached for her hand and held it.

"What are you going to do now?" he asked.

She grasped his hand. She knew what she said next meant there was no option of disappearing again, that she was throwing herself on the mercies of a system she didn't understand, that it would mean a hundred more waits in a cold hut in a car park. That at the end of it, they still might want different things, or different paths. But it was as clear to her as a reflection in the evening sun.

"I'm going to try to get you out," she said.

Chapter Fifty-Six

Arthur dreamed of Gertie. It left him with a companionable feeling, as if they'd just returned from one of their long walks down the coast. He opened his eyes, saw the plaster of the ceiling, and savoured the feeling until it was gone. Then he propped himself up on the pillows and stared at the room. Gertie's picture was hanging opposite, and he had another of them both at the side of the bed. But no, something was wrong. He sat there for a moment, and then realised he was plonked right in the middle of the bed. He shuffled over to the left-hand side, his side. That was better. In a moment she'd return with the tray, the teapot, the mugs and the little pot of milk, and set them down on the table.

The doctor's appointment was next week. He'd asked for a check-up, and he was going to be clinical about it. He remembered this. He forgot that. Sometimes he trembled. Get it over and done with.

With Gertie, there had been no warning – just a shudder that woke him up that night, and caused him to reach for her instinctively before he realised what was happening. He'd often wondered what life would be like if she had survived the strokes. How he'd have coped.

Now he wondered about her. Could she have ever accepted being chained to a frame, being spoon fed by him while her knitting lay where she'd left it, half done, on the chair?

Outside the window, a bird began to sing. Maybe the doctor would be sensible, and see he was just getting old. Well, if that was true, he'd better not waste time in bed. Margaret would be here soon, and expecting lunch. He got up and threw on his dressing gown.

*

Sue was already in the kitchen, with a big pot of that scented black tea she had bought when they visited her tarty friend in Preston. She had a stack of paper in front of her. She'd been making models for days. They still didn't know about the application to remain, so they had adopted a kind of fiction where they never spoke about it and she kept on practising her English and talking about jobs. She had written to her mother, he knew, a very long letter that she'd stayed up all evening squinting over. Now she got up every morning to check the post.

"Hi," she said. "My Regret is coming for lunch?"

"That's right," Arthur said. He helped himself to a bowl of cereal and ate it in companionable silence. Afterwards he began making lentil soup, the one described in a particularly dog-eared page of Gertie's recipe book, and Sue helped, if helping was the right word for surreptitiously adding things when she thought his back was turned. The doorbell rang. Arthur peered carefully through the spyhole and saw it was Margaret, her foot tapping impatiently on the doormat, hands no doubt twitching for her own set of keys. He let her in.

"That smells good," she said. She peered in the saucepan. "Did you put butter in?"

"There's nothing wrong with butter," Arthur said.

"I know," Margaret said. "I was asking because I like it."

She sat down at the table. "I see the O'Briens have sold next door. Have you met the new neighbours yet?"

Arthur had deeked the moving van in the drive, but he hadn't introduced himself yet. It felt disloyal, somehow. But when he'd spoken to Angela on the phone, she'd whispered, in that diminishing voice of hers: "Go on, I'm nosy."

"I'm going to put a note through their door," he said.

Margaret looked sceptical, but she nodded and turned to Sue, who had emerged from the cupboard with a pair of scissors. "How's the application?"

"Stressful," Sue said. She had learned that word the previous week, and now she used it all the time.

"The police came round yesterday," Arthur said. "It's going to court. Sue's giving evidence against the boss."

Sue spread the paper out on the table. "Not boss," she said. "Only driver." The police had arrested a young Chinese lad in his early twenties – the lawyer had shown Arthur the picture. She picked up the scissors and began to cut. "Maybe I should get another fake passport," she said.

"Well, hopefully the application will be successful, and you'll get a real passport," Margaret said in the tone Arthur recognised from when she spoke to him about safety handrails.

Hopefully. But nothing was certain. All they had was the time between now and the time when they knew she could be taken away. There was only this moment – this kitchen, with the clatter of pans, the snip of scissors, the steamed-up windows shielding everyone from the winter outside.

"I'll lay the table."

She was helpful like that, Margaret, even if she did always use the wrong china. Within half an hour they were sitting at the table, all three of them. "The soup tastes interesting," said Margaret.

"Delicious," Arthur said. It was the only word he could find to describe the feeling he had, but it was something else, really: hot soup on a cold winter's day, and the three bodies clustered around the kitchen table; and his desire, however long it stayed in his memory, to savour it.

Chapter Fifty-Seven

My Regret was at the door. "Suling, do you want a lift anywhere?" she asked.

"Old Uncle is driving me," she said. She stood at the open door and waved My Regret off, and not long after she had disappeared, Old Uncle appeared wearing his jacket.

"Ready?"

She hoisted her bag onto her shoulder, picked up the barbecue lid and the plastic shopping bag full of paper models, and nodded. "Ready."

He drove out of the quiet street, down to the crossroads where she had paused and anguished, and turned down the coastal road. It was one of those days that flipped like a card – one moment the sun dazzled the mirrors, the next the windows were slurred with rain. The wind had shaken the trees bare. The road twisted and turned through the hills until it reached the open expanse of the bay, and Old Uncle accelerated. After a while he said: "Where?"

She pointed at the turn ahead: "There."

He turned off onto the gravel lane, and they got out of the car. The wind slapped and shook them – she offered Old Uncle her arm, and he took it. The tide was out, and the marsh grass rose in the breeze, like the hackles of some enormous beast. They walked along the marshland where it hugged the shore. When they reached a rocky outcrop, the wind died down a little. Old Uncle pointed at some twisted trees above them.

"There," he said.

He had tried to describe the bench to Suling over several cups of tea. It was intended as a kind of shrine to his wife, she grasped that immediately, but all the same it had seemed a strange idea to want to sit on your loved one.

She squatted on the marsh grass. She had seen pictures of Gertie with her short, curly hair and big smile, but now she felt her, striding out towards the horizon. Out here, the bench suddenly made sense. Once you sat on it, you saw the world through her eyes. Perhaps she should ask if the cocklers' names could be on it too. But would they want to stare out at the place that claimed them? No, the place for their bench was on a mountain path, halfway between the fields and the warm, blue sky.

Old Uncle had gone into the gap between two rocks. "Here," he called over the wind. She followed him and saw two dirt paths crossing. The perfect spot.

"Got everything?" he asked.

"It's here," she said, putting down the bag where the paths met. She set down the barbecue lid and emptied the branches she'd gathered onto it. Then she arranged the kindling, and after a few attempts, lit it.

Old Uncle spread out a blanket and eased himself onto it. They sat watching the fire, the clouds streaking across the sky behind it. The day had flipped again – now it was grey and moody. Old Uncle disappeared beneath his thick scarf and hat. She was glad for the two jumpers under her jacket. The wool was coarse and itchy against her bare skin, but it was her armour against the world.

She stared out at the marbled sand of the bay. It was not good or bad, just the blank poster for a calligrapher's message.

Hopeful, scared, angry, greedy – out there, you could see human character as it really was.

The fire bloomed in the wind. She reached into the bag and drew out the first paper object – a car. They would probably want two in heaven these days, she thought, and tossed it onto the flames. It glowed for a moment, and she hoped that somehow the cocklers knew she'd sent it. Then it was gone.

Next she pulled out a TV, a paper box she'd taped together the night before, but they would know it was a TV. She committed it to the flames. Then she pulled out a house, her third attempt, the kind everyone dreamed of building in their village. It too sank in a blaze. She hoped that wherever the cocklers were, they were finally enjoying the fruits of their labour. That they had big houses, with gardens and court-yards, and they too had built a fire in it and were warming themselves by it.

She thought about Changfa, of the house he had imagined within the walls of the detention centre, and Cockler Number One's siblings, who must be wondering why their money hadn't come. She thought of Kee Teh, who had drunk all his dreams, and Miss Tiger Stripe, drunk on them. She thought of her mother, and the letter winging its way towards her, the words crossing a thousand borders closed to her. She thought of the jobs she might do if her application succeeded, and the jobs she might do if it did not.

They sat there watching the fire, until it had died down to the embers, and the sky had faded to grey, and then Old Uncle shook out the barbecue lid, Suling picked up the bag, and they walked back to the car to go home.

Afterword, by Hsiao-Hung Pai

Morecambe Bay, February 5, 2004. It was a Lantern Festival that fell on the fifteenth day of the Chinese New Year. Most Chinese workers would have taken time off to celebrate and rest – including the cockle-pickers at Morecambe Bay. All except for Ah-Ren's team of more than forty workers, who had a production schedule to keep to.

Like other Chinese recruiters who worked for the local gangmasters, or labour providers, twenty-nine-year-old Ah-Ren, officially known as Lin Liang Ren, was at the bottom end of the supply chain. The local gangmaster known as "John" was paying him £15 per bag of cockles. Discontented with the profits he was making, Ah-Ren wanted to take over John's team and be a proper gangmaster like him, so he could work directly with the clients. He pressurised the workers to go out to pick cockles that night, keen to maximise production to meet the high demand from the multinationals.

Back then, there were tens of thousands of undocumented Chinese migrants working across Britain, among them around 80,000 migrants from Fujian province. They worked in industries like catering, food-processing, construction and seasonal agriculture, where they earned half or even less than half of Britain's National Minimum Wage and enjoyed no rights nor entitlements. They were the hidden workforce that you wouldn't see when you ordered a Chinese takeaway or purchased your supermarket salads. They were marginalised and isolated even from the British Chinese communities, who were, in the workers' eyes, made up of bosses who exploited them and lawyers who made big profits sorting out their immigration status.

Since the early 2000s, cheap Chinese migrant labour had been much sought after by local cockling businesses in Merseyside and Lancashire. Local gangmasters brought in teams of Chinese workers via their contacts in the Chinese communities. Chinese workers had been identified as a disciplined and cheap workforce. They were earning £5 to £8 for a 25-kilo bag of cockles, depending on recruiters.

By early 2004, there were more than ten teams working in Morecambe Bay, each with forty to fifty Chinese cocklers. Production demands were high and competition fierce. Their exploitation was made possible not by snakeheads, but by gangmasters and the supply chains for which they worked.

Checking tidal times the day before setting out to work is essential in cockling. But local gangmaster "John" had passed on this task to Ah-Ren, who had passed it on to his own assistants, who knew nothing about tidal charts and gauged the tidal times only by "common sense". Other teams also worked the same way.

Knowledge of geographical and weather conditions is also essential: understanding the location and behaviour of the quicksands and shifting gullies; knowing how fast the tide comes in. Safety equipment is a must. A suitable communication device, a location device, ideally a GPS, or at least a compass is required. None of these basics had been explained to the Chinese workers – not by the local gangmasters, nor by their recruiters.

On the night of February 5, as the timetables had shown, the tide moved fast and conditions were extremely unsuitable for working. When Ah-Ren sent his team onto the sands, there had been one hour left before the tide would start coming in.

He should have told the workers to come back to shore before 7pm at the very latest.

By 8:30 pm, friends and families started receiving calls from workers who were stranded in between the gullies. These were their last calls. The workers tried calling emergency services, but none of them could say any more than 'Help us! Help us!' 'Sink in water!' Ah-Ren's assistant Tian Long called him. 'Think of a way to save us!' he pleaded. Ah-Ren rushed back to the shore and dialled 999, but when the operator answered, he panicked and lost his English.

Twenty-one bodies were recovered from the bay in the days that followed. The twenty-second body wasn't found until autumn 2010. The twenty-third was never found. Twenty-two of those who lost their lives were from Fujian. They were workers and poor farmers who had borrowed heavily to come to Britain to find a livelihood. The families sought compensation after the drownings, but as their loved ones were deemed to be working without papers, they were not eligible.

Following the Morecambe Bay disaster, in March 2006, Lin Liang Ren was given a fourteen-year prison sentence for twenty-one counts of manslaughter. No one else was held responsible. Not the local gangmasters, not the suppliers, and certainly not the multinationals.

In response to the tragedy, the Gangmasters Licensing Act was passed in June 2004 and came into effect in October 2006 with the establishment of the Gangmasters Licensing Authorities (GLA). However, the Act only covered labour providers in a limited list of industries, and the GLA was underfunded and understaffed. Above all, the regulating of labour providers did not benefit Chinese migrant workers because it specifically excluded the protection of undocumented workers (who are called "illegal" under the Act). The GLA was later transformed into Gangmasters and Labour Abuse Authority (GLAA) which began operation in October 2016. It has become part of the government's Modern Slavery initiatives, which work alongside immigration and border controls by which "illegality" and migratory status is often put before workers' interests.

This is the background underlining why it is important to keep talking and writing about the Morecambe Bay tragedy. Over the years, Chinese workers in Britain have moved from sector to sector, as a result of the toughened immigration policies and the increase of immigration raids. The shellfish industry and agriculture don't tend to use agencies that bring in Chinese workers anymore, for fear of heavy fines. Internal border controls have become tougher, whilst work conditions have not improved for migrant workers, often Chinese or Vietnamese. State and society have still not moved on from keeping migrant workers as a subordinate workforce subjected to exploitation and living a kind of parallel existence from the mainstream.

I think this is where good fiction can come in. *The Bay* centres on the unlikely friendship between Suling, a cockler from Fujian, and Arthur, a widowed pensioner, two people who belong in parallel worlds. Their imagined crossing of paths brings out both the social contradictions and the potential solidarity between them. I recall the families and friends who were left behind by the tragedy as well as those in the local community who felt a strong connection with the bay and were scarred by the disaster. These voices often got lost in the stereotypical media representations of the Morecambe Bay tragedy as a story of snakeheads and evil traffickers.

These lost voices can be brought to life in fiction.

Hsiao-Hung Pai, October 2022

Author's Note

The Morecambe Bay tragedy happened when I was fourteen, and at first I didn't associate what I read in the papers with the sleepy corner of the world I had visited every year to see my grandparents. I don't remember anyone mentioning the connection to me either. Perhaps that's because my grandmother was already showing the first signs of Alzheimer's and my family were preoccupied with other things. Or perhaps it was simply too disturbing to discuss on a holiday, in a place where my grandparents had fallen in love, and chosen to retire.

I had always known that the bay was dangerous – the irony of my grandparents living in Grange-over-Sands was that we never stepped out onto the sand at all. Instead, we watched it from the promenade and the fells. Sometimes it would be a desert, sometimes a glimmering sea. The whole town was defined by it, as was Arnside, and further away, Morecambe. On a clear night, we could see the lights of Blackpool Tower.

When I finally put two and two together and worked out the bay and Morecambe Bay were one and the same, the tragedy had vanished from the headlines. I was left with the feeling of not having observed enough, of having been lulled into complacency by the old stone walls and the villages proclaiming themselves "Winner of Best in Bloom". I started a short story exploring the contradiction, but couldn't find a neat conclusion. Instead, I began to read. I read the newspaper reports again, all depicting the incident as a terrible accident, and then I read Hsiao-Hung Pai's book *Chinese Whispers,* which jolted me into thinking in a different way about not just Morecambe Bay, but the whole society I was living in.

Pai, who went undercover to report on her subject, spent weeks socialising and working alongside undocumented Chinese migrants who could very easily have ended up drowning in Morecambe Bay. In her reporting, the cockle pickers who died come across as ordinary, hard-working people at the blunt end of enormous supply chains. I was working in London at the time I read her books, and often walked to work through Chinatown, picturesque with its archway and lanterns. Through Pai's reporting though, I learned about another side of Chinatown, one where desperate people gathered to find work and waiters survived on tips alone.

The question of how much Britain relies on cheap labour reared its head again with Brexit. At the time, I was writing an early draft of the novel and working at *The New Statesman* magazine, where journalists were dispatched to report back from "forgotten towns". By then, my grandparents had died. I often wondered how my grandfather – an Irish Catholic who gave his Filipino neighbours lifts to church – would have voted. All I did know was that his views were complex, and nothing like some of the stereotypes that were now flying round as the recriminations began. I went back to the draft and tried to put myself more firmly in the shoes of someone who had seen their town crumble in a time that was supposed to have been a period of economic boom. At the same time, when writing Suling's part of the story, I tried to push against the prevailing mantra that there was something wrong with being an economic migrant. With both characters, I found myself returning to the same question: why shouldn't someone want more?

Twenty-three people are believed to have drowned in Morecambe Bay on February 5, 2004. A smaller number made it back to shore and survived. Although I tried, I didn't manage to contact them for this book. Their identities have always been protected, and rightly so. Although in the past one survivor has given interviews about his experience, someone close to him told me he no longer wished to relive these upsetting memories.

For this reason, it is doubly important to make clear that, while undoubtedly provoked by a real and terrible tragedy, this is a work of fiction. If those who experienced the real thing ever do choose to tell their stories, I hope that they will be heard. What struck me when researching the book was that the tragedy could have happened many times, in many places, or could have been prevented with a little more communication and empathy. My book explores the space in between these two possibilities.

As the book is fiction, some of the complexities of the cockling industry and undocumented workers were surrendered to the demands of the story. For those who are interested in learning more about the tragedy, the film *Ghosts,* based on Hsiao-Hung Pai and others' reporting, is a faithful recreation. *The Gathering Tide,* by Karen Lloyd, tells the story from the perspective of local cockle pickers, as well as telling many more stories of Morecambe Bay. *Sand Pilot of Morecambe Bay*, the memoir of Cedric Robinson, the former Queen's Guide to the Sands, is a beautiful and moving insight into the bay and its dangers. His successor, Michael Wilson, who was kind enough to read a version of this manuscript, leads regular walks across the bay.

For more on China's young, rural migrants, Leslie T. Chang's book *Factory Girls* is an in-depth and engaging account of the women in China's factory cities, and possibly my best ever thrift-store find. Sheng Keyi's novel *Northern Girls* captures the same voice in fiction. The charity Paper Republic is an excellent resource for anyone keen to read more modern Chinese authors, while the Beijing-based journalist Karoline Kan's memoir *Under Red Skies* gives a sense of the pace of change experienced by Chinese millennials. I'm particularly indebted to Hsiao-Hung Pai, who not only was kind enough to reply to the email of an unpublished stranger, but read two drafts of the novel and gave me invaluable feedback on both. Her books *Scattered Sand* and *Invisible,* covering the lives of China's rural workers and sex workers in the UK respectively, were also illuminating. Thanks also to two Chinese academics at British universities, Jianan Zhang and Dr Lei Peng, for their sage advice on names and language. I'm also grateful to my dear friend Christina Lam, who mastered English at the age of seven, and shared her memories with me during the writing of this book.

The town, too, is an imagined composition, based on several towns around Morecambe Bay, although the conditions of the terrace itself are based on newspaper reports of the cockle pickers' accommodation in a deprived neighbourhood of Liverpool. The lido, however, really exists – those who would like to see it reopened can support the campaign Save Grange Lido – and the old stone hospice can be found on top of Hampsfell. The detention centre is based on my visit to the now-defunct Oakington detention centre, and my conversations with former detainees. Reading Wendy Mitchell's memoir about living with dementia, *Somebody I Used to Know,* was both helpful for writing the novel and a moving insight into what my grandmother, who never complained, might have experienced. Thanks to the Lakeland Dialect Society and The University of Leeds Dialect and Heritage Project for dialect advice.

Today, you are more likely to hear about Chinese migrants propping up the economies of the North-west's university towns than dying in rural coastal areas. The system of exploitation, though, continues. Although successive governments have tried to tackle modern slavery, on October 23, 2019, when I had all but finished the first full draft of the novel, thirty-nine Vietnamese men and women were found dead in the back of a lorry in Essex. Sadly, government rhetoric on "cracking down" on immigration only pushes those who could lose everything further into the arms of gangs and smugglers. "Stay invisible," Changfa warns Suling at the start of the novel, but if we truly want those at risk to seek help, we need to make it safe for them to step into the light.

Acknowledgements

Many of the best novels I've read have never been published. This one might have met a similar fate if not for the help and encouragement from some very specific people.

I will always be indebted to my high school English teacher, Allan Crosbie, who made me believe I could be a writer, and submitted my poems to the Foyle Young Poets award. The prize, a week on an Arvon Course, transformed my life in more ways than I can count. Bobbie Darbyshire's Clapham writing group helped me turn a rambling short story into a first draft. Many thanks to Ellen MacDonald-Kramer, Joanne Rush, Karen Wallace, John Keenan, Anand Bhopal, Dima Mekdad, Curtis Chin, Sophie Wawro, Joseph Pierson, Sarah Butler, Christina Lam and my sister Claire Rampen for reading drafts and giving me valuable feedback. Alice Malin was generous enough to read it twice, once for a tight deadline. I am particularly grateful to Emma Bamford, who not only read a draft but persuaded me to enter the First Pages Prize, which led to recognition in the Bridport Prize and the Bath Novel Award. Thanks to the organisers, judges and readers, especially Emma Healey, Kate Simants, Sarah Butler and the Literary Consultancy. In the challenging year of 2020, having this kind of encouragement meant the world.

Writing a novel was, nevertheless, a crash-course in rejection. Thank you to my agent, Euan Thorneycroft, for his belief in the book, and to Sara Hunt of Saraband, in association with New Writing North, for taking the plunge and publishing it. The New Writing North Awards is a fantastic programme and I feel so honoured to be part of it.

For my family, the novel-writing process meant putting up with a hermit who didn't want to answer any questions about what she was doing. Thanks for your tolerance and patience. Finally, I am grateful to my husband, Jamie Kenny, who read a draft and became the novel's biggest cheerleader. You are the best reader anyone could wish for.

Julia Rampen, October 2022

JULIA RAMPEN is a Scottish-Canadian journalist, podcaster, editor and writer based in Liverpool. She is the Media Director for IMIX, a charity that supports refugees and migrants in telling their stories to the media, and co-founder of the storytelling platform Qisetna: Talking Syria. She was formerly the digital night editor of *The Liverpool Echo* and digital news editor of *The New Statesman*. *The Bay* is her first novel.